THE
REVIVALISTS

A NOVEL

CHRISTOPHER M. HOOD

HARPER

An Imprint of HarperCollins*Publishers*

THE REVIVALISTS. Copyright © 2022 by Christopher Hood. All rights reserved. Printed in the United States of America. No part of this book may be used or reproduced in any manner whatsoever without written permission except in the case of brief quotations embodied in critical articles and reviews. For information, address HarperCollins Publishers, 195 Broadway, New York, NY 10007.

HarperCollins books may be purchased for educational, business, or sales promotional use. For information, please email the Special Markets Department at SPsales@harpercollins.com.

FIRST EDITION

Library of Congress Cataloging-in-Publication Data has been applied for.

ISBN 978-0-06-322139-0

22 23 24 25 26 LSC 10 9 8 7 6 5 4 3 2 1

FOR DAPHNE

I long—I pine, all my days—
To travel home and see the dawn of my return.
And if a god will wreck me yet again on the wine-dark sea,
I can bear that too, with a spirit tempered to endure.

—*The Odyssey*
(trans. Robert Fagles)

THE
REVIVALISTS

Dad, it's me.

Hannah, it was Hannah, Hannah's voice, except it sounded wrong, cottony, no audible eye-roll as talking to me so often inspired. Her words collapsed at the end, the *me* a whisper, as though we were talking on the telephone, as though she was holding the phone up with her shoulder as she reached for the tea on a high shelf, and the squeal of my ham radio was the kettle on her stove.

"Hannah, what's wrong?" Her breath was so loud I could hear it, even through a continent's worth of crackling space. I could hear my heart too, thrashing in my chest. "Hannah, what's wrong?"

I turned toward the stairs. "Pen! It's Hannah!"

"Nothing's wrong."

I wanted to ask if she was high, but she was three thousand miles away, and her voice could disappear at any moment, she could stop transmitting and fly away. Anytime we managed to connect over the radio it felt so tenuous, a single strand of spider thread reaching across the country, and if I spooked her . . .

"Where are you?"

Penelope was thundering down the stairs, and I couldn't hear what Hannah said.

"What? Where are you?"

"I'm still in Bishop," she repeated.

Penelope was next to me now, her head pressed to mine, temple to temple, both of us straining to hear. "Tell me you're okay," she said. "Baby, talk to me."

"You're both there."

"We're here," we said in unison.

"You don't have to worry about me anymore." Her voice picked up speed, with the rhythmic cadence of someone reading aloud. "I've found the answers, and it's brought me peace. This sacrament requires sacrifice . . ." She stumbled over *sacrifice*, her tongue thick, and Penelope burst in.

"No no no! Baby, you aren't doing this."

She kept droning on. "My previous life must be thrown on the fire. I am baptized anew."

"Don't you dare." Penelope had a grip on my forearm, her fingers tightening hard enough to hurt.

"I ask you to respect my choice . . ."

I felt like I could hear someone else in the background, a murmur saying the words just ahead of her. "Who's that?" I said. "What's going on!"

"Because it is done," she finished. There was a pause, and we all sat in silence for a moment. Then Hannah said, "I love you guys" in a little mouse squeak, and a man's voice said, "That's enough," and the voices disappeared and the static surged, the alien whines and breathy crackling I listened to all day in the kitchen, hoping that what had just happened would happen, that Hannah would use again the radio frequency we'd shared with her before the phones died. I just never thought that she would use it to recite the terrible Revival pablum intended to cut us out of her life for good.

"Hannah? Hannah!" Penelope was shouting into the handset. I stood in the kitchen, empty-handed, my mouth hanging open. It was hopeless, there was nothing we could do. We could call into the void, we could send our voices to California and beyond, there could be someone on a sailboat in the Pacific listening to us, laughing at the panic in our voices, but none of it mattered if she wasn't listening.

Penelope tried a new frequency, though it was useless, and another after that, finally just spinning the dial and dropping the handset. I was standing behind her, dumb, the kitchen tile cold under my bare feet. Her head fell, her palms flat on the countertop. *"I am baptized anew?"* she asked, not looking at me but at the radio staring back at her implacably. "Jesus, what the fuck is that. And they gave her something, you know they did. Did you hear her voice? It sounded like she was underwater."

It was late evening in the early fall, the leaves on the Japanese maple in the front yard were still green, not yet a bloody red, and the sun was coming through the front windows behind Penelope, bright enough that I couldn't see her face, not really, though I didn't need to. I knew her expression. I knew what she was going to say before she said it. She was going to say *I told you this was going to happen.*

And I guess she was right. The room spun around me in a long arc, and I felt the same light-headed nausea that came whenever I saw my own blood flow.

"We are going to get her."

That's what she said. It was the way she said it that captured all the rest, her conference-call-Zoom voice, which made her sound like a different person, like she was squashing potential dissent before it could germinate. I wanted to feel nothing but joy at hearing Hannah's voice again. I wanted to feel closer to Penelope too, united on a quest to rescue our daughter. And I did feel both of those things, but I felt resentment too, and even a thought it would have been impossible to share with my wife: Is it really so bad if Hannah joins The Revival? What options are left? If they had food and shelter and safety, The Revival sounded pretty damn good to me.

Let me say this now, at the outset, before all that follows: I don't expect sympathy. Whatever was to come as we crossed the country to rescue our daughter, our living daughter, I was already shamefully gorgeously lucky: there were two people I loved enough that losing them would break me, and they had both survived. What were the odds? I didn't know. Hannah's was the only voice from more than a few miles away that we'd heard in months. Progress hadn't just reversed; it had leapt backward in time. It wasn't just that the phones were dead—there were no telegrams, no smoke signals, no Pony Express. The Big One could have struck California, dropping half of it into the sea, and we wouldn't have known. Even New York City, only twenty miles south, was a mystery. We heard rumors. The fear that the virus was traveling through the ventilation systems had driven people from the buildings to die in the cold streets now snarled and impassable with abandoned cars, just when the subways stopped for good. Was the Central Park Reservoir, drained, really being used as a mass cremation site? I doubted it, but who knew?

Whatever the odds, our survival felt luckier even than that. No family got through this unscathed. We should have been shouting *Hosannah!* in spasms of gratitude that we even had a daughter left to join The Revival. But you don't have to be a psychologist to know that's not how people work. I was ready to altar-sacrifice everything for our daughter. And rational Penelope? Who could swim in an IPO prospectus all afternoon and surface in the evening with a single crystallized number? Who actually read actuarial tables? Who'd run from all the uncertainty and prejudice and chaos of her early years and found refuge in the mathematics of money? Penelope was a feral creature when it came to Hannah, and always had been.

When the virus rose and lockdowns began, all anyone could talk about was COVID-19. It had been only a few years, after all. *I can't do that again*, we all said, *I just can't.* But if COVID-19 had been Death in a black hoodie with a scythe, this new virus was the reaping industrialized, a combine, massive, its maw chewing through the population of the world. Most viruses had the good sense to temper their ravenous desire to reproduce reproduce reproduce, keep enough hosts around to live on in perpetuity, but not this one, this one didn't want to cull the herd, but eradicate it, a sated wolf killing for the kill, dying gloriously and taking all those hosts with it. This virus was Edna St. Vincent Millay, burning the candle at both ends, leaving only the lucky immune few, and then disappearing, burned on its own pyre.

It emerged from the melting permafrost in Iceland, and social media immediately dubbed it Shark Flu, blaming the Icelanders' strange practice of eating fermented shark meat while drinking in bars, a story no one even had time to debunk, it all spread so quickly, a hemorrhagic fever that seemed to attack the very boundaries between the body and the world it inhabited: every deadly disease is horrible, but one that loosens your bodily integrity? Blood leaked from places it shouldn't, people died gasping, organs weren't *actually* melting, but that was the sound bite that played endlessly in our minds, the simile a doctor used on CNN: *It's like the organs melt.*

Every day for twenty years, the *New York Times* flew onto our lawn, grenade-style, a man I never met but sent twenty dollars to each year at Christmas reaching his left arm from the driver's-side window and sending the blue-plastic-wrapped paper in a long arc over the roof of his faded Toyota to land on our grass or in our hedge. Shark Flu started as a sidebar, below the fold, but daily the news got worse, the headlines more apocalyptic. The virus had a two-week dormancy in the body, contagious but asymptomatic, then broke

5

free like a racehorse from the gate. People died in days, sometimes hours. Iceland locked down. *Thank God it's an island*, everyone said, but it was an island upon which thousands upon thousands of flights between North America and Europe had stopped to refuel, and the Shark Flu was already out and running, every plane carrying stowaways, hidden not in the cargo holds but in the blood. Masks we all had, but with this disease, any mucous membrane would do, your eyes were enough, their glistening wet a breeding ground, virus landing and rising like a cloud of mosquitoes from a puddle.

Hannah was in California when it began, studying sociology at Irvine. We told her to fly home, who cared about classes at a time like this? But she was stubborn, and the instructions from the administration veered wildly. At first, it was *Everyone has to go, classes are canceled*, but the situation was changing so quickly, the virus as contagious as measles, deadlier than Ebola, and that deadly two-week grace period meaning it was always two steps ahead. The police are always trying to catch up to the criminals. Before anyone could leave, the pendulum swung, and they locked down the campus. No one allowed out of their dorm rooms.

She called us sobbing, and we were in the car fifteen minutes later, headed west. The rules of the road seemed to no longer exist. Cars swerved into the median grass and accelerated, intersections hopeless, and all it took was one screaming, doors-opening argument between fellow motorists to ripple backward for miles, stopping everything, inspiring more people to attack one another. We persisted, though we could see as we finally approached that the bridge we still called the Tappan Zee was blocked. Perhaps our story might be enough to break through the quarantine. The car was silent, both of us staring ahead, knowing what was happening, but not willing to vocalize it and make it true. When finally it was our turn at the head of the line to plead with the granite faces of the state troopers, the National Guard with their gas masks and armored personnel carriers, it went as well as it could have, meaning, it did not go at all. They might as well have been animatronic for all we were able to crack the veneer, their arms endlessly pointing us backward.

Did we drive south and try the GWB? Yes, we did. And it was only when we'd driven *back* north, to the Bear Mountain Bridge, that we finally found a cop who broke character just enough to tell us that everything in the country was locked down just like this, they were trying to use the Hudson River like a firebreak, as it were, that the individual states might as well have been forty-eight separate countries for all that we'd be able to travel between them. At 4:00 a.m., we were back in our driveway, staring at the house, the car still running, both of us too shattered to even open the doors.

Even as a young child, Hannah had a stormy inner world, but we had always been invited inside to share it. Then puberty blitzkrieged our home, and, seemingly overnight, we became onlookers to her life, supplicants grateful for whatever morsel she deigned to share with us. Now, trapped in her dorm room with a few packs of instant ramen, braving little runs down the hall to the bathroom, she was our little girl again, on the phone with us all day long. I'd be upstairs lying down, and though it had been only a few hours since I'd heard her voice, I'd find myself tapping her name on my phone, the clipped ring in my ear telling me she was already talking to someone, and then before I could leave a voicemail Penelope's voice would float up the stairs *I'm already on with her!* and I knew she was sitting downstairs in the bay window looking out over our little front lawn, her legs drawn into her body, listening to Hannah on her cell, knew Hannah was saying *Dad's calling again. Aren't you guys in the same house?*

At first it was a game, being locked in the dorm. Beer pong tables set up in hallways, kegs smuggled in, weed stockpiles raided. Then the first student died, and the hallways emptied in a finger-snap, people creeping out to go to the bathroom, running back to their room at the first sign of movement. *No one has come to help,* Hannah cried on the phone. *There's a body in the room next door!* And no one was coming. All my professional calm flew out the window as I sobbed on the phone with her. There was no one *to* come. Hannah was alone in her dorm, terrified and sobbing and hungry, and we were three thousand miles away, and there were no airplanes, no trains, no buses, and the American freedom of the road was a quaint memory, like a gas station sign on a restaurant wall.

Then Penelope spiked a fever. The boundaries of our house had somehow been breached. I tried to keep the raw panic from my voice when Hannah called, but Penelope was almost immediately delirious, the sheets were soaked with sweat, Hannah was sobbing *Mom has it? She has it?* and I would have tried to keep a level head, to say *We don't know that yet*, but now Hannah's voice was Doppler-shifting in my ears, the phone suddenly slick in my hands, and I don't know what I told her, but I found myself running down the hallway to vomit. A horrifying day passed of which I remembered only strange hallucinatory images—the walls bending trapezoidal, insects crawling down those same walls and onto me, sliding underneath my fingernails and into my body with audible little pops, like my phone's haptic feedback when I tapped it. I saw Penelope smearing into abstraction, I saw my own father, now ten years dead, smoking a pipe in our living room. If I'd been capable of taking my own temperature, I wouldn't have known what the number meant.

A day and a half passed like that—Hannah told me later how long it had been—and then we were better. It was just that simple. As though we'd swum a few body-lengths underwater and emerged into the sunlight while everyone else dropped to the bottom like stones. It was nothing that we'd done, we were just dippers, the lucky winners of the immuno-golden ticket. Dippers were all the medical establishment talked about in the final days that a medical establishment existed. We held the promise of a cure, Icelandic doctors with long unpronounceable last names explained that several patients had dipped and survived, but almost immediately those doctors were dead themselves, and then the hordes were descending on the under-staffed emergency rooms, and it was no longer relevant whether the application of twenty-first-century medical science was the equal of the virus because we no longer lived in the twenty-first century. We might as well have thrown leeches at the problem, the mobs beyond triage, the hospital staff dying in the hallways and ready rooms.

The fever Penelope and I had endured, those were the last visions most people had: whatever they saw in their delirium was what escorted them to the grave. And the vast majority of the lucky few who came back from their hallucinations must have found reality to be even worse: they returned to this world to find that their spouse, their children had not been so lucky. When I thought about what that would have been like, finding Penelope's cold body in a pool of . . . It would have been better to die myself.

Hannah was still in the dorm, she was hungry and thinking of venturing out, the rooms along the hall had gone frighteningly silent. I wanted to help her come up with a plan, but Irvine could have been a planet circling a distant sun for all I knew of what was happening there. I hung on her every call, lived for them, and then one afternoon, I was outside and Penelope didn't even have to call my name, I just heard the terror in her voice and ran. My hip caught the edge of the sofa, throbbing as I lurched sideways the last few steps.

"You're not making sense!" Penelope was saying. She placed a palm over the phone before hissing at me, "She's got it, I know she does. *She's got it.*"

I could hear the warped babble of Hannah's voice. My breath was ragged from running and now from the panic surging uselessly in my blood.

"He's here," Hannah said. "He's come to visit me at school," her words slurring together, and I knew that my girl was seeing someone in her delirium, but I didn't know who, and then she said, "I gotta go," all in one word, *Igottago*, and we were crying into the phone *no no no* but there was only silence where her voice had been.

For a long day, I thought those were the last words I would hear my daughter say. We kept calling her back, so frequently that later she told us she'd thought her ringtone was a bird caught in her room, frantic to get out. She'd never bothered to set up a greeting on her voicemail, so we didn't even get to hear her voice, just a canned female robot reciting her number, again and again. Then the ringing stopped, straight to the recording, and we knew her phone had died. Penelope and I were broken, neither of us slept, even the most basic communication between us fragmented. A half hour could pass between a question and answer. We retreated, finally, into silence, huddled on opposite sides of the crater, the aftermath we would live with forever if we chose to live on at all.

And then the phone rang, and it was Hannah. She'd dipped.

Impossibly lucky. That's what we were. All around us, the world narrowed. Radically. The paper stopped arriving—whether that meant our driver was dead or the *New York Times* itself was dead, I did not know. The television stations stopped broadcasting. Was the president somewhere in a secure bunker, still leading the country? Maybe. How would I know? She no longer seemed relevant. I remembered years before when a twelve-hour ice storm in Atlanta sent it into brief barbarianism: fistfights and babies delivered on the highway. Lenin said every society is three meals away from chaos. That seemed to imply hordes in the streets, revolution, torches. What it actually meant was silence. It was October when the virus first emerged in Iceland, December when everything stopped. No one walking. No planes in the skies, no cars on the roads. No water from the taps, no power from the grid.

That the phones would die was the one thing I foresaw. For the most part, I muddled through the world as simply as a protozoan: sitting in one place until something jabbed me and I reacted. But I knew, I *knew*, as soon as Hannah recovered from her fever, that all the lines of communication were doomed, and so I swallowed my pride, my professionalism, my ethics, and ventured out to the home of a client. He was a science teacher in Hastings, and I knocked and knocked before I broke in, my chest clenched tight, waiting to find his body around a corner. There was no answer to my voice calling his name. And thank God, no corpse, no sign of anything beyond the empty abandoned house and his cat, wild and skinny, yowling to be released. I opened the door and it darted out like an arrow. If my client had died, he'd died elsewhere.

I took the ham radio that he'd told me about, session after session, in his on-the-spectrum sincerity—*I am an enthusiast*, he'd said earnestly, telling me just how far his rig could reach, the friendships he'd made across thousands of miles—loading it into the back of my Subaru along with his books explaining how to use the thing, his spools of wire, his little kit of connectors and doohickeys, all labeled and placed in a plastic bin with little dividers. His handwriting scrawled across each straight-edged piece of masking tape. I even climbed onto his roof to take his antenna.

So before the phones could die, I was able to give Hannah a frequency we would monitor, made her repeat it endlessly until I felt even her rebellious hippocampus wouldn't be able to forget. Only a couple of days after that, the ascending lines disappeared on our cell phones, replaced by NO SERVICE, and the landline went static, and when I thought of how close we'd been to losing contact with her forever, it made me sick. We would have spent the rest of our lives waiting for a knock on the door that would never come.

My little girl. I remembered when she first began going to kindergarten, when the realization that she had her own life apart from us filled me with pride and poignancy, and now the thought of her wandering the ruins of California alone would have torn me apart with emotion, except I was distracted, overwhelmed by the bare needs of survival. After a mild December in Dobbs Ferry, January brought *cold*. How cold, I didn't know. We didn't have a thermometer. Who did? We had phones that usually told us the temperature, but those phones were now useless bricks. Cold enough, suffice it to say, that many dippers must have survived the virus only to freeze to death.

Modern life was built on redundancies—we preached to our children that mistakes were just opportunities for learning. Now a mistake could kill you. I hadn't reached out to our heating oil company to arrange a delivery a week before they ceased to exist as a company. They just came because our tank was running low and we were on the schedule. So the fact that we were topped off with as much oil as we were going to ever have was a crowning piece of luck. Maybe it was why we survived. I set the thermostat to forty-five degrees and we dragged our mattress down to the living room in front of the open fireplace.

With the money Penelope had made over the years, we could have moved to a palatial home, one we never could have heated after the apocalypse, but we'd always felt attached to this modest Tudor on a tree-lined side street, unremarkable, not much in the way of styling, no dark wood beams or artfully unstuccoed patches of brick. Just plain off-white walls, a steep roof punctured by a brick chimney, and one bay window for a grace note. But it was ours, we'd bought it when I was still a grad student in psychology and Penelope was pregnant and working at Merrill Lynch. The only house Hannah ever knew, her home, perhaps why we'd never moved. She had her own room across the hall from ours (though she'd shared our bed for years as a child). Downstairs, the kitchen wasn't large, but we all found ourselves there at day's end, Penelope leaning against the refrigerator with a glass of white wine as I chopped carrots and onions and Hannah perched on the counter, ankles twined, her conversation growing and deepening as the years passed by, her childhood passing too fast, a flicker of years I could barely remember, so that even now, I found myself plugging in my otherwise-useless cell phone, just to page through old pictures of our daughter.

It was a good house, a sweet-souled house. If it had been able to speak, it would have said *Come on in, put your feet up.* That winter, it tried to adjust, to give us what we needed. Sure, the faucets might have gone dry, but giant buckets under the drainpipes outside could collect snow and meltwater from the roof. Penelope's fund had been on Tesla early, riding the stock skyward, and we'd gotten one of the first Powerwalls, the roof's southern exposure obliging for solar. So now, even in the strange new world, we had juice for the furnace and the radio, whose antenna I'd crawled onto the roof to install. The lights we left off, relying on candles instead. No need to advertise our luck to anyone who might be out on the prowl, looking for something better and willing to do God-knows-what to get it.

The house did all it could for us. The kitchen stove was gas, not electric, so when the gas stopped flowing, we started cooking where we slept, in the living room before the fire, canned food warming in a pot, slices of Spam spattering in a cast-iron skillet over the embers. We were still human beings, after all: the coffee must be made.

Which meant the coffee must be found. I crept out to the grocery store to plunder the shelves, what once would have been called looting but became a government recommendation before the government disappeared, though they called it Existing Resource Management— when there is no one to take your money at a grocery store, do what comes naturally. And when there is nothing in the grocery store, there may be accessible stockpiles in Formerly Occupied Homes. (Of course, when Black people tried to Manage Existing Resources, it was still called looting, so Penelope let me do the honors.)

Every trip was fraught, trembling, a T-shirt wrapped around my face, sweatshirts piled on under my coat, because if the chill gripped me, it might never let go. Luckily, there wasn't much snow, just brittle cold, so I could rattle a shopping cart along the pavement, the AR-15 we named Arnold, though it didn't merit a person's pronouns—*it* was an *it*—poking out from the basket like a roll of wrapping paper. I had no ammunition; Arnold was just for show. I wasn't trying to steal from anyone, and even entering an obviously empty house took everything I had. There was the fear of what I would find, and even worse, the moral injury as I walked through someone's life, past their photos on the wall, past the toys in the corner, to steal from their pantry. One thing about the apocalypse: there was plenty of food. Canned, dried, boxed. Who was left to eat it?

I say that, but the shocking thing about the end of the world was how many of us were left to see it. Just in Dobbs Ferry, there had to be hundreds. You would walk down the street on your real-life scavenger hunt and see movement in a window, although in the cold dark days before it became clear that the virus was gone, people were still so afraid of contagion that actual human contact seemed wildly reckless.

In every dystopian nightmare story I'd ever read, the world immediately seemed to crawl with sadistic, sociopathic warlords, as though they'd been sitting in caves, waiting for this moment, passing the time wrapping baseball bats in barbed wire until they could descend into violent chaos. I could speak for only Dobbs Ferry, our sleepy suburb in Westchester County, but this vision seemed to be bullshit. The virus didn't care if you were a prepper. It left behind a perfect cross section of society: children and the elderly, men and women and, Hannah would be quick to remind me, nonbinary and trans people too. Most terrified, lonely, and suffering through an unimaginable trauma. Were people hungry, cold, tired? Sure. Was there violence? Sure. Was human nature ugly sometime? Yes. But there was also loneliness, boredom, love.

I'd be rummaging through the bare ruined choir of the Stop & Shop, earplugs shoved into my nostrils to muffle the stench of the meat and fish rotting behind their counters, when a noise would alert me that I wasn't alone. Someone was in the cereal aisle, doing the same thing I was, and when we pushed our carts around a corner and encountered one another, we kept our distance, hands held up in greeting, but I also wanted to stride over and pull them in for a hug, the desire for human connection was so tangible.

The skin on my fingers and knuckles cracked from the dry cold, so I stained my gloves, my clothes red without realizing I was bleeding. When I rummaged through the pharmacy at the supermarket, the Band-Aids and antibiotic cream I needed were some of the only things left. The pills were gone. At the same moment that life became wildly difficult, for many it also probably lost its meaning.

The tasks I had to accomplish were a gift, searching for food, raiding the woodpiles stacked by our vanished neighbors, taking care of my wife. You have to understand, the end of the world was particularly difficult for Penelope. I was equipped, somehow, for the long hours of rumination, the emptiness. All through my youth, I wandered through school like it was a dream. Not drunk or rebellious, just . . . distracted. The grades I received always came as a surprise, good or bad, a thing that happened to me rather than something I'd worked to achieve. Where was I? Somewhere else, drifting along. If I'd never met Penelope, I probably would have achieved what seemed to me the stubbornly bland existence my sister had found in Oklahoma with her husband. She and I were mildly estranged, spoke once a year, dutifully and awkwardly. I hadn't seen her in a decade, and now, if she was alive, I would probably never see her again.

Penelope was a marvel, a perpetual motion machine. When she was twelve, she filled out the paperwork for Prep for Prep in secret. Her parents didn't trust the idea of a White private school, so Penelope fought her way to Horace Mann on her own, and when she was there, she fought her way to Amherst, and to Merrill Lynch after that. When I met her at a party, we were both sophomores, but I was stumbling through classes at UMass I might as well have selected with a dartboard. Let me be clear, she never applied pressure, she didn't care what classes I took, what I did. That was up to me. But meeting her was like throwing open the sash of a window I hadn't realized was closed. I became a psychology major, found myself applying to graduate school.

Years later, when I was studying for my licensure exam, I explained my strategy: a 71 was the same as a 100, all you had to do was pass, and my goal was that 71. Any studying I did beyond that was lost time, useless. I rolled over, half asleep, thinking what I'd said was so obvious that she must be nodding. Something in the silence made me open my eyes and turn back. One eyebrow was raised, her eyes saying I was a stranger in her bed, and then she gave me a little smile and said, "There it is," and turned away to sleep. That was our private joke, what she said when I was having a White male privilege moment.

Her strategy was frontal assault, overwhelm the opposition. Just our morning routines told the story: I could shuffle out of bed, shower, or even forgo it, pull on a blazer, and there I was: charmingly rumpled White middle-aged male psychologist. She was up at five, her makeup alone took forty-five minutes, and it wasn't vanity. It was survival. What did the world think of a Black woman who stumbled into work, hair untouched? Her opportunities came because she'd given them no option but to come. In the face of her intellect, her preparation, her *will*, White people gradually lost the skepticism in their eyes, the skepticism they would have denied vociferously if brought to their attention. In its place, like a magic trick, she got to see the dynamic flipped: clearly she was the product of affirmative action. The color of her skin was not a hurdle, but the very reason she'd managed to get where she was. Or, perhaps worse, their eyes glowed with self-congratulation. *Look how good I am to be collegial with this Black lady. But, of course, I don't see color. That said, would you mind if the photographer we brought in to shoot for the website gets some shots of you with a client?*

Penelope worked until she broke, the breaking a reality she successfully hid from everyone but her family. She didn't vacation so much as collapse, Hannah and I running down from our rental to the beach, towels waving like flags behind us, while Penelope lay in bed, watching television, maybe reading a book, maybe just staring. She slept for hours during the day, then began yawning before we'd finished dinner.

Now, in the January cold, that collapse came in earnest. The sudden meaninglessness of little colored paper wasn't the problem. We lived simply relative to her financial peers, paid off our mortgage early, filled up our 401(k) and investments. She didn't really care about what money could buy. What she cared about was *purpose.* When Merrill felt too mercenary, she'd gone out on her own, found like-minded women of color, started a fund with a social-justice slant, worked twice as hard. She volunteered. She did a TED Talk on race and personal finance.

Money wasn't spending power, it was a voice. And then money ceased to exist. The young women she mentored were dead. A few years before, her mother had died of COVID-19—horrifyingly, Penelope hadn't been allowed to see her before she passed, saying goodbye via iPad instead—and all her remaining unprocessed grief now emerged as though from hiding. She disappeared. Not literally. She was there, on the mattress by the fireplace, but days went by when she couldn't be roused. I sat with her, my hand's pressure endlessly circling her back. I braided her hair, something I hadn't done since she taught me in college. I made what food I could find, brought it to her, rejoiced if I could get her to take a bite or two. The sun's angle worked through the room like a protractor as the days rose and fell.

She dropped from our shared life like a stone into water. She could barely speak, ate only when I insisted, could stare drowning at the wall for hours. Sometimes I could see her there, wavering on the bottom, and sometimes the light broke off the surface and she was just gone, in a different world. There was nothing for her to do, and all her life, she'd *done something.* If I was from Venus, wanting to slow things down, talk it through, think about our feelings, she was a Martian: onward into the fight. I understood, I tried not to judge; we all had to survive the apocalypse in our own way. But I was so terribly alone.

And then Hannah brought us back together, though not in the way that either of us wanted. The days were blurring together into a miasma of cold and silence. Perhaps it was late February? All the ways I'd marked time—the Knicks schedule, reading the paper, scrolling through Twitter before climbing out of bed, thinking *How many clients do I have today?*—all of them were gone, leaving behind only one: the planning of meals. But instead of parsing what ingredients a recipe demanded I pick up on the way home, I was evaluating a dent in a can of soup, wondering if it meant botulism. That would have been the savage punch line to a civilization-ending joke: to survive the virus and the winter, only to kill ourselves with Campbell's Chunky Clam Chowder.

I was deciding to go for it when there was a crackling hiss and then Hannah's voice was speaking in the kitchen, as though she'd arrived home from school and was already raiding the fridge. Penelope was up and halfway there before I could move. The radio had worked! I was weeping, overwhelmed. When the clamor of our greetings died down, Hannah told us that she'd gone with her friend Angie—*You remember Angie, right?*—north to Bishop on the eastern side of the Sierra Nevada mountains. *It's just impossibly beautiful up here*, she said. We didn't get a lot of details, but she gave us just enough about the horror of Irvine and Southern California that I could tell she was setting us up for what she said next: Angie had decided to join The Revival, and Hannah was thinking she might do the same.

She could have told me she was flying to Jupiter and I would have celebrated. Just to hear her voice. What did I *want* her to say? Obviously, that she had gotten her hands on a car and was halfway home, radioing in from St. Louis. But I would take this gratefully, and when Hannah said she had to go, when the radio went silent, I expected Penelope and me to be united by our shared relief and joy.

In retrospect, I should have seen it coming. As with most marriages, ours was both cemented and threatened by our child, our parenting. We loved Hannah beyond measure, a love that brought us closer together when she was swaddled and tiny, her lips pursing as she sucked in her sleep. When she grew up, that same love threatened to tear us apart. When Hannah began picking her own classes in high school, for example, some of her choices were idiosyncratic at best—she wanted to drop science junior year because it conflicted with ceramics—and my indulgence of her thought process felt to Penelope like an utter, almost criminal, abdication of my parental role. I thought I was just being realistic: she wasn't going to listen to us anyhow, our meddling was doomed to failure, but it went beyond that too. I trusted Hannah to make her own choices.

Trust or neglect? There was no way to know which one of us was right other than to watch Hannah's life unfold and endlessly parse our influence on it.

Relationships were hard, marriages were hard. I had this conversation with clients in my office a thousand times. But the truth was that my own marriage had always felt relatively easy. We fought, of course, but our seismometer for conflict was calibrated finely. Couples we knew had screaming matches, threw pots and pans, would have risked arrest had they not lived in the privileged embrace of million-dollar homes. We were so attuned to one another that a raised voice or narrowed gaze was enough.

My role in our marriage was accommodation. Penelope charged forward, and I traveled in her wake, borne along by her energy and drive. It was a gift, she'd never stopped surprising me, until Hannah began to grow up and this essential disagreement emerged, this grit caught in the oiled mechanism of our marriage, heating it up, threatening that it could blow. They were dangerously similar, mother and daughter, both forever on quests the other saw as illegitimate. When I tried to point this out, they united in a shared refusal to be psychologized by me.

Now, even after civilization had fallen, the scar tissue from our old fights was revealed instead to be a scab, torn free, fresh blood welling beneath. I couldn't understand why Penelope was so upset about The Revival. I mean, my God, Hannah was alive. Shouldn't we be celebrating that? The truth was that I thought I did understand, but when I suggested to Penelope that being upset about our daughter's decisions might just have been her way of finding some normalcy in the wake of apocalypse . . . Well, I learned not to say that again.

Penelope was up from her hibernation, animated not by love for me or a newfound commitment to life, but by utter bafflement at the choices made by her family: What the hell was Hannah thinking? What the hell was I thinking? She could draw a direct line from my appeasement of Hannah's poor decision-making all the way from childhood to this very moment, though whether she said that explicitly, I couldn't remember. All I know is that it felt titanically unfair, and soon we weren't fighting about The Revival at all—we were fighting through ancient arguments resurrected like zombies, lurching through our home and trying to eat our brains.

What was The Revival anyway? I tore through a stack of old *New Yorkers*, looking for the article I'd read about the rise of cults in the post-Trump years. Or had it been the *Times* magazine? It took me two days, but I finally found it in a year-old copy of *The Atlantic* in the abandoned town library.

Their philosophy seemed relatively simple: the problem of modern life is *choice*, coupled with the relentless veneration of the self. The answer to the problem is erasure. Be not the fish but the school, be not the bird but the flock. The sense of commitment to something larger than you. You sacrificed your individuality and in return were given a group identity. I understood the appeal, in a way: hadn't monks and nuns been doing this for centuries? Millennia? But the writer of the article pointed out the essential difference, the thing that the Catholic Church had figured out: cloistering people only worked if you forbade them from having sex with one another. Whatever the intent of The Revival, they seemed to be already devolving into what most cults became: machines for the subjugation of women. A member of The Revival gave his or her body to God, and, conveniently for the male Revival leaders, God wanted those bodies to procreate. The beautiful and refreshing simplicity of sacrificing one's self remained beautiful and refreshing only when expressed and understood in abstract philosophical terms. But nobody lives in abstractions, and when the fracture between theory and practice becomes irresolvable, out comes the Kool-Aid.

The person dishing out the Kool-Aid, the leader and patient zero of The Revival, had all the classic cult leader symptoms: the charisma, the false humility, the messianic insanity. He called himself The Nameless One. It was too perfect, the ultimate humblebrag. He wasn't really nameless. He was *The* Nameless *One*, there was only one, could be only one, and he was *it*. Just meeting him through the type on the page, my hands wanted to throttle him.

I had wanted the article to be reassuring. That was why I'd spent hours rummaging through yellowing magazines, so I could bring something home to Penelope and say, *See? It's going to be fine*. But then I found the real horror: The Revival took seriously and literally the words of Jesus when he said, "If you come to me but will not leave your family, you cannot be my follower." They required a clean break, had developed their own patter for the final conversation between the convert and his or her family of origin, patter I tried to tell myself we would never hear because Hannah was too smart to fall for any of it.

I felt committed to my role in the argument, which didn't leave much room for my own surging worries about The Revival, but it didn't matter in the end. I had been right all along. After two weeks of Penelope and me living like strangers in the house, bound together only by our shared need to survive, Hannah's voice called to us again from the kitchen. Penelope came running down from upstairs, where she'd been spending much of her time despite the chill.

Angie had gone all the way. "I can't even call her Angie anymore," Hannah told us. Her new name was something that sounded like *Eggnog* over the radio, and it wasn't until days later as I shuffled my shopping cart along that I realized they just reversed people's names. Hannah's skepticism was alive and well, we could hear *that* clearly.

"Get out of there," Penelope said. "You have to get away from them."

"You know they're the only reason we're talking, right?" Hannah said. "You guys gave me this radio frequency, but, like, who has a *radio*? It's not like I can swing by the radio store. The Revival has one so the flocks or whatever can communicate with each other."

She'd found a spot to crash just outside Bishop, some house she called *Revival-adjacent*, whatever that meant. We worried too much, she'd be in touch when she could, and oh God you should see what these Revival people *wear*.

In the end, we had to settle for skepticism over distance. We had to trust Hannah, which was the same place we'd always been in. Penelope and I could argue, our voices could empty of things to say, and all along Hannah would simply do what she was going to do anyway.

Her transmissions were infrequent, and in between Penelope dropped back into silence, as though each spasm of anger was the body's twitch before it fell asleep. We never got to reconcile, she disappeared even more deeply into herself, and the winter was unrelenting, the chill driven by the wind, and the flurries that spun over the frozen ground.

Weeks passed, and then the cold began to lift, and birds to sing, and on the first sixty-degree day, I opened the windows, but with the heat, the smell began to rise from the Carlson house down the block, sticking in my nostrils, an odor as nauseating as it was horrifying in its implications. They'd never been popular, leaving their minivan on the street instead of the driveway, which was scattered with kids' bikes and scooters, a drooping rim and backboard. A trampoline competed for yard space with an inflatable Santa or skeleton or turkey, depending on the season. In the summer, they shot fireworks off their back deck, as though willfully defying the fastidious norms of our neighborhood. One summer, an *aboveground* pool appeared. Cue whispered conversations and shaking heads as people with better, WASPier taste power walked past the house.

They almost made it through the virus, the Carlsons, hunkered down all together, the parents, all the kids, the grandparents too, I think, maybe even an aunt or uncle in the mix. I'd seen them in the windows, the bustle of movement, an occasional child's face pressed up against the glass. They made it long enough that when they all fell ill and died, the people who were supposed to clean up the dead were dead themselves. If the Carlsons lost just one child in normal times, the whole neighborhood would have drawn them into an embrace, their pain would have been the subject of hushed conversations in every kitchen on the block. Now their monumental tragedy was just an unheard cry added to the wild noise, though when I allowed myself to think about what it must have been like in that crammed house as the virus struck, I lost my balance, the horror of it, I was too light-headed to move.

But the sun came up, the weather turned. Spring. I stepped out the door into the first truly warm day, strode down the driveway. I stretched. Looked around, as though I were pondering mowing the lawn. Maybe a barbecue later. Crocuses were breaching the ground, the forsythia blooming yellow on the hedges. Robins hopped through the grass, and a timid bunny crouched on the lawn across the street. These were the strange moments, the waking-from-a-nightmare moments, when feeling trembled in the phantom limb of our previous lives. Like Penelope talking in her sleep, scheduling something, even in our postcalendar world: *Tuesday's no good*, she'd say into the darkness. *Let's try next week.* And though she'd woken me with her voice, though sleep grew a more vanishing target each year, I swelled with love for her, reached out to rub the small of her back. *What is it?* she would ask. *Nothing*, I would say. *You were talking in your sleep.* And she'd settle herself deeper into the blankets and ask, *What was I saying?* but she was asleep again before I could answer. The embers glowed in the fireplace, and her breathing settled deep, and the world felt whole.

Taste could do it too, summon a whole lost existence. I'd go out to Manage Existing Resources and find, say, boxes of organic butternut squash soup. Warmed over the fire, the first closed-eye spoonful could make you weep.

The birds sang, a squirrel leapt from the roof onto the drooping branches of a tree, which dropped but held his scampering weight, the cloudless sky's blue lightened as the sun rose higher, and a door opened in the cottage a few doors down. Carlos stepped out onto the stoop. His hands were in the front pockets of his jeans, his shoulders heavy. I found myself waving, and we stood for a long moment, staring from half a block away. I'd seen him going out for supplies, alone, after his wife died. I'd seen the candlelight flickering in his windows.

He slouched down the steps and out into the street.

"Hey Bill."

"Hey Carlos."

He was standing fifteen feet away from me when he asked, "You guys dip?"

"Yeah, we dipped."

"You?" I asked. He nodded, and walked the last few steps up to me. We stood side by side, looking at the neighborhood, the hillside beyond, bristling with trees, still bare but with green buds to promise leaves soon.

"I'm sorry about Jen," I said, and he nodded.

"Thank you."

"How are you holding up?"

"Good, good," he said.

I didn't say anything. With the failure of water to flow from our showers and taps, self-care had gotten harder, just when it also felt meaningless. I could smell him, and was suddenly aware that he must have been able to smell me too.

"I'll hear her say something," he said. "And when I'm half asleep, I keep reaching for her, and then I realize all over again that she's gone."

"I'm so sorry."

"I don't sleep much, I guess. It's too cold anyway." He looked back at his house. "And there's too many memories in there."

We both turned at the sound of a car downshifting out on Broadway, the squeal of tires. A red Maserati skidded onto our street and lurched to a halt in Al's driveway.

"Of all the people to survive the apocalypse," Carlos said.

The trunk popped, and Al climbed out of the driver's seat. He pulled a golf bag out onto the driveway. He saw us and paused, staring, then darted inside.

"I guess he's not feeling neighborly," I said.

A few seconds later, he emerged, carrying something. When he was halfway to us, I made it out. A six-pack.

"Usually I'm a Coors guy," he said when he got close, "but it's still beer."

He tossed cans in sun-glinting arcs toward us. Carlos caught his, smothering it against his body, but I just jumped out of the way. The can popped when it hit the asphalt, a jet of beer and foam spraying as it rolled away from us.

"What the fuck, man!" Al said. "They ain't making any more of that!"

"Should we be doing this?" I said. "The virus . . ."

"What about it? You seen anybody sick lately?" He held a beer out toward me, but I still hesitated.

"I haven't seen anybody period," I said.

He nodded. "Yeah, well, I been driving around, I talk to people. I think that shit is gone. It did what it came to do. And that's it, man."

"I don't know," I said.

Carlos cracked open his beer and took a long swallow. "Fuck it," he said. "We all dipped. Anybody who's still alive dipped."

I'd never been one of those guys who played golf to get away from his wife. Penelope was the sun at the center of my orbit, but I did have my poker buddies, a friend I ran with on occasion, fellow psychologists I would join for a drink some evenings. They were dead, or gone, my world had collapsed into the gravity of my family, and there was suddenly nothing I wanted more than to be a guy having a beer with other guys, and I grabbed one from Al and drained half of it in a single pull.

"Sorry it's warm," he said.

"It's great," I said. "Thanks." Warm Budweiser was a pretty good substitute for piss, but the birds were shining, the sun was singing, and I stretched tall, my shoulders rolling back. I'd been hunched over for a long time. Carlos held his can up. Cheers.

"New car?" I asked Al.

"Hell yeah. I'm riding in style now," he said.

"Where are you coming from?"

"Winged Foot."

"Seriously?"

He ripped a belch that sounded like a chain saw.

"First warm day, I always play golf. I got halfway to Dunwoodie when I said *What the fuck are you doing?* Drove to Winged Foot, parked right in front of the clubhouse, played eighteen."

"How was it?"

"Fucking great. Virus took out all the elitist pricks, and now I get to play in their little paradise." He drained the last of his beer, twist-flattened the can, hurled it at the rabbit still nose-twitching in the grass across the street. We all stood silently. I took another swallow. Al opened another, then tears formed at the corners of his eyes. Carlos and I stared at him.

"I don't know," he said. "It was kind of depressing actually. I only played nine." He laughed nervously, then cleared his throat, shook his head, and drained half a beer. "Ahh, the course has gone to shit anyway."

The breeze shifted, and his nose twitched. "What the fuck is that smell?"

"The Carlsons' house," I said. "I think it's coming from there."

We all turned to look.

"You mean . . ." Al said, and then his voice petered out.

There was a long silence as we all stared at the darkened windows, the looming mute bulk of the house.

"We should do something," I said.

"I ain't going in there," Al said.

The house stared back at us.

Carlos broke the silence. "We should burn it," he said.

We both turned and looked at him. "Wait until a rainy day," he said. "To make sure the fire doesn't spread, jump to other houses."

"We can't just burn a house down," Al said.

"Why not?"

There wasn't an answer. And so when it rained the very next day, it seemed like a sign. We met outside, Al and I in raincoats. Carlos had an umbrella.

"Can we siphon some gas from your car?" Carlos asked.

"I'll do you one better," Al said. We walked to his garage, and he came out with a big plastic gas container that must have held five gallons. "You know Timmy, works at the Mobil station? He cracked open the underground tank. And he emptied the minimart and brought it all home. Fucker's got Cheetos for years. Now Timmy's the richest guy in town. Who would have thought."

We filled smaller buckets with gas, my eyes watering at the smell, and carried them carefully down the street. The rain was cold, raw, and I thought about Penelope still curled on the mattress, staring into the fire.

Carlos, Al, and I stood on the street in front of the Carlsons'. An inflatable reindeer lay like a russet smear on the leaf-strewn green of the lawn. The trampoline canted to the side, one leg broken. That close, even in the cold rain, we could smell the house.

"Walk the perimeter," Carlos said. "Try to slosh it onto the wood and not just the foundation."

Al and I set out in opposite directions and we met in the back, by their porch. When we got to the front, Carlos was on the stoop. He had wrapped a T-shirt around his nose and mouth, and he broke the glass, reached in, and turned the knob. The door swung open like a mouth. He stood for a second, framed by it, then swung his bucket from behind and tossed it in, the gasoline splashing in a long arc.

He walked back to us.

"Did you"—Al paused—"see anything in there?"

Carlos shook his head. We all stared at the house.

"Who wants to do the honors?" he asked.

"I can do it," I said.

"Shouldn't we say something?" Al asked.

Carlos spoke in Spanish, so quickly I couldn't follow any of it until he hit the last word. "Amén."

"You don't need to light inside," he said. "I think it'll catch."

"Okay," I said. "Here goes nothing." I had the stick lighter that I was using to start our fires in the hearth, and it felt slippery in my hand as I walked. I held it up to the house and nothing seemed to happen, a long pause, and then sudden long flames were licking up the siding in an iridescent swirl. Absurd panic surged in me. There was no way to undo what I'd just done, the smoke was rising into the rain now, I could feel the heat against my body. My breath raced, and I backed away, found myself next to Carlos and Al on the street. We stood and watched, moving farther back as the smoke boiled upward, black now, and I thought about the Carlson children, all five of them, five, had there really been five? They'd become a single mass at some point, riding their bikes down the street like fighter pilots in formation, launching water balloons at passing cars, fighting on the lawn in a swarm of shouting arms and legs.

We'd retreated all the way across the street when the gas inside caught with a smothered explosion, the glass shattering in the windows, and flames breaking through the roof. And we watched, though it was cold, and the water had broken the will of my raincoat, until the roof fell into the second floor, which fell into the first, and the blackened beams reached like arms out of the smoking rubble, hissing in the rain, and now the smell was no better than before, but it was different, and the Carlsons had been laid to rest, cremated like the rest of the infected, and every time it rained in the coming months, the stink of ruined wood ash would return like tinnitus you could forget for a time, then catch again, a high-pitch squealing in the ear that would last forever.

We walked back to our separate homes without a word, even Al.

If the world had ended with a meteor strike, we would have seen wondrous things as we died—the tidal wave, the rain of fire, a pestilential sky. T. S. Eliot was right, though. Not with a bang, but a whimper. Blood should have plummeted from the clouds, the sky should have torn asunder, the sun disappeared in perpetual eclipse. Instead, it rose every morning as if nothing had happened, just another day. The differences were strange: a red fox trotted down our street in plain view, braving the packs of dogs that had formed in town, still collared, but feral now, hunting in strange packs of labradoodles and mutts and golden retrievers and an occasional bulldog huffing along behind.

Summer came. I hoped it would jolt Penelope from her hibernation, and it did, to a degree. She'd help tend the garden, sweep the house, but there were still days that stretched into one another where she could barely get herself upright. And even when she was moving, she was distracted, her responses to my questions coming late, if she heard them at all.

It was only when autumn began to chill the air and we had a mission, after Hannah radioed to recite the terrible Revival patter, that Penelope came back from wherever she had gone, acting as though she'd never left, as though the months in between had passed in an eyeblink, and I hated the resentment that swamped me in response. The more loving she was now, planning our drive, cooking, holding me tight, wanting to have sex for the first time in I couldn't remember how long, the angrier I felt, but there was no room for talking. She was a whirlwind. We were going to leave everything behind to save our daughter, even if she didn't want to be saved, even if making it across the country seemed like launching an arrow into the sky and hoping it hit a target beyond the horizon. The more that Penelope willed this outcome into being, the more I felt myself collapsing into doubt, as though her rise caused my fall. I felt hopelessness descend like a cloud. How could we possibly rescue Hannah in *California?* We hadn't left our *town* in months. And hadn't she already cut herself off from us as the cult demanded?

And yet, when I stared into the fire as Penelope stirred baked beans for our dinner, all I could hear was the voice that had escaped at the very end of Hannah's transmission, so young, our daughter's voice breaking through the brainwashing and the drugs, whatever she'd gotten herself into.

I love you guys.

CHAPTER 2

Hannah's voice over the radio tearing our life from its moorings and setting us off on our journey came on a Tuesday in September, a fact I knew because I'd spent the whole summer seeing clients again. After the long dateless winter, calendars were once again relevant. It sounds absurd, but it turned out nothing demanded a therapeutic response more than apocalypse. I'd always idly assumed that therapy lived at the peak of Maslow's Hierarchy of Needs, a final stage of civilization, but I'd been wrong: it was actually down at the bottom, in the mess, with food and water and breath. It was human connection, without which what was the point?

For years before Shark Flu, I'd begun to stagnate, my practice a subway turnstile of intake, treatment, termination, twenty years in the same space, the dust gathering in the corners, how many boxes of Kleenex? I bought crates of them at Costco. When Hannah was young and I was just starting on my own, the first clients who ventured up the stairs almost brought me to tears, just the idea that they would entrust me with their secrets, their anxieties, their fears, their inner worlds. Eventually, like a marriage tiring, the sessions felt like endless iterations of the same formula, and I began to wonder if the entire therapeutic constellation was doomed by solipsism. Penelope had always been the breadwinner anyway, my practice almost cute compared to what she brought home. I thought about giving it all up, but the idea of hobbies filled me with existential despair. I golfed occasionally (never with Al), meant to run more than I did, liked to cook when the spirit moved, knew gardening required a daily commitment that I would only maintain for a week. Was this a midlife crisis? I had already turned fifty and could have bought a sports car, but didn't see the point. I stared at the remaining decades of my life with jealous dread. I would fight like hell to have every day on the planet that I could, and I had no earthly idea how I would fill those days.

I never had the balls to try something new. When the virus came, I still had a full caseload, twenty-eight people, and the post-doc I supervised in my practice flew back home to Wisconsin before they grounded the planes, leaving her clients to me as well. During COVID, I'd done all my appointments via telehealth in my office, but now even walking downtown seemed too dangerous, so I spent the early weeks of the national quarantine upstairs in Hannah's room, pulling down her posters to make a white wall behind me for Zoom after Zoom, with phone calls in between. Penelope said *You have to stop. You have to take care of yourself.* She was frantic too, the two of us trapped in the house. And then, horrifyingly, the calls slowed, no one picked up when I opened the video session. My caseload dropped from fifty to twenty-five, from twenty-five to ten, before the Internet and electricity failed. Were the rest of my clients dead? Were some just hiding, afraid to come out? Or were they sitting numb in the crater left behind by loss?

I knew how hard life could be, the inequity inherent in Fate or chance. Even before Shark Flu arrived, the virus too small for any of us to actually *see*, my clients battled invisible enemies, obsessive-compulsive disorder that forced them into endless handwashing, depressive thinking that told them, on a loop, of their own worthlessness, panic attacks that sent them to the emergency room. Now public health had caught up to the inner nightmares—it all came true. I used to spend my days doing exposures: let's talk about spiders, then maybe look at a photograph or two, and then eventually, *Do you want to look at this spider I found in my house?* I drove to the airport to watch planes taking off with a client, to sit by a gate as though we were readying to board, focusing on our breath. I walked people down the street to the coffee shop where we touched all the door knobs, then ate a croissant without washing our hands first, just to show them that nothing terrible would happen. Now, the coffee shop was gone, along with the planes. The spiders were still around. The spiders were thriving. The end of the world was stressful for anyone, but the clinically anxious? All the mindfulness techniques I'd taught seemed irrelevant—how could I caution against catastrophizing in the midst of catastrophe? All I could do now was listen, absorb the pain, show people they were not alone.

All winter, as society fell, my practice lay dormant. I thought it was dead, but it sprouted again in the spring, like the first green knuckles breaking the flower beds' soil. And it began in the most surprising way.

I was out Managing Existing Resources, lost in thought, when a police car came up behind me like it was doing a traffic stop on my shopping cart. The blue lights strobed the world around me, and I jumped, then Jimmy's voice came over the loudspeaker.

"Bill, I need you to put your gun on the ground and step away from it please."

"Is this not okay?" I called out. "I thought everyone was doing this now."

Very slowly, I took Arnold out of the shopping cart and placed it on the pavement. I stepped back, and Jimmy got out of his car.

He looked awful, his face puffy and red, eyes bloodshot. "Hey Bill," he said. "Could you please come with me back to the cruiser?"

"Did I do something wrong? I don't even have bullets for it, actually. It's just for show."

He just sat down in the driver's seat. I'd known Jimmy for years—he picked up Hannah once when she was smoking weed in the park with her friends, and instead of arresting or citing her, he brought her by the house with a warning. "I figured," he said to Penelope, "you could probably figure out a better lesson to teach her than I could."

"You figured correctly," she said, although we both knew that Hannah would absorb however many phone-less days we threw at her without it penetrating her armor of stubbornness.

Now I was scared, though, climbing into the backseat of the cruiser. Jimmy turned halfway around and looked at me. His nostrils were flaring with each breath and his eyes were wild. If I ran, I didn't know how far I could make it. The vinyl seat creaked as my weight shifted.

"I don't know how this works," he said.

"How what works?"

"This is, like, confidential, right? What we talk about?"

"What do you mean?"

"When I talk to you. This. Whatever you call it."

"A session? You want to have a session with me?" I almost laughed out of relief, but his face kept me quiet.

"Yeah."

"I mean, sure." I smiled. "I'm not sure who I would tell."

He just looked at me.

"Tell me what's going on," I said.

He seemed to lose his voice. When he finally spoke, I had to lean forward to hear him.

"My mom and my sister went to take care of my grandma in P.R.

35

right before everything fell apart. I haven't heard from any of them in months."

"That's hard."

He nodded.

"Not knowing can be so difficult."

He nodded again, then started crying. "I shot somebody," he said. "It wasn't my fault. I don't know. Maybe it was my fault."

"Oh," I said. "Jesus." Fencing off my own feelings to keep them from trampling the therapeutic space was so ingrained that he couldn't notice how I shrunk into my seat, how he'd hit one of my deepest fears. I'd suffered a recurring dream since I was a child: I seemed to have killed someone. How, I wasn't sure. The dream was the aftermath, the pure, hopeless desperation of searching for the person alive, just so I could know I hadn't killed them.

Then a girl in my high school class killed a man walking on the roadside just weeks after getting her driver's license. She came back to school after being cleared of any charges, walking the hallways like an untouchable ghost. I didn't want to stare at her, but I couldn't stop. She had crossed over the river, a living embodiment of the dream.

Jimmy was a cop and he'd shot someone. I could feel myself pulling away from him. The endless parade of headlines flashed through my head, photograph after photograph of police officers who'd shot people for running away, for talking on a cell phone, for reaching for a wallet, and Jimmy's face could bleed into theirs, I could feel the way I looked at him changing, but also I was here in his car, a therapist talking to a man in crisis, the tears breaking from his eyes, his face dirty enough that each one left a line down his cheeks.

"He was White," Jimmy said abruptly. He could feel my reaction.

"Okay," I said. I tried to breathe. I tried not to lean away.

"You heard about the sexual assaults in Hastings?"

"I did, actually." A client had told me about them, her face filling the Zoom screen on my computer just days before Zoom ceased to be. The virus wasn't the only reason she was afraid to leave the house. There were people taking advantage of the chaos to do terrible things.

"I increased night patrols in response . . ."

"You were patrolling all winter?" I interrupted.

"Someone has to, right?" It was the kind of thing people said to brush off a question, but his eyes were serious. He was really asking me.

"Yes, that's right. I'm grateful that you're doing it."

He nodded, and when he continued, the tempo of his voice changed, staccato.

"The alleged perpetrator was a White male, twenties, wearing a dark hoody. At 22:30, I was patrolling Clinton Avenue when I encountered a person matching the description leaving a house. I exited the cruiser, identified myself as a police officer, and called out for him to stop where he was and raise his hands. I hit him with the spotlight. He turned, at which point I saw that the suspect was armed with a shotgun. I instructed him to drop his weapon. But he didn't."

"Did he, the person you shot, did he make it?"

"Oh no. He's dead. That's for damn sure. I didn't flinch. Three shots to the center of mass. And he *dropped.*"

Silence filled the cruiser. I felt the gears slowly shifting into motion in my head.

"You served in Afghanistan, right?" I found myself asking.

He could see where I was headed with that. "I just fixed Humvees," he said, and now he was sobbing. I climbed out and sat in the passenger seat next to him. When his breathing slowed, I spoke.

"Taking a life is a profound act," I said. "I'm glad you're talking about it. You don't want to keep that inside. Even when it's done in the line of duty, or in self-defense, it's a reckoning, and you have to work through it."

I could see him swallow. "If I discharge my weapon, I'm supposed to get therapy, to go on paid leave. But there's nobody left. It's just me. And when I tried to talk to this state cop I know, he laughed at me."

Speaking the last part, his voice dropped to a whisper. He looked at his hands.

"Why didn't he just drop the gun?" he asked.

"I don't know."

"He started to raise the gun, to point it at me. I didn't have a choice."

"Sounds like you didn't."

"Yeah." His fingernails were ragged, and he picked at them.

"What is it?"

His voice was so quiet I had to lean forward. "It all happened so fast. What if he didn't?"

"Didn't what?"

"Didn't raise the gun. What if I'm making it up. I'm so tired, and all I can think about is my sister and my mom, and I don't trust myself. What if he was innocent?"

"Well, he didn't drop the gun, right?"

"No."

"When you told me to put my gun on the ground, did I do it?"

"Yeah."

"He didn't."

"I don't know. I guess."

He was shivering, his knee chattering against the steering wheel. He was still wearing his uniform, dirty though it was. The lights were still on from when he pulled me over, the world outside pulsing in red and blue.

"Jimmy, I notice that you were using 'cop talk' when you told me the story," I said. "Why did you do that?"

"I don't know."

I didn't say anything more, just waited.

"It's how you're supposed to talk about it," he finally said.

"When?"

"What do you mean, when?"

"You probably don't talk about it that way in the locker room or at the bar," I said.

He laughed. "No. You don't want to know how we talk." He paused. "How we talked."

"It's the way you talk when you're on the record, talking to your superior, or filling out a report?"

"Yeah."

"Because you're a cop, and that's what cops do after they discharge their weapon in the line of duty."

"Yeah."

"There's supposed to be an order to this."

"Yeah."

"When you're a cop, you know you're putting your life in danger, right?"

He nodded.

"But almost as hard is that you're putting yourself in a position where you may have to take another human life."

I could see his Adam's apple pulse as he swallowed.

"I think you should fill out a report," I said.

"What do you mean?"

"Go down to the station and fill out whatever paperwork you're supposed to fill out after something like this."

"There's no one to read it."

"I know. But you're a cop. You're not just a guy on the street with a gun. And what do cops do when they have to discharge their weapon in the line of duty?"

"Yeah," he said. "I'm a cop."

"Fill out the report. That's all you have to do. Just fill it out. If you need to show it to somebody, you can show it to me."

Would he do it? I didn't know. It usually took many sessions to get someone to make a change, to start to incorporate some of my suggestions. But what did I know about dystopian psychology?

He offered me a ride home, but I gestured to my cart, and he nodded. The cruiser started to pull away, then he lowered the window and leaned over.

"I'll let you keep the gun," he said. "But do me a favor and leave it at home, will you?"

"Sure thing." I didn't know why I was taking it along anyway. It just seemed like what people were doing.

Jimmy's last words before I got out of the car were to ask how he could pay me. I told him he already had, that I felt honored he'd been willing to talk to me, and I wasn't just blowing smoke.

I was so deep in thought walking home that I didn't see Penelope sitting on the stoop in the sun until I was turning up the walk.

"Hey," I said. "It's good to see you outside!"

She smiled, a little distracted smile, but a smile, and nodded to the cart.

"Not much luck?" she said.

"Well . . ." I took the paper bag from the cart and emptied it onto the flagstones. "If we're patient . . ." Seed packets piled on top of one another, scattered, the luscious photos on each blending into a confusion of squash and tomatoes and corn and beans and carrots and flowers I'd added because I'd hoped they'd make her happy.

"Wow," she said. "Where should we plant them?"

"The front lawn gets the best sun."

She nodded. A little breeze was stirring, just enough that the branches on the trees were moving. Above them, the clouds were so slow that they seemed locked into place.

I sat down. "Jimmy just stopped me."

"Jimmy."

"The cop. The one who brought Hannah home?"

"Ah, right. Why did he stop you?"

"He wanted a session."

She looked at me with a raised eyebrow.

"He knows I'm a psychologist, and he wanted to talk. He just didn't know how to do it, so he stopped me and we had a session in his cruiser."

"That's sweet." She was looking across the street at the maple trees just starting to bud, but her eyes were wide and blank. Maybe she was looking into the space between, maybe she was looking at nothing.

"I'm thinking of restarting my practice," I said.

Her pupils refocused and she looked at me.

"There's so much need out there. I could do some good." We were both quiet. I went on. "You know when you're cooking and you can't smell it at all because you've been in the kitchen the whole time, and then you step outside for a minute, and when you go back in, the aroma just hits you?"

She nodded.

"That's what it felt like, doing therapy again. I don't know how people would pay me, I don't know if anyone would come, but my office is still there. It sure seems like the virus is gone. Why wouldn't I see clients again?"

"I think you should."

The way she said it, we could have been talking about beans or soup for dinner. I knew she'd been essentially comatose for months, I'd been there, I'd nursed her, I'd held her close to me as the fire died down and the night got colder, but now, now the sun was so bright, and my excitement so vivid, I couldn't understand why she wasn't sharing it with me, why she seemed so absent. Resentment tinged what I said next.

"You probably think that's dumb."

There was a long pause as she stared beyond the trees and houses and town. I waited.

"I've been thinking about suicide," she said, then patted my knee. "I'm not suicidal, that's not what I'm saying. But I've been thinking about suicide."

She had her feet only one step down, so her knees were drawn up almost to her chest, and she held them with her arms while she talked.

"I never understood it. I judged it, actually. Not in a religious sense, obviously, but in economic terms. A pure waste. And it never seemed to be the people who were really suffering. Those people fought and fought to survive, and then somebody with everything to live for just ends it?" She shook her head. "But then I had this realization this winter, and I've been trying to figure it out for months. I realized that if it weren't for you and Hannah, I would kill myself."

I was aware of myself breathing, the air moving through my dry mouth. I wanted to reach out for her hand, to hold her, but she felt so far away.

"Like I said, I'm not suicidal. I have you, and I try to trust that wherever Hannah is, she's okay. But just knowing that otherwise, I would do it . . . It's so strange. It's just . . ." She made a little face, a thinking face, a face I knew so well. It was entirely unselfconscious, like when a spreadsheet wasn't immediately offering up a truth she knew it held.

"I remember talking to Hannah about asteroids," she finally said. "She was . . . seven maybe? And somehow asteroids came up, and I asked her if she knew what an asteroid was, and she didn't even look up from her drawing, she just said *It's a rock in space*, and I was so surprised, I said *Yes, that's exactly right*, and then I asked her *When did you learn that?* and she looked at me like I was crazy and she said *I've always known that.*"

"I remember that," I said.

"It was like that. I just knew that if you and Hannah died, I would kill myself. And if that's true, then I feel like I don't know myself at all." She looked at me. "What is it?"

"You're scaring me."

"I don't mean to."

"Don't you think I need you too? And Hannah?"

"Of course. I never said you didn't."

We looked at one another.

"This isn't about you," she said.

"No, this is about *us*."

"Not really."

"How is this not about us?"

"In this scenario," she said, "you are dead, remember?"

"I'm allowed to be scared if my wife suddenly starts talking about the conditions under which she would take her own life."

"It doesn't feel sudden."

"What?"

"I spent the whole winter thinking about this."

"And you didn't mention it to me? It's relevant to me."

She put her face in her hands.

"I'm sorry," I said.

"Look," her voice came through her fingers, "I'm doing the best I can. Can't the takeaway from this be how much I love you? That you're the reason I'm alive?"

"Yes, yes. Of course."

"And yes, you should restart your practice. There are a lot of people trying to figure out a lot of hard things right now, and you could help them." She stood up. "Do you know how to plant a garden?"

I shook my head. "I mean, first we have to dig up the grass."

"Let's walk down to the library. I'm sure they have gardening books."

The conversation didn't feel complete, but I didn't know what would make it so. We all have our roles in relationships. Penelope's

43

was to be practical, bulletproof. After Trump got elected, we went to a Christmas party with some of her old colleagues from Merrill Lynch, and half those guys had voted for him, and half of *those* guys weren't even ashamed of it, they laughed about it, gloated even, said *I tried to vote for him twice.* I wanted to toss my eggnog in their faces, but she laughed it off. Once you've been shredded at a performance review, told *Our clients are accustomed to a certain level of service* and known they were really saying *How are* you *going to take them to get hammered at Scores the way they expect, Black Lady?* then why would bullshit at a Christmas party stir you up?

On the way home, I made the mistake of saying *How can these guys not bother you?* Usually only Hannah had the power to trigger Penelope, but my blunder did it. I was her husband, the love of her life, and mistaking her gritted teeth for genuine acceptance . . . did I understand anything at all?

This was a gift Penelope gave me: she jarred me loose from my assumptions. She didn't get angry often, but when she did, it was real, it was sharp, like a dagger, and she never wielded it carelessly, unlike my family growing up, whose prime directive was *Repress your feelings*, and as a result, we all—my parents, my sister, myself—wielded only prop swords, soft-edged, harmless, unless you hit hard enough to bruise, and so we all just bludgeoned each other constantly, without pause or thought. I never would have found psychology if it weren't for Penelope, and the shocking realization that my tacit rules were not universal.

My aversion to actual conflict ran so deep that every time we fought, I found myself wondering if her next words would be a demand for divorce. Instead, there were apologies, and better yet, laughter, revealing that the yawning abyss between us wasn't that deep after all. It was just a fight. Couples had fights. It felt like magic, this realization that we didn't have to climb an insurmountable slope after all—there was no slope. We were on flat ground together. It was just my mind that hadn't been right.

I had moments of doubt, moments when I knew why I'd fallen in love with her, but wondered why she had chosen me. I asked her once, and she laughed and said, "Everyone loves a man who listens." Her voice sounded like she was quoting someone, and I cocked my head, and she said, "James Baldwin." I'd never been able to find where he said it, but it was true: I could listen to her all day. And I knew that her father had said nothing when he retired from the MTA, just kept putting his boots on and leaving the house early, only now he was spending his days with the woman it turned out he'd been seeing on the side for years. Even more than by the realization of his infidelity, Penelope was crushed to learn that her mother had known all along. So I understood that part of her decision must have been simple— she found someone who not only *would* never do such a thing, *could* never do it either. My God, it seemed like so much to manage! One life was hard enough, let alone two. When news of some couple's infidelity broke among our friends, we would look at one another and say, "Who has the *time*?"

In the end, twinned stars rotate around one another because of their shared gravity. I loved her because she loved me, and she did the same, and marriages were not just alliances, both parties with their eyes on goals the other could help further. The marriage contract was unlike any other. Our love was as foundational a part of our reality as any of the laws of physics, an action as well as a state of being. I loved and I trusted that I was loved in return, just as she did.

Penelope didn't bullshit. If she said she'd been thinking about suicide, she meant it. And I understood what she was saying: if she did take her life, by necessity I wouldn't be around to see it, unless we fell into a *Romeo and Juliet* scenario. But it shook me nonetheless. She'd disappeared into herself all winter, and now part of me was angry.

Why had she left me alone to face the failure of everything around us? When I wept on our mattress before the fire, she roused enough to hold me, but that was all. Where was the way we talked with one another? Usually, she knew my moods better than I did. Her voice, her reasoning was how I managed myself. Without her, I ended up stumbling down the icy street, trying to say out loud whatever words she would have said to me in comfort and reassurance and, above all else, understanding, but I could only manage a strangled *You're okay, you're okay.* And all the while, she'd been staring into the fire, cocooned in blankets, changing into some new form. Who was this new Penelope?

Maybe new Penelope and old Penelope weren't that different. Maybe she'd just applied her analytical mind to the end of the world and come up with the only answer that made sense. And I didn't want my anger to send her back into hibernation, so I tried to let it go, though I could feel that it wasn't gone, just retreating somewhere deeper inside.

We walked together to the library, hand in hand, with wandering steps and slow, and filled the shopping cart with books: gardening, but also novels, books we'd always said we were going to read but had never gotten around to. I remembered that the hardware store on Main Street just down from my office sold hammocks, and so we went inside and picked one out—they were all still there, no one else seemed to have thought to Manage hammocks as an Existing Resource. That afternoon, we broke ground in the lawn, dug up the grass, my hands blistering on the shovel.

Is it terrible to say I was happy that summer? So much grief and loss, a world so consumed by it that if you weren't constantly rending your clothing, pouring ashes over your head, you had to be an asshole. But Hannah was alive in California, the garden was growing, I came home from seeing clients, and even though Penelope largely fell back into bed, some days I found her outside weeding, sweating through one of my old T-shirts. I'd planted by height, the corn all the way back along the house so it wouldn't shade the rest. Looking out from the living room, we could have been in Iowa. Carlos helped out, even Al. Our lawn always seemed tidy, petite, but transformed, it began to *produce*. The wheelbarrow was full every day.

Reopening my practice meant throwing open the windows in the suite, dust spinning wildly in fresh shafts of sunlight. The postdoc's office was a little smaller than mine, but had better light, and that was what mattered now. Most of my clients were gone, I knew that, but I got some gas from Al and drove to the homes of those who might have survived, ringing doorbells and knocking on windows, half expecting to find nothing, but they were there, eight of them came to the door, wary, blinking, shocked. And five of them started coming to my office again, sitting in the waiting room in their ragged clothes, paging numbly through the last issue of *People* magazine to ever grace the world, though they knew each article and photo by heart.

One client suffered from seasonal allergies, and his red eyes and sneezing nearly sent me into a full-blown panic attack when I first saw him in the office. But he explained—*Where could I get antihistamines now?*—and I worked to get my breathing under control. I'd worked with him for years, slowly doing exposures so he could master his crippling social anxiety, and now he joked that he was doing the same for me. It was true: this was the world. People got sick, people had allergies. A runny nose didn't mean that Shark Flu was back. It had dipped into and out of our lives, vanishing as quickly as it had come.

Our challenge was navigating the wreckage it left behind. Some clients walked in crying, lay down on the couch crying, and fifty minutes later, stood to walk out crying. Others discussed the loss of their entire family with a disassociation born of a circuit breaker, the fuse that regulated their emotions blowing, leaving behind a gaunt, wide-eyed blankness. But they came, and others came too. HIPAA compliance was no longer a concern, but I kept my notes locked anyway. I was a professional, after all. The value of money was sentimental, at best, but there was barter. People had things to exchange. My clients paid me in canned goods, eggs, sometimes a useless twenty-dollar bill they extended and I took. I took whatever they gave me. And there were referrals, of all things, people they told who came too, and, of course, Jimmy. Jimmy braved the office. I saw him once a week.

When the garden burst forth, I gave my clients vegetables—zucchini, corn, tomatoes. I fed the body and the spirit. There were days when I caught myself whistling as I walked down the hill toward Main Street and my office. The world had not died, people were emerging from their hiding places, again, the amazing thing about the end of everything was how many of us were left to see it, all saying the same thing—*Everyone's gone*—but here we all were, saying it to one another.

So this was what Hannah was taking from me. Was I angry at her? I don't want to say yes. She didn't intend to wrench our lives out of place, but loving her had always meant accepting her terms. Even as a child, when we'd tried to lay down the law about mealtime—*We will not be making anything special for you, we eat as a family*—she simply stopped eating until we were scared enough to make mac and cheese, again. I knew people whose children strove endlessly to please; Hannah lived as though our approval was irrelevant. During the college process, we were treated to increasingly dire emails from the counselor letting us know that Hannah had failed to meet another deadline, Penelope wild in the kitchen, the scenarios spinning in her head—what was Hannah going to do when all her friends were off at school and she was home? Maybe that's what she needed, a wake-up call. And then letters arrived at the house, Hannah had applied on her own, somehow gotten into Bennington. And her response to our joy and pride was to go to UC Irvine instead, fly to the other side of the country, where now we would have to leave behind everything to look for her.

Yes, I was angry at Hannah. Parenting means sacrifice, but this? I was leaving behind the life we'd built here, built twice actually, once in the former world, once in the decapitated one. I was leaving behind clients who depended on me. They'd lost parents, siblings, children, friends. They slept alone in houses that once rang with voices, they slept in cars because they couldn't stand being in those houses and only a car calmed their fear of being trapped and not able to move. They crept out of wherever they were hiding, took the risk to come back to therapy, to talk to someone again, and now I was going to leave them. I would say that I was going on a trip, that I would be back, but what were the odds? It didn't feel like a trip. It felt like I was an astronaut, reading and signing a paper that stated I understood there would be no rescue if something went horribly wrong, that I would die in the vacuum of space. And there was no one to refer them to. There had to be other psychologists who'd survived, but where? Who?

The heartburn I occasionally suffered came back, eye-watering pain in my chest, the taste of vomit lingering in the back of my mouth, it didn't matter what I'd eaten, whether I'd eaten. If I abandoned my daughter to a cult, what did that say about me? If I abandoned my clients, what did that say about me? It felt like a heart attack, but I knew this feeling, this feeling was an old friend, my stomach pulsing acid out toward the rest of my body as though out of hate. I couldn't sleep for the pain.

Penelope was up all night too, packing, planning, as though she'd stored sleep all winter to use now. We could take her Tesla or my Subaru wagon, and the choice was clear. At least with the Subaru, we could take jugs of gasoline along in the back, explosive gallons hidden under the tent, the food, the clothes, the endless supplies she realized we needed and sent me out to procure: a portable water filter, sleeping bags, a road atlas of the United States. It was all happening so fast. I stayed in bed later and later in the morning, though I wasn't sleeping at all.

She found me staring out the window at the leaves starting to color on the trees as though I might be quizzed on it later. I had to pee, it didn't matter. I wasn't moving.

She had brought coffee.

"Is this your way of telling me to get out of bed?"

"If I was going to tell you that, I would just tell you," she said. "This is my way of saying I love you."

"I know. I'm sorry."

She lay down and spooned me from behind, her arm around me, hand flat against my chest.

"I hate that we have to go," she said.

"What I do may not be groundbreaking," I said. "I'm not doing any research, I never wrote a book. But I've always been ethical. I'm a good psychologist."

"I know you are."

There's not much more to tell you about the conversation. I'd love to say that we found an answer, there in the bedroom, as the sun rose and fell, that we resolved the moral dilemma, that all was well. We didn't. I just had to go into the office and tell my clients that I was leaving, that I would be back, but I didn't know when, that I was sorry, but that we would make a plan for them before I left. And the social niceties remained, they understood, most of them, or said that they did. A couple walked out without speaking. When I told Jimmy that we would need to put treatment on hold, he said, *I don't know about any treatment. We were just talking.* I told him, sure, he was right. We'd just been talking anyway.

One of my clients, I'll call her Susie, she was lying down on the couch holding a pillow to her chest when I told her, and she stared at the ceiling for a long time. The room was still. Traffic noise had been the only problem with the location, but now, with the windows open, the only sound was the birds. She'd endured a decade of emotionally abusive marriage, started seeing me when she was summoning the strength to divorce him for real. And then her son, the jewel in all that squalid mess, died early in the pandemic.

She didn't collapse into nothing. In that terrible long divorce, she'd found something indomitable deep inside. Some of my clients were coming now in rags, unwashed. I had to throw the windows wide. She was dressed, clean, wore the same perfume. Though she had been on a sliding scale for years, she'd always paid me for every session. And now she was lying on the couch looking at the ceiling.

"Is it okay if I still keep coming?" she asked. "Maybe I can just be here by myself, maybe that will help."

Her voice was so small, I couldn't help it, I started crying. I gave her the key to the office.

Back home, the car was full, jammed. I'd gone with Al down to the Mobil station to see Timmy, the richest guy in town. He looked at me wary-eyed as I explained the situation until I said Hannah's name.

"You're Hannah's dad?"

"How do you know Hannah?"

"She used to hang out."

"Oh." I didn't know what that meant.

"Bring by some containers, I'll give you as much gas as you want."

"Really?"

"Hannah was always cool to me," he said. "Go save her."

A whole world bloomed that I'd never known. Where had Hannah been when she was out? We'd assumed she was with her Horace Mann friends, but I realized now, as though I'd been blind my whole life, that of course Hannah hung with the townies, she didn't give a single shit about social status, never had.

Her name was a magic talisman. We had all the gas we could want, and he threw in four quarts of 10W-30 and a big bag of barbecue chips.

Our neighbors came to see us off with parting gifts. From Al, two cases of Natural Ice beer and a big jug of Jack Daniel's. From Carlos, a medal on a gleaming Cuban link chain he said we should hang from our rearview mirror.

I started to protest, but he said, "It's not real silver. Stainless steel." He winked, then said, "San Cristóbal will protect you on your travels. Or at least, he won't do you any harm."

We told them the garden was theirs. And Carlos we told to move into the house. Electricity, the fireplace.

"Take care of her for us," we said.

He was on the stoop waving when we pulled out of the driveway. We made it two blocks when blue lights whirled in the rearview mirror. "It's just Jimmy," I said to Penelope. I lowered the window. In a moment, there he was, bent over, leaning on his elbows to see in the car.

"Hey, Penelope," he said.

"Hi, Jimmy."

"Good luck. I hope you find her."

He turned to me. "Did you bring the gun?"

"Yeah, it's in the back."

"Have you ever fired it?"

"No, like I said, it's just for show."

He pulled his sunglasses away from his eyes.

"I hear things," he said. "It's messy out there. You can't depend on anybody but yourself. Do you know what I mean?"

"I think so."

He just looked at me, at Penelope.

"All right," he said. "Here's what I want you to do. Get started.

But when you get away from the city, once you're into some country, find a field or quarry or something and practice."

"We don't even have any bullets."

He walked to his car, came back carrying an armful of small cardboard boxes that he started handing to me through the window.

"You do now."

CHAPTER 3

I don't know if it was Jimmy's gift that silenced us or just the end-of-the-diving-board feeling that filled the car as I drove away. The wheel turned as though on autopilot away from the river and toward the Saw Mill Parkway. We could have been headed to Whole Foods, maybe the Container Store, the window open for my elbow, Penelope at my side. Maybe we'd get dinner after. Restaurants. I'd almost forgotten restaurants. There were no other cars, it could have been an early weekend morning when the world was sleeping in, except the sun was high overhead, and no one was coming to fix the potholes that were already deepening in the asphalt. Penelope looked out her window at the world unfolding, the tree branch in our lane I maneuvered around, the dark storefronts. The door of a dry cleaner nudged open, and a raccoon nosed out and sauntered across the road. Three thousand miles stretched ahead of us and the back of the wagon was packed full enough that the rearview mirror was useless, except as a place from which San Cristóbal could dangle. Jimmy had told us the

Tappan Zee was blocked, so I turned south onto the empty parkway and accelerated. Penelope spoke for the first time.

"How fast should we drive?"

"I don't know, what do you think?"

"I mean, we can go as fast as we want. I'm just worried there could be something in the road."

There could be something in the road. My palms went wet and slick on the wheel so quickly that they slipped, and my breath caught in my throat. My foot came off the gas. The car drifted, slowing, toward the shoulder. Thirty-odd years I'd been driving without thought, my brain churning through some problem at work, or refighting an argument with Penelope, or wondering when, exactly, the Knicks game tipped off that evening. All the while, the car flying through space, seventy miles per hour, eighty, canting on corners, the stomach lift of the road's rise and fall, all the while blithely secure that in the unknown ahead, an empty clean lane awaited me. How utterly, breathtakingly stupid. How had I survived before the Shark Flu? How had any of us? Before Penelope spoke, my muscle memory had been about to engage the cruise control, which now seemed tantamount to suicide. The car came to a stop on the road edge.

"Jesus Christ," I said. "You're right."

A helpless feeling welled up in me, and I froze. All through the winter, I'd never really panicked, instead just doing the next thing: finding food, chopping wood, carrying water. I had feelings, of course, but they never lasted, as though the breeze outside was spinning the snow up and around my blank mind. And now, when I was behind the wheel, on the precipice of the journey, I could feel my lungs gasping for breath, my heart thudding, my forehead wet with sweat.

She didn't say anything. We sat in silence on the roadside.

"If we have an accident," I managed to get out. "There's no one to call." A vision of us spinning off the road into a ditch from which we would never emerge seemed so real in my brain that I could almost feel the world rotating around us.

"I know," Penelope said. "It's scary."

"I just need to get myself together."

"Do you want to stop? We barely started."

"No, I don't want to stop." The enormity of what lay ahead loomed, like standing at the base of a skyscraper and craning your head back to see it yawning forever above you into the sky. Though we'd been packing the car with water filtration pumps and iodine, an entire box of first aid supplies, though I had a fucking *gun*, I realized now that my unexamined inner vision had included us zipping along the freeway, windows down, music on the radio, road tripping. And now I found myself flayed by the wild uncertainty of it all. We couldn't even make it down the Saw Mill Parkway to 95 without fear of what might be waiting in the road. Fallen trees, pileups of abandoned cars, emboldened deer, who knew. And one accident would be all it took.

The noise started as a distant whine, it could have almost been a mosquito, but it deepened, a ripping snarl, and echoed as a motorcycle whipped into view on the far side of the median. We'd been puttering around Dobbs Ferry for so long, I'd forgotten anything could move faster than a feral dog chasing the neighborhood fox. The rider was in a crouch, black helmet with a smoked glass visor, a blur that was gone as soon as I could make it out, though I could have sworn he turned to look at us as he flew. It could have been a vision, except that the roar was still audible in the distance.

"Well, okay," Penelope said.

We looked at one another, and she laughed.

"Want me to drive?"

"Yes."

We met in front of the car, and neither of us moved aside. She walked right into me and wrapped her arms tight around my chest.

Her head rested against my collarbone, and I put my face down and breathed her in.

"Ready?" her voice asked.

"Let's go."

We drove toward the George Washington Bridge, a gentle nausea settling in with the swooping turns of the parkway, the road unfurling. We could have been driving in to see a show—the West Side was so inaccessible from Grand Central that we always took the car. Penelope eased left at the exit—the signs all remained, of course they did, but they were like relics of a forgotten world. The stoplights weren't working, but there wasn't much to watch out for.

"Remember when we took Hannah here to see that allergist?" Penelope asked.

Columbia Presbyterian's bulk was visible on the hill above us.

"Did we think she had allergies?"

"We were wondering about asthma."

"God, right."

Penelope put her turn signal on before hanging a right up the ramp to the GWB, and there it was, silver against the sky, and we swayed left to take the upper level, the bridge intact and waiting, and we'd gotten halfway across when Penelope let the car ease to a stop.

"What are you doing?"

"Just listen." She turned off the engine and opened her door. We both stepped out and there was a high whistle, the wind singing between the cables, that must have always been present beneath the diesel rumble of trucks. We looked at one another over the roof of the car.

Onward across the bridge, the mile-wide toll plaza welcoming you to New Jersey, the seemingly accidental snarl of roads in Fort Lee: offerings on the altar of traffic, like Ozymandias in the desert, empty. Not that there weren't any other cars, but the ones we did see felt like events. A Ferrari weaving and gasping as the undoubtedly new owner struggled with the clutch. A station wagon in the right lane, clown-car packed, faces pressed against the windows. A convertible despite the chill, a hand waving at us casually as it passed.

What joy to have been wrong! I could feel myself cracking open in bloom. We were already breezing through Jersey—there was the colossal emptiness of the American Dream mall, which was once called Xanadu, all the names seemed cursed, the cantilevered slope projecting from the back that I and everyone I knew said was an indoor ski slope "like they have in Japan," though none of us had been inside to see it. Giants Stadium. The distant towers of downtown Manhattan reaching upward like fingers brushing the sky. Vees of migrating birds arrowed along above us, and I kept the window down as long as I could until Penelope told me she was cold.

"If all goes well," I said to her, "we could be in California four days from now." I'd calculated the gas. We had fifty gallons in the back, and that got us halfway at least. In the distance, Newark Airport looked like a child's diorama. Planes, little Matchbox cars. Penelope turned onto 78, and now we were headed west. California filled the windshield, if we could only see far enough. I pulled out my phone and plugged it into the car charger.

"Do you think we might find cell service?" Penelope asked.

"No, I don't." I hit the button for the stereo, the Bluetooth linking right away.

Marvin Gaye filled the car and I spun the volume knob to the right. *When I get that feeling . . .*

"It's our wedding song!" I cried.

"You're crazy." She was laughing.

What few clouds there were hurried across the sky as though trying not to ruin anything. It was the best time of year, when everything wobbles between summer and fall, the air a little crisper, the sun still warm. I lowered the window again. Penelope was driving easy, slowing down before the blind turns, but she had one hand on the wheel, the other holding mine, and her fingers were drumming time to the music. Whatever I'd downloaded before Spotify failed, that's what we had. It was going to carry us across the country.

"Oh my God." I had a moment of brilliance. "I forgot the car has a CD player." When was the last time I had listened to a CD? Were they even still making CDs? "We can Manage the Existing Resources of a music store." But what would we choose? Penelope's taste in music was awful, shockingly so, since her judgment seemed so unerring in everything else. If she had to listen, she'd always choose jazz, but not real jazz, smooth jazz, perhaps some treacly R & B. Hannah and I played hip-hop on the Bluetooth speaker in the kitchen, thirty years leaping between her songs and mine, and Penelope just shook her head and took her wine to the couch by the fireplace.

Marvin Gaye, part of our narrow common ground, was singing "Trouble Man" from the car's speakers, and I was thinking I guess now it's just death and trouble, taxes are gone forever, when Penelope hit the brakes hard and I slid in my seat and she said, "What the hell?"

We shuddered to a stop in the middle of the road, a few yards in front of a yellow-orange portable road sign. It had a solar panel on top, and words were crawling across it. That would have been startling enough.

. . . METER. DETOUR TO 80 . . .

It hung on the sign then flashed three times.

. . . FOR SAFE TRAVEL WEST.

My hand reached out and turned off the music as the sign went blank, then began again with the beginning of its message.

59

DANGERDANGERDANGER...

...NUCLEAR INCIDENT AT...

...THREE MILE ISLAND...

...MAINTAIN 50 MILE PERI...

...METER. DETOUR TO 80...

It went through one more cycle before we managed to say anything.

"Where is Three Mile Island?" Penelope asked.

"Jesus, somewhere in Pennsylvania. I don't know."

We stepped out of the car into the silence of the empty highway. I had the atlas in my hand and I spread it out on the hood, my finger ranging across Pennsylvania as though the place names were written in Braille.

"There." I stabbed. "Near Harrisburg."

She looked down, then back up. I could see her swallow once, hard.

"The wind is coming from the west," she said. "Right?"

The clouds were still racing along, and suddenly the air felt charged, malevolent. My throat was thick.

"Get in the car!"

I jumped into the driver's seat. Penelope was already in the passenger seat. I stepped on the gas.

"Where are you going!" Her voice cracked, hitting a higher pitch than it ever did.

"287!"

"Shouldn't we just turn around?"

"287 is right up there." I pointed. "We'll take it north to 80."

"Just go. Go!"

Now we were headed northeast, 287 wandering up through Jersey, and I was doing it fast. Silence filled the car as fully as music had just minutes before.

"God," Penelope said. "Imagine if there'd been no sign. If it hadn't been working. Does it work on a cloudy day?" She was holding one hand over her mouth as though afraid of what she was saying. "I think I'm going to throw up."

"Do you want me to stop?"

"Jesus, no. Keep going."

The trip, which only moments before had felt like a lark, now loomed like a whirlpool into which we would inevitably be drawn. Hopeless.

"We aren't even out of Jersey," I said.

"Just get to 80. The sign said it was safe, right?"

"I mean, can we trust the sign?"

She didn't say anything. We were holding hands again, but it couldn't have felt more different, and I was driving fast enough that I had to take mine back, hold the wheel with both. Morristown flew by, the road wide and empty. The car clock said 5:58, and the sun was starting to go down.

"We'll find a place to camp in Pennsylvania?" I asked.

"Let's just keep going. We should get west of Three Mile Island. We can just sleep in the car if we have to."

"Yeah, you're right. Of course."

We were on 80 now, the windows were up, but Penelope was still shivering.

"I can turn on the heat," I said.

She shook her head.

"Put on a coat," I said.

"Okay," she said. "I will." She didn't move. The car ate up the miles, but even farther north, on the road the sign said was safe, my fingers were cramping, and I felt like I could sense the radiation slowly degrading my DNA.

"We'll feel better once we're in western Pennsylvania," I said. "Pittsburgh. Or whatever."

She nodded.

"We'll feel better," I repeated.

We were driving into the sun as it fell. I had the visor down and sunglasses on. Penelope was holding up a hand against the light. The highway, which had been sliding through wild farmland, suddenly cozied up next to the water.

"Delaware River," I said.

Penelope nodded.

"The Water Gap is just ahead and then we'll be out of New Jersey."

She nodded again, I was looking over at her to see if entering Pennsylvania was scaring her, when I heard a flat percussive clap in the distance.

"What was that?"

I was slowing down and the cliffs of the Delaware Water Gap were looming in front of us, the sun hanging between like a marble, the highway snugged up next to the river and preparing to S-curve through the gap, and there was the crack again, a gunshot, only this time I felt like I'd heard the hornet whine of the bullet, and Penelope was shouting something and pointing ahead where, blinking against the light, I could see a roadblock, a man with a rifle pointed at us, another man standing with a palm flat outstretched.

I hit the brakes so hard the antilock kicked in and we shuddered to a stop.

The two men walked toward us.

"Oh, Jesus. Penelope, what do I do?"

She didn't say anything, and her eyes were wide. My hand pushed the transmission stick into reverse, but would he just shoot us? The car was silent and we were both frozen as they approached. The guy with the gun stopped in front of us, his weapon lowered but still at his shoulder.

The other guy tapped on my window. They were both wearing

camouflage, I could see that now, and as I lowered the window, I saw a name above his shirt pocket. DeGrassi.

"Turn off the ignition, please."

I did.

"What the hell were you thinking?"

"What?"

He had a wide, tan face, and he didn't have to be smiling for his teeth to show. His jaw hung low, like he breathed through his mouth.

"It's a fucking roadblock, Jimbo. We almost had to shoot you."

"I didn't see it."

His face got even wider with astonishment. He turned to look at the other guy. "He says he didn't see it."

The face above the gun shook back and forth in derision.

"I'm sorry," I said. "We'll go. We'll go back."

"Nope."

A little sound escaped from Penelope. I could feel her next to me, even as I looked up at DeGrassi. He was craning his head to look behind me into the backseat, piled high with supplies.

"It's not safe," he said. "We'll escort you through in the morning. You try to go anywhere when it's getting dark, you won't make it."

"What?"

"There's bandits in the hills, they're stopping all the cars. We're rooting them out. But until then . . . we escort folks through in daylight."

Penelope spoke for the first time. "You're military?"

"United States Army, ma'am. Chuck will take you over to where we're encamped."

He turned back to the roadblock and whirled a hand. The sun had fallen while we were talking, and headlights came on behind the barricade. A Humvee bumped out across the curb, its long whip antenna flopping. It slowed down as it neared us, and a head stuck out.

"Just follow me."

I waved and pulled around. The guy with the gun still stood in the middle of the highway. He had never said a word.

We weren't going fast, and we didn't go far, pulling off at the first exit.

"This is good, right?" I said to Penelope. "They'll escort us through in the morning."

"I suppose," she said.

We were pulling into the parking lot of a TA truck stop. NORMAN KNIGHT TRAVEL CENTER, the sign said. PIZZA HUT. TACO BELL. COUNTRY PRIDE RESTAURANT.

"I mean, it's the army."

She just stared ahead. There were a couple of Humvees in the lot, and a scattering of cars. Most I would have bet hadn't moved in months, but a couple were packed like ours. I pulled in next to a Porsche Boxster with a bumper sticker that said MY OTHER CAR IS AN X-WING. Beyond the gas pumps, where semis would usually be parked, there was a tank, motionless as a sculpture, its long cannon angled upward.

The guy driving the Humvee hopped down to the ground, walked over to us.

"Toss me the keys," he said.

"What?"

"It's for your safety," he said. "We don't want anyone leaving the truck stop until we're ready."

"We're not going anywhere."

"I just need the keys."

"I don't understand."

Penelope's hand gripped my thigh. I looked over. She gestured. "Give him the keys."

I raised my eyebrows, and her eyes got wider. "Just do it."

"Sure thing," I said. I pulled the car key off the ring and tossed it. He tried to grab it one-handed, but missed, and it skittered across the pavement. His posture was all casual as he knelt to pick it up, like he'd meant to do that.

"Come on inside," he said. "You can meet the colonel."

"We'll be there in a second," I said with a wave. I turned to Penelope.

"This doesn't feel right."

She shook her head.

"Why did you say I should give them the key?"

Her bag was sitting on the floor of the car, next to her feet, and she bent down and reached inside. "Because I've got mine," she said, and there in her palm was the second Subaru key.

She shouldered her bag, and I followed her out of the car. As soon as I closed the door, the Humvee guy squinted at the key in his hand, held it out, and pressed a button. The horn honked once, the car was locked. Penelope looked at me.

He waited for us at the door, his arms crossed.

"Lemme just take your temperature." He pulled an ear thermometer from his pocket and gestured toward us.

I stepped forward, but Penelope put a hand against my chest. "We'll just stay outside," she said.

"Come on."

"I don't want that in my ear," she said. "It was just in your pocket."

"It'll just take a second."

"No."

"Okay, *fine*." He shoved it back in the pocket. "You guys dipped, right?"

"We're here, aren't we?"

He rolled his eyes and pushed his way through the doors. Penelope and I looked at each other and then followed him in.

At first, I thought it was just the setting that made this "military encampment" laughable. The wide tiled entry was dark, as were the empty shelves of the convenience store, the Pizza Hut and Taco

Bell, but somehow they'd gotten the overhead lights in the Country Pride to blaze. Penelope and I paused in the wide doorframe, like kids entering a school cafeteria for the first time. At one table, a man and a woman were hunched together, speaking a language I didn't recognize. Russian? They looked up at us blankly, and I knew one of the cars in the lot was theirs. Squeezed into another booth, a sweating bearded White guy sat alone. He stood up when he saw us and waved. A black sweatshirt reading HAN SHOT FIRST stretched over his belly.

I waved back.

Leaning against the empty salad bar station was a silver-haired brush cut with a tight mustache. He wore an olive-green T-shirt, camouflage pants tucked into tall boots. Two leather straps circled his right thigh, holding up a pistol in a holster. The only other time I'd seen that was on an action figure I had when I was a kid.

The Humvee guy saluted the salad bar guy who hip-pushed himself upright, hands still in his pockets, his pelvis canted forward GI Joe angle, *I-love-the-smell-of-napalm-in-the-morning* angle. He returned the salute. I could see something red folded in his back pocket.

"At ease," he said.

"They were trying to get through," with a head swung back at us.

"Those the shots I heard?"

"Weren't stopping at the roadblock, Colonel."

The colonel turned to us. "You think we're kidding around here?"

After a second, I realized it was a real question. "No," I said. "It doesn't seem like you're kidding around at all."

"You're goddamned right." He stared at us for a long time, past curiosity, past intimidation, into parody. Penelope and I looked at one another.

"Follow me," he said. He waved with his hand and walked to a window at the far side of the restaurant, where the cliffs of the Water

Gap were just visible in the failing light. He pointed. "They're in the hills. Even if it were broad daylight, you couldn't see them. Dug in deep. We've got superior firepower, but every one we eliminate, seems like two more pop up."

The guy who'd tried to take our temperature had walked over with us. "It's like in that movie, with the guy from *Avatar.* Where he fights the Hydra."

The colonel looked at him. "Aren't you on KP?"

"No, it wasn't the guy from *Avatar.* It was the one with the Rock in it."

Another look from the colonel and the guy turned and walked off.

"This is a natural choke point," he went on. "Controlling all access."

"To Stroudsburg?" I asked.

He looked at me hard. "We could let you go through, let you get picked apart, that's what you want."

I held up my hands. "I didn't mean anything by it."

"To the whole West," he said. "The Delaware Water Gap is the key to the West."

His arms were crossed, and he stared out the window as though he were Eisenhower surveying the beaches at Normandy.

"Did the Pentagon send you?" It was the Han Shot First guy talking. He'd come up behind us. "To secure the Water Gap?"

The colonel looked pleased with the question. "No, those desk jockeys don't know the situation on the ground. We took operational initiative."

"Were you all from the same unit? You know, before?" His belly under the sweatshirt seemed even more pronounced, and I realized he was borrowing the colonel's hip tilt. A couple more guys had walked up to join the conversation. They were wearing red berets like the one in the colonel's back pocket.

"The mission brought us together," said the colonel.

I could see how desperately Han tried to look casual as he asked his next question. "Are you recruiting?"

The Colonel gave him a long up and down, like he was going to put a number grade on a girl.

"We require military experience," he said finally.

"Starfleet don't count," said one of the other guys, and he and his buddy cracked up.

Han was trying not to look crushed. He knew enough not to correct them.

"I need to go to the bathroom," Penelope said. "I'm just going to go outside, okay?" She was holding my hand and she gave it a hard squeeze.

"Me too," I said.

"Outside?" The Colonel laughed. "We've got working facilities right here. Running water. Just the men's room though. You'll have to tough it out."

"I should get food from the car, though," I said.

"You've got food?" He turned, his eyebrows raised, and then he smiled and waved a hand. "We have enough. Relax. Pick a booth. Your server will be over shortly." He laughed.

As though on cue, headlights blared through the windows. A Humvee was bouncing into the parking lot. Guys piled out, and in a moment they were walking into the Country Pride, chests out, barking at one another. They held the door open for two of their comrades dragging a deer carcass. Hollers rang through the entryway.

"Good work, gentlemen!" the colonel called. He looked at us and laughed. "See what I mean?"

Penelope's hand was threatening to squeeze mine into a pulp. We retreated to the dining room and slid into a booth as far from everyone else as we could. There were salt and pepper shakers still half full on the table, an empty napkin holder, plastic menus. I looked at

Penelope to ask if she was okay, how she was feeling, but two little vertical lines had appeared in her brow. She was thinking, not feeling.

"Okay," she said. "Let's go through this rationally. Ignore the military bullshit. We were stopped by men with guns and they took our car keys. The only evidence we have that it's not safe is what they tell us. They are holding us, and they won't let us leave. And there is no fucking way I am eating that deer."

I drummed my fingers on the tabletop. "I'm not sure they're planning to eat it either. Did you see his face when I said we had food in the car?"

"Do you think there are actually any bandits in the hills? Isn't that what they said, *bandits*?"

I shrugged. "Who the hell knows."

"We never should have come in here." She looked around at the folksy wallpaper, the plastic tables, the six-foot anthropomorphic chicken statue, holding a wing aloft to welcome diners. They'd given him an eye patch and a bandolier of ammunition. The deer had been dragged off somewhere in the back.

We sat at the table and hatched a plan as the sky outside lost the last of its color.

A couple of the guys were hanging in the lobby when I approached, laughing by the rack of brochures for local attractions, guns hanging on straps from their backs. How do you break into a circle of the cool kids?

"Hey," I tried, "can one of you guys open up our car for me?"

They didn't look up.

"Sorry to interrupt, I just need to get . . ."

"What?" he said. "What do you need from the car?" He drew out the word *need*.

"We wanted to thank you guys. I mean, if the bandits had gotten us . . ."

"Don't worry about it."

"I have beer. For you."

Now I had their attention. One of them put two fingers in his mouth and blew a loud whistle. "Hey," he called. "Tell Ryan to get the keys!"

He turned to me. "I'll take you out."

"Thanks, man," I said. "It's just Natural Ice, but it's still beer. Glad to share."

"Yo!" he called. "Tell Richie this guy's got Natty Ice!" He clapped a hand on my shoulder. "It's his favorite."

"Wow. What are the odds?"

We walked out under the stars, the great hunched knobs of the Water Gap looming in the darkness.

"Sorry it's going to be warm," I said.

"We'll toss it in the freezer, if it lasts long enough."

"We just really appreciate the sacrifices of those in uniform." I worried I was laying it on a little too thick, but he seemed to soak it up like it was his due.

"Sure," he said. "Don't worry about it."

"I'm Bill, by the way."

"Hawk."

"Cool name."

He nodded. We got to the car and he held the key up to the glimmers of light from the restaurant.

"It's the button on the left," I said.

He pressed it, and I could hear the doors unlock as the horn sounded across the lot.

I rummaged in the backseat.

"Careful," he said. His gun had migrated from his back to his hands.

I tucked the jug of Jack Daniel's deeper under the sleeping bags. We'd debated busting it out, but Penelope and I had decided that we didn't want to see these guys truly hammered. The beer would do.

"How many guys do you have?" I asked him. "Is one case enough?"

His eyes were wide. "How much do you have?"

"Two cases."

"Better grab both." He looked like a kid about to open a Christmas stocking.

I grabbed our road atlas, hoisted the beers, and we began walking away from the car. After a few steps, he remembered the key, began searching for the button to lock the car.

"The alarm has been acting up," I said. "You might want to lock it manually instead."

"Don't worry about it," he said.

"I'm just saying, we never use the buttons at home. Not unless we want to get woken up in the middle of the night."

He looked at me, his eyes narrow. Without breaking his gaze, he held the key out toward the car, stabbed a button, and the horn echoed. I could hear the doors lock. I shrugged.

Inside, there were whoops and shouts. A dozen guys were there, and the colonel stepped forward. "One case for the freezer," he said. "And one for now." Fist bumps were flying my way as they tore open the case, and one of the guys held a can out toward me.

"No," I said. "I'm good. It's all for you."

I got the grand tour. The generator humming out back, the freezer with deer carcasses hanging, none of them dressed out yet. A storage room had turned into their lounge, with a flat-screen. DVDs were scattered and heaped around the TV, brightly colored, and even from a distance I could tell that they'd been liberated from the shelves of a Lion's Den Adult Superstore.

The Subaru horn wailed in the lot, long high-pitched sirens mixed with a low thudding beep.

"There it goes," I said.

We were walking back out into the lobby. The siren stopped, and then the guy in charge of the keys came back in from the lot.

"Sorry about that," I said, but they were already cracking new beers.

I walked back to Penelope where she had shifted to a booth right by the window, closer to the car.

"So far, so good," I said.

"It's like being trapped in a frat house," she said.

"You didn't even see the back."

"Yeah?"

"The smell in that room was ungodly."

She shook her head. I reached for her hand over the table and we looked at one another for a long moment.

"Again?" she asked.

"Sure."

She snaked her hand back under the table, and pressed the alarm button on her key. Again the horn wailed out into the night, and again one of the guys walked outside.

Slowly, evening turned to night. Han Solo had gotten his hands on one of the beers, and he stood on the edges of the group. The other table, the Russians, whoever they were, hadn't moved since we'd arrived.

Twice more, Penelope hit the button, and finally as the guy headed out toward the lot, the colonel called out to him, "For fuck's sake, just turn off the goddamned alarm."

"Give it here." The guy who'd walked out to get the beers with me grabbed the key, and this time, when the alarm fell silent, there was no solitary horn, and I knew that he'd locked the car manually instead.

Penelope and I sat with the atlas as the empty cans grew, dead soldiers scattered around the lobby floor. If anyone had come over, I would have flipped west, shown them we were planning the rest of our journey, when in actuality we were memorizing the layout of the local streets, the road on the other side of the river that snaked through the gap.

Finally, the television blared in the back room, the boom–chukka–thud of the soundtrack spliced together with moans, and all the guys but one disappeared.

Penelope had a lifetime's practice of keeping her anxiety from showing. The sharks she'd worked with could smell an atom of blood in the water. I knew the truth, knew she was not, in fact, bulletproof, but now there were actual bullets all around us. Her face looked scared, and that scared me. My forehead was wet, and like a feedback loop, she saw it and said, "God, you have to calm down."

"I know."

"Wipe your face."

I pulled up the bottom of my shirt and while I was blotting my forehead, I took some deep breaths, feeling the cloth pulling in and out with the movement of my lungs.

"Okay," I said.

"You ready?"

I shrugged and stood. This was the moment when, if I were a secret agent, I would do something debonair and devil-may-care. I winked at her.

She laughed. And that was all I needed.

The lone sentry was gazing longingly at the door to the porn room when I walked up. "Hey," I said.

He nodded. He looked younger than the rest, his mustache downy. "Thanks again for the beer," he said.

"Anything for the troops," I said.

He accepted the absurdity of this statement without question.

"I'm afraid my wife is having a little trouble with the . . . ah, noise," I said.

"The Black lady is your wife?"

"Yes, she's my wife." I kept my face still.

"Oh."

"Would you mind if we stepped outside?"

73

I was a little taller than him, and Penelope was walking up to us, both of us doing our best to look quietly but respectfully disappointed in his life choices.

"Give it to me!" a woman's voice called from the television set, her timing perfect. "I want that cock in my ass!"

His eyes widened.

"Oh God," he said. "I'm sorry."

"That's okay," I said. "We'll be right outside."

We were still standing in the puddle of light from the restaurant when he opened the door and called to us.

"They don't mean nothing by it. It's just . . . you know."

"No problem!" I said, and Penelope waved. He looked relieved, gave us a smile, and stepped back inside.

"What do you think they're going to do to him?" Penelope asked.

"I don't know. Let's just worry about getting away first."

We gave it a good show, looking up at the stars, pointing at constellations. What a beautiful night. Eventually our feet wandered to the farther corners of the lot, dark, but away from the cars, and when we were sure he couldn't see, I looked at her and squeezed her hand, and we ran for the Subaru in a looping arc.

She slipped the key into the lock and looked at me. I swallowed and nodded. This was the crux, when we had to rely on luck. A turn of the key, and the doors unlocked with a snick. She held the door handle and I crouched, ready to dive. "One two three," she said, and swung open the door and I threw myself into the driver's seat, scrabbling to turn off the dome light as it began to shine out in the darkness like a beacon.

No cries of alarm came from inside, no clatter of movement.

I climbed out, and Penelope sat down at the wheel, made sure the headlights were off before putting the transmission in neutral and the key in the ignition.

"Ready?"

She nodded, and I put my shoulder to the car and pushed. For a long second, I thought nothing would happen, but then momentum gathered and it was moving and we were headed away from the truck stop and I jumped into the passenger seat and Penelope turned the engine over and he never even stepped outside to see our darkened car slide away into the night.

CHAPTER 4

Penelope crept along without headlights. The rectangles of window-glow from the truck stop disappeared as we turned the corner, and there was no moon yet in the sky. Tree shapes blocked out the stars on the sides of the service road, which felt impossibly narrow, a thread we could fall from anytime, but for the silver glimmer of the guardrail to our right. Then the guardrail disappeared. She slowed to a stop. I could hear her swallow hard.

"We've got to keep going," I said. As soon as we'd pulled around the corner and out of sight, my mind had filled with a sequence of events so vivid they had to be true: the cry of alarm from the sentry going unheard until he ran inside to break up the masturbatory celebration. Armed, angry, priapic men pouring from the Country Pride and into Humvees already skidding out of the lot, headlights blazing. Now any pretense of the public good would be abandoned. They would shoot us and dropkick our ragdoll bodies into the Delaware River.

"I can barely see!" Penelope said.

I stuck my head out the window, away from the matte glow of the dashboard.

"Drive!"

I called out directions until the guardrail appeared again, and she went faster. The road turned away from the wide blank of the highway I'd been able to feel to my right.

"There's going to be a hard right soon."

"I should turn on the headlights."

"No!"

"Why?"

"Then it's a fucking race!"

"What?"

"Once you turn them on, you can't turn them off! You won't be able to see anything!"

"Fine! Do you want to drive?"

"There's the right! There!"

The trees along the road had disappeared, and the farther we got from the truck stop, the more my eyes adjusted. She bumped over the curb.

"Keep going!"

Now we were driving underneath the highway toward the river, the darkness total, and then out the other side, and Penelope slid to a stop and said, "Which way?"

The road parted in front of us, and signs loomed overhead, but I couldn't make them out. The map we'd looked at in the brightness of the Country Pride swam in my head.

"I don't know."

"I don't know either."

We'd gone a half mile, maybe, from the truck stop, still on local roads, and half of that was snaking around the cloverleaf, so they were still there, maybe a quarter mile away. The car windows were down. If they were squealing out of the lot, would I hear them?

"Okay," I said. "Hit the lights."

She turned the knob and the parking lights came on and that was enough for us to see the choice before us: left toward the local bridge and on into Pennsylvania where we could cross through the Water Gap without running into their roadblock again, or right onto 80 East.

80 East. The highway home, beckoning us to fly, a hundred miles per hour, faster, the Subaru at the limit, leaving the Humvees and the danger and the journey behind, back to the pointless comfort of our little home. We could sleep in our bed, eat the last vegetables from the garden, hope the jet stream wasn't strong enough to carry Harrisburg's radiation all the way to us. Carlos might not be thrilled to leave our comforts behind, but we would all settle back in, the folks of the neighborhood, preparing for another winter, this one colder as the oil tank ran empty, more wood burned in the fireplace. And then spring would come again, and we would plant the garden, and the days would rise and fall and none of it would mean anything, just us living out the remaining years on our lease before the big sheriff showed up at the door and evicted us from this world. Was I enough to keep Penelope alive until he came for her, or would she leave early, leave me alone? Even if Penelope stayed, I could feel the awful blankness of waking without Hannah, the darkness we were driving nothing compared to what waited at the house, the aching purposelessness of it all. It wasn't even a choice, *home* was a meaningless word. And yet, a part of me layered deep in shame wanted to run, wanted to say "Go right!" and soar along the highway, wanted to say "You've done all you could" to her, to me, and be right. We'd done all we could. How could anyone expect us to do more?

"Left," I said, but she'd already gone left, hit the gas, and it was only a moment before another sign swam overheard, green and wide, another forking of the road, this one not profound but absurd: we could take a right to continue on 611, or we could go left and take 46 East to Buttzville, New Jersey.

Penelope was going faster now, and we slid under an underpass before we hit the turn.

She went left.

"Right! Go right!"

She swerved, the Subaru throwing me nearly from my seat into her lap as we almost sideswiped the jutting knuckle of the guardrail divider.

"Didn't you see the sign?"

"I'm a little distracted!"

It didn't matter. Now the bridge stretched out before us. But we would be naked as we drove across it, nowhere to hide.

I didn't have to tell her to cut the lights. We sat in silence as our eyes adjusted to the dark, and then she put it in drive and pulled her foot back from the brake and we began easing across the river I could hear now through the open window, the quiet rush and gurgle of the blood-dark water, Penelope trying to keep the yellow center lines beneath us so we wouldn't inadvertently plunge. I craned my head back to the right, but I could see nothing of the truck stop in the distance.

At the far side of the bridge, we slid through the empty toll booths, and we were in Pennsylvania, we'd finally made it out of New Jersey.

"What do you think?"

I knew what she was asking. "I think we're okay."

She hit the headlights, and we blinked for a moment in the brilliance, and the first thing I could make out were white letters, body high, standing up from the grass, as though sending us a message.

D R J T B C

If it was a sign, I didn't know how to interpret it. Penelope swung down a ramp to stay on 611. Power lines stretched overhead, the cracked asphalt of the two-lane road, a handmade sign for Cortland Steel by a chain-link fence, a donut shop in a low brick building, its ragged sign proclaiming AMERICA RUNS ON DUNKIN'. We drove past the faded storefronts of a downtown that must have been suffering before the virus struck—bank, market, post office, antique shop. KEEP PENNSYLVANIA BEAUTIFUL. As quickly as it filled the cone of light our car made, it was gone, the trees closing back in, a railroad track twinning us on the right. We passed a pullout, Point of Gap Overlook, and then the road began to narrow, stone crags marching in on our left. Penelope was holding the wheel with two hands. The clock on the dash read 11:58, and I was about to say, *Can you believe we were still in Dobbs Ferry this afternoon?* when she hit the brakes.

"Fuck," she said. "It's them."

A panel van blocked the road ahead, PLEASE STOP FOR THE TOLL spraypainted on its white side in black letters bleeding at the bottom.

"Shit, shit, shit . . ." She was slamming the transmission into reverse when I saw movement in the side mirror: a figure carrying a pistol was stepping out of the woods and into the road behind us.

We froze.

The figure grew as it walked closer, then disappeared from my mirror. A sharp rap, and there we were again, a gun tapping the glass, our car stopped, only this time it was a woman gesturing to Penelope to roll down the window.

"Well, hello," she said. "Do me a solid, keep your hands visible?"

The pistol's matte finish shone dully in her hand, her long index finger conspicuously straight rather than tucked in against the trigger.

I placed both of my hands on the dash. Penelope didn't move, action in stillness, one hand on the wheel, the other on the transmission.

The woman gestured toward the open mouth of a pullout next to the van, a sign reading RESORT POINT OVERLOOK.

"If you don't mind," she said.

I could see the calculus running through Penelope's mind, the pistol, the car squealing into reverse, the narrow road, our plummeting odds no matter which option we chose. Her hands tremored.

The woman switched the pistol to her off-hand, reached in with her right, and placed it softly over Penelope's on the wheel.

Penelope jerked her hand away so fast it nearly hit me in the chest.

"Whoa," the woman said. "Easy."

"The Shark Flu," Penelope managed to say, and that was when I realized that I'd been out in the world, scavenging, seeing clients, building my tolerance for human contact in the postvirus world, but this was the first time in almost a year that Penelope had been touched by someone other than me. I'd been so caught up in my own shit, I'd never really considered it. Uncomplicated love for her swelled in me, the way it always had when I'd thought about Penelope as a child, before she'd met me, before she'd remade her own life, earnest, driven, young Penelope, the world all before her.

"Honey," the woman said. "I've seen a lot of people coming through here, and nobody's been sick. Not for months and months. Not since the winter."

Penelope managed a nod.

"So . . . what do you want to do?" the woman asked.

"What do you mean?"

"Well, you can pay the toll or turn around."

"We can turn around," Penelope said. It was a question, but her voice was flat.

"It's a free country. If you want to take this road, there's a toll. You don't want to take this road, that's your business." She slapped the roof and walked back toward the woods.

Penelope's jaw was set. She swung the car backward in a half arc, then we lurched around the way we'd come, the tires squealing on the pavement. For a moment, the headlights centered the woman, now sitting again in an aluminum lawn chair under the tree's apron. Her hand rose in farewell.

I didn't say anything as Penelope whipped along the road, hugging the corners. When we got back to the little town, she swung into the parking lot of the PNC Bank, then hit the brakes. The headlight's beam glittered against the spiderwebbing cracks in the plate glass behind which an ATM machine canted drunkenly. She cut the ignition and pulled the key. We sat in darkness and silence, the fan still whirring underneath the hood, and then she slowly slumped forward until her forehead rested against the steering wheel, her hands dropping to her lap.

"I'm so tired," she said.

I could feel my own exhaustion like a figure backlit behind a curtain, as the adrenaline started to fade. Though seeing clients already felt like something I'd done in a former life, I had a bag of apples in the back one had given me for payment. I opened the door, the dome light dizzying in its sudden brightness, and popped the back hatch, digging through until I found a jug of water and the fruit. When I sat back down in the passenger seat next to Penelope, the light slowly dimmed above us, and we ate, passing the water back and forth.

"What do we do now?" she asked.

I took a swig. "We could always take the lonely road to Buttzville."

She looked at me for a moment before she broke into laughter, and hearing her laughter delighted me so much that I began to laugh, which made her laugh even harder.

Finally she said, wiping her eyes, "It's not even that funny, but for some reason . . ."

Maybe it was eating something, maybe it was just the laughter, but I felt myself lift a little.

"I remember this time when Hannah was young," I said. "We were in the kitchen, laughing at something, who knows what, and she came in and heard us and just immediately collapsed into laughter, I mean, the three of us were weeping we were laughing so hard, and when she could finally get her breath again, finally talk, she said *What was so funny?"*

Penelope smiled and put her hands on the wheel. "Okay," she said. "Let's go."

"Which way?" I asked.

"We pay the toll."

"Yeah?"

"I don't even know how we would go around, and who's to say we wouldn't run into the same shit. Or worse."

So we drove back, only this time when we got close, Penelope rolled down her window and called out *Hey* to the woman in the lawn chair.

"Back so soon?" She stood and ambled over to the car.

"What's the toll?" Penelope asked.

"That depends."

"Depends?"

"We believe in a progressive toll structure, in keeping with a socially just philosophy."

"What?"

"Pull up," she said. "They'll look at what you've got and work something out. You don't like it, you can drive back."

Penelope turned into the lot. A low stone wall stood between us and the drop to the river, and at the far end, the flicker of a campfire rose into the trees above, rouging the leaves, the canopy alive in the wind moving through the water gap. Penelope turned and slid between the white lines of a parking slot until the nose of the Subaru sniffed the stone wall.

We sat in silence, looking at the river and the wide bulk of the I-80 bridge. The moon was rising now, and in the new light, the lurking hunch of the opposite hill was just a shape cut out of the sky.

A person rose from the campfire and walked over toward the car, her hair up in a rough ponytail. She bent down at our window and smiled.

"Headed west?"

Penelope nodded.

"You want to hop out, we can look at the car, figure the toll."

It was cold outside, a chill I hadn't noticed standing in the parking lot of the truck stop, my heart thudding. I pulled a jacket from the backseat, handed Penelope her sweater.

"I'm Sienna," the woman said. "Mind popping the back?" Penelope and I exchanged a look while she poked through our supplies.

"Lot of gas," she said. "Where you headed?"

"California."

She whistled. "How come?"

"We're going to get our daughter," Penelope said.

Sienna closed the hatch with a thud. "Toll's one of your containers of gas, a box of food."

I didn't know what Penelope was thinking. I didn't really know what I was thinking either. After the chaos of the day, my immediate impulse was to cry *Deal!* in a spasm of gratitude. Then we could all hug. Conflict avoidance, an instinct as early and primal in me as hunger.

"I don't love it," Penelope said.

"I imagine not."

"Why should we give you anything?"

"Our road."

"Why?"

The woman seemed unfazed by Penelope's questions, and I smothered my urge to intervene, to say *Honey, give the nice lady our gas and food and keep driving.*

"Why does anyone own anything?" she said.

"Usually they purchase it. Ownership is a legal instrument,"

Penelope said. She had to look up at Sienna, who might have been taller than either of us.

"Possession is nine-tenths of the law," Sienna said. "Right now, I'm thinking it's a hundred percent. Though we did purchase it."

"You did. With what?"

"Blood." Her voice was matter-of-fact as she said it.

"Whose?"

"Ours, other people's. The greater good requires sacrifice, especially now."

"How is this the greater good?"

"Well, survival is good, for us. And we maintain a progressive toll structure that contributes to the community."

"The woman on the road said that too. How is this progressive?"

I kept watching Sienna, who wasn't obviously armed, for signs of anger, frustration, but she seemed amused, maybe even pleased.

"We take what people can afford to lose. In some cases, that means less than nothing. Some people that come through are scraping bottom so hard, *we* give *them* a hot meal, a gallon or two of gas, send them on their way."

Penelope's eyebrow was raised. "Why would you do that?"

"We're a feminist collective dedicated to the survival of a liberal social philosophy in the new world."

"Seriously?"

Sienna shrugged. "It's what we believe."

"Maybe we should go negotiate with the military on 80."

She laughed. "Good luck. They'll take everything you've got."

They looked at one another while I looked between them.

"The toll is the toll," Sienna said. "But we've got some venison on the grill, and you're welcome to spend the night here, under our protection. Maybe you could throw in some of the corn I saw in the back, we could break bread together. In the morning, you're on your way. What do you think?"

Penelope looked at me. I shrugged.

"I have one question first," Penelope said.

"Shoot."

"Did you put up the highway sign on 78 telling people there was a nuclear accident and directing them to 80?"

"Nuclear accident?" Sienna's face looked genuinely surprised. "No, we did not. What did it say?"

Penelope looked at me. I cleared my throat. "It said there was a *nuclear incident*, I think was the wording, at Three Mile Island. That you should stay fifty miles away. It detoured us here, to 80."

Sienna thought for a moment. "That is just what you would say if you wanted to scare people off," she said, nodding. "Of course, it's also what you would say if there was a horrible nuclear accident that would melt your organs like candle wax."

"We weren't going to roll the dice," I said.

"It could have been our friends across the river," she said. "I don't know."

"Can we have a minute to discuss?"

"Take all the time you like."

She started to walk away, then turned back. "This goes without saying, but you should know, before you get any exciting ideas, we do have weapons on you from the woods, for our own protection." She smiled and walked back toward the fire.

We stood on opposite sides of the car, looking over the hood.

"I don't know," I said. "I mean, we could go look for another way into Pennsylvania, but who knows what we'll find. Maybe all the roads are like this."

"I think she's telling the truth," Penelope said.

"About what?"

"That the colonel would have taken all our stuff, or at least a lot more than she will. That she doesn't know anything about Three Mile Island."

"So you think we should pay?"

"I'm fucking starving," Penelope said.

I laughed. "Enough to eat a deer?"

She just rolled her eyes.

I pulled an armful of corn from the back, and we walked to the campfire, where four people sat in the flickering light, Sienna, two other women, and a man. They rose as we approached, introduced themselves with names I forgot as soon as they were mentioned.

"Corn!" one of them said. She grabbed an ear and pulled down the husk, leaving it attached at the bottom.

"From our garden," I said. "Here, I'll help shuck."

"Don't rip off the husk," she said, "Just pull the hair, dip the ear in the water, then wrap it back up." She pointed to a bucket near the fire.

"And pull up a log," someone else said. "Make yourself comfortable." We sat. Sparks whirled up and spun overhead. Thick chunks of wood were licked with fire to one side of a glowing heap of coals, over which meat sizzled on a makeshift grill. Corn was now being tucked into the ash to cook. If I closed my eyes, with the heat on my face, it could have been a camping trip with Hannah, there could have been s'mores in the offing. It was just like that, only instead of a guitar hung around her neck, the woman sitting on the stone wall opposite us had an Uzi.

The man with them prodded the coals with a stick.

"I thought you were a *feminist* collective," Penelope said.

"We are."

"What about you?" She was looking at the guy. He didn't answer.

"He's cool," the woman shucking corn said. "Men can be feminists too."

"I know that," Penelope said. "I'm just trying to get my bearings here."

The guy just kept staring into the flames.

"So you met the Water Gap Militia?" Sienna asked. She was

sitting cross-legged, and in the firelight I could see her face more clearly. She was older than I thought, she was our age.

"We ran into the roadblock," I said.

"Almost literally," Penelope added.

"The sun was setting," I said. "You could barely see it."

"Sunset?" Sienna said. "Took you a while to make it over here."

"They took us to their . . . base," Penelope said.

"No shit?" Everybody around the fire perked up. "How'd you end up over here?"

"We escaped."

The woman with the Uzi let out a full-throated laugh. "They're such a joke," she said.

"We were pretty crafty," I said.

"Yeah?"

"Well, we gave them beer and snuck away while they were watching a porno."

The circle of people collapsed into laughter. When they finally mastered themselves again, Uzi asked another question.

"Did you meet *The Colonel*?"

We nodded.

"I'll give you one guess what he was doing before Shark Flu."

"Marines?" I said.

"Home Depot."

"And you must be the bandits they warned us about," Penelope said.

"Bandits." Uzi laughed. "Usually they just call us murderous cunts."

"They said they were . . . eliminating you. One by one."

More laughter. "They tried at first, but we 'eliminated' a couple of them and then they stopped trying."

"Are any of them actually military?"

"Who knows. Reserves, maybe? Maybe they were clerks."

There was a metal baking pan sitting on the stone wall, and the woman who'd shucked the corn pulled the meat from the grill with a big fork and put it there to rest. Another chunk of wood went on the fire. The breeze lifted and for a moment I was blinded by the smoke before it died and I could see again.

"You said you were going to get your daughter." Sienna was looking into the flames as she said it.

"That's right," I said.

"How do you know she made it?"

"Shortwave radio. I put an antenna up on our roof."

"She lives out in California?"

"She went there for school."

"Which one?"

"Why do you want to know so much about our daughter?" Penelope interrupted.

Sienna looked at her. "I had a daughter too."

They held eye contact silently. The only sound was the popping of the fire. I could see moisture boiling into whitish foam from the split end of the wood. The log settled a little, and sparks spiraled upward.

"She joined The Revival," Penelope said. "We're going to get her out of there."

"Revival. The . . . religious group?"

"You can say cult. It's a cult."

"Sorry."

"It's all right."

"Why did she join The Revival?"

Penelope was sitting just far enough away from me that I could shift my body and watch her as she spoke. I didn't know what she was going to say.

"She's always been . . . looking for something," Penelope said. "And I've never been able to figure out exactly what. I wanted to succeed so badly when I was a kid, it was all I thought about. I tried to instill that drive in Hannah, but . . ." She shook her head. "I don't want to give you the wrong idea. It's not like she's a slacker. I hear other parents talking about their kids, and they say, *oh, they're aimless, oh, they have no ambition, oh, they're going to end up back at home*, but that's not her. She's chasing something. I just have no idea what it is."

The moon had fully risen now, an oblong hole punched in the sky, and I could see Penelope's face like it was day.

"To be honest . . ." She laughed a hard little laugh that I'd never heard from her before. "Sometimes she makes me feel . . . conventional. Like maybe I never thought about anything for myself, just chased the rabbit like a dog."

Penelope stared into the fire like it might hold an answer. "How can you love somebody so much," she said, "and not understand them at all?"

Sienna was looking into the fire too. "My daughter was autistic," she said. "She lived in her own world. It didn't matter. She was my daughter."

The silence darkened.

"I don't know if she really understood what was happening to her when she got the virus. It broke my heart. She was so scared and she didn't understand. Other parents, they say things like, *Just take me instead, and let my daughter live*, but if I died then who would take care of her? That would have been worse. We had to live or die together. The other options were impossible. I couldn't stand to watch her die, and I couldn't stand the thought of her alone and frightened."

Her voice was steady, but the lines on her face deepened as she spoke. "In the end, it doesn't matter. We don't choose anything. I watched her die."

On the far side of the fire, the Uzi woman swung the gun around behind her so that she could squat next to Sienna and rub her back.

"They're just little boys on the other side of the river," Sienna said. "They may be cretinous buffoons, and their camp a whirlpool of degradation and filth. But they're also just frightened boys play-ing soldier because it's their way of making meaning out of all this horror."

She clapped her hands together as though cleaning dirt from them, then rose to standing from cross-legged without using her hands.

"Time to eat," she said.

CHAPTER 5

After dinner, we retreated to the car, slept there with the seats cranked back rather than digging out the tent. I woke first in the early morning darkness, the car hot despite the cracked windows now steamed enough that my fingertip left a line behind, a drop of water pearled on the tip. As though I could taste salt in the air, it brought me back to Martha's Vineyard, where we rented a house in Oak Bluffs for years when Hannah was young. I'd never been there before, the ferry as much a novelty to me as it was to our six-year-old daughter. Penelope had gone for weekends with friends from Amherst and determined then and there that if she had a child, she would provide this gift, this island where the Black upper classes congregated in the summer months, all the more so after she married me and knew that this theoretical child would grow up biracial, navigating turbid, contradictory waters. Martha's Vineyard would be part of Hannah's exploration of her heritage.

For years, we spent three weeks every August, and I was remembering now a late afternoon after we drove to Edgartown and tried

Jet Skis, or Hannah and I did, and afterward, mother and daughter walked for ice cream, and exhausted, I fell asleep in the car, waking as I did now to the heat and sweat, my mouth metallic and grainy.

A wave of sadness swept over me, so intense and sudden that my eyes dampened and a drop broke loose and ran to my lip and I tasted the salt water. My memories of Hannah's childhood had always warped time, seeming to come from a previous life even though I could swear they'd happened just the other day, but now the scissor-snip of the world's end made me feel all the more how lost those memories really were. She was a child no longer, this was her world now, this was what she'd inherited. Even if we made it across the country, which felt impossible—we'd been traveling for an entire day, and we'd barely made it out of New Jersey—what were we going to do when we found her? Put her in the trunk? Give her a talking-to? Bring her back home so she could live in her old room, listen to music in her headphones, roll her eyes when we called her down for dinner? Would we give her a curfew, an allowance?

We were being selfish. Was this trip really about Hannah? Or was it just Penelope and I, fighting our impending uselessness and eventual death, trying to find a purpose when all purpose had been lost?

The therapist in me said, *This is not the moment to trust your feelings. You're tired and hungry.* I could still diagnose my own perseveration, even if I couldn't escape it. I needed to wake Penelope, maybe she could help me find the exit ramp from my own thoughts.

I turned and found her eyes already open in the half dark.

"Hey," she said. "How'd you sleep?"

"I was just thinking about Martha's Vineyard," I said.

Her face softened. "You know what I remember," she said. "When you used to snorkel out from the beach and come back with hermit crabs for Hannah."

There it was, a sweet memory, and it was true, I'd flap-walk out with flippers, a net, and a mesh bag, then scan the sandy bottom for hermit crabs, whelks, scallops, even the occasional spider crab. I'd bring them back up onto the beach, where Hannah played under the umbrella, and the memory of the pure joy and wonder on her face kept me out there, facedown on the water forever on barren days as the tide turned and the waves built, until my net was full. Of course, eventually she began not to care, to say things like a distracted *Oh, more hermit crabs?* or a whining *Dad, not now, I'm reading.* I'd felt her innocence running through my fingers like sand, no matter how tightly I squeezed my hand.

My mind could ruin anything. There were times I envied Penelope's disposition, the long swells of her emotional tides, even if at bottom it meant months of near-silence. My moods swerved: jagged, raw, dependent on sleep and blood sugar and my brain chemistry that seemed so much more volatile than hers.

"We need coffee," I said, and stepped out of the car. I walked out toward the red flicker of the campfire coming back to life.

A container of gas, a box of food, and less than an hour later we pulled out of the lot and onto the road before the sun had risen beyond the trees, the light still soft, though dawn's rosy fingers had already faded from the sky. The road hung above the river, notched into the hillside, with a thin scrim of trees separating us from the drop. To my left, rocky crags piled up like Jenga stacks, hemming us in. Penelope was quiet as I drove into the gathering light. A few fall leaves whirled in the car's wake. An old-timey sign welcomed us to the Borough of Delaware Water Gap Business District as the land around the road began to widen.

There were houses, a sudden confusion of little streets, a giant weeping willow. A downtown, but without the promised businesses. I stayed on what seemed like the main road. Faded patio furniture on concrete terraces, American flags, a blue recycling bin upside down in the middle of our lane. A hulking restaurant was the first sign of commerce that we saw, the Sycamore Grille, a red, white, and blue OPEN flag still fluttering, a message board anchored in the sidewalk with removable letters like those in a theater marquee instructing us to LIVE EVERY HOUR LIKE ITS HAPPY HOUR!

The road forked to either side of a pizza place's triangular lot. I stopped. Racks of orange canoes like missiles in a launcher stood outside a river outfitter.

"Which way to the highway, do you think?" I asked.

Penelope looked around her seat, bent to peer under, then back up at me.

"The atlas," she said, and I knew exactly where it was: on the table in our booth at the Country Pride restaurant.

"Shit."

I took the right fork. The highway was in that direction, and I hadn't gone long before we saw signs for I-80 and gas stations staring at one another from opposite sides of the road. I pulled into the Gulf.

"Maybe there's an atlas in there."

Penelope watched me walk inside. The door was unlocked, the shelves empty, the refrigerator cases, everything. There was still a sign telling me I needed to be eighteen years old to buy cigarettes, twenty-one to buy alcohol, but neither was there to be bought. I walked back out.

"I'll just check across the street."

Penelope nodded from inside the car.

The Sunoco was dark too, I could see that as I was crossing the road, and the door swung open just as easily, but even before my eyes adjusted, I could tell something was different. A revolving wire postcard caddy stood by the entrance, telling me in yellow bubble letters to RAFT THE GAP! There was no fluorescent hum, no sound from the cold cases, but they were full, actually *full*, the American Dream, a blizzard of sports drinks. Bags of chips swelled from the racks. Stepping inside was like falling into a lost world.

A voice called out, "Hands in the air, *now!*"

I actually jumped, I said *Gaaah*, threw my arms up, half turned in time to see a man behind the counter collapse into laughter. He pointed at me.

"You should have . . . seen your face!" He could barely get the words out, pointed at me, then threw his arms up in imitation, bugged his crossed eyes, stuck out his tongue.

"I'm pretty sure I didn't look like that."

"You did!"

"Well, you scared the hell out of me." I lowered my hands.

"Sorry, buddy." He didn't appear very sorry. His beard draped over his chest like a necktie. He ran his hand over it before speaking again.

"What can I do you for? You want twenty bucks on pump five?"

"Wait," I said. "You have gas?"

"Hell no. That's been gone for months." He was laughing again. "You're just coming by to swap your propane tank out anyway, right?"

"You have propane?"

"Powerball ticket," he said. "That your poison? I hear nobody's won the jackpot in months. It's gonna be *huge!*"

His self-amusement was beautiful, in a way. How long had it been since I'd had an interaction that wasn't, in some way, dolorous? A year ago, if I'd walked into a gas station and found this guy, I would have been looking for the exit. Now, he seemed like a gift, someone sent to remind me all was not dread.

"Actually, I just need a road atlas," I said.

"Well, hell, why didn't you just say so! Just got a new shipment last week. Hot off the presses!" This sent him into guffaws sustained enough that he had to wipe his eyes.

"Good one," I said.

"Lemme get you an atlas, we can talk payment." He lurched off his stool and stepped around the counter, revealing that he was not wearing any pants over his gray tighty-whities.

I knew he had a joke loaded and waiting in the barrel, just waiting for me to acknowledge what was manifest before me.

"Looks like you forgot your britches," I said.

"You know what this is called?"

"What?"

"Redneck air-conditioning!"

"Well, the price sure is right," I said. This barely qualified as a joke, but he nearly wept.

"The price is right," he repeated weakly, and I knew that would be a new addition to the repertoire. Some things would never change. This was who he was, he'd been this guy his whole life, working at the Sunoco, cracking jokes, probably working through new material each night at the kitchen table to use the following day. A world-ending virus had come and even that broke like a wave against his humor. Nothing could tear it down. Someday, decades in the future, he would die laughing.

No sooner had I thought this than his eyes widened, he went pale, and his mouth fell open. He was looking over my shoulder, and I spun to see Penelope in the doorway of the minimart, Arnold at her shoulder. She was shaking, the gun barrel swinging in little circles, her chest heaving with her breathing.

We all stood frozen in place and silent.

"No, no, no," I started to say, but the guy spun and dove for the counter. Simultaneously and instantly, I knew two things to be true: one, he had a gun back there somewhere, and two, the AR-15 my wife was carrying was still unloaded, useless.

Two steps to the door and I grabbed her arm, tugging her, running through the shade of the high awning over the pumps. A gunshot sounded behind us, and she wrenched herself free to turn back, swinging the rifle around.

She pulled the trigger and nothing happened. Her eyes went so wide they looked circular, and I pulled her again, across the street, sprinting now, into the Gulf station lot. She threw herself inside the car, the gun clutched to her chest. I stomped on the gas, the engine already running. We bumped over the curb and skidded onto the road and I was weaving as I accelerated and one final bang sounded behind us.

I had two hands on the wheel, squeezing so hard my fingers hurt. A traffic circle loomed, the car canted drunkenly to the right as we squealed around and onto the on-ramp for 80 West and we were driving, fast, down the highway. Two miles, and she was still cradling the gun in her arms, her breath still coming in ragged gasps. I put a hand on her knee.

"I thought I was going to lose you," she said. "I looked over . . . and I saw you jump and your hands were in the air . . ."

"I'm okay, we're okay."

"But what if I hadn't been watching? I mean, what if I hadn't looked up when I did?"

I didn't say anything.

"I can't lose you."

"Hey," I said. "Deep breaths. We're okay. I'm okay."

She looked down at the gun. "Why didn't it fire?"

"It's not loaded."

"It is!"

"No, I've never loaded it."

"I loaded it. That's why it took so long for me to get over there."

The gun suddenly looked very different cradled in her arms in the passenger seat.

"Jesus Christ," I said. "Is the safety on?"

"It is now."

"Was it on when you tried to fire it?"

"I'm not an idiot!" She was looking down at the gun, the little thumb catch above the trigger loudly marked with white-lettered SAFE and red-lettered FIRE. "I don't know. It all happened so fast."

"Well, we're safe now, that's what counts."

We were passing through the outskirts of Stroudsburg, the road hemmed in by lane dividers. A sign for the Olive Garden flashed by, and we were through town. The highway widened, trees replacing concrete, the median wild and unmowed and starting to encroach on the shoulder. Penelope was staring straight ahead at the road unfurling in front of us, the two little lines appearing between her eyebrows, which meant she was deep in thought. The highway was rising into the Poconos, and the occasional overeager tree had already flushed red against the yellowing background. She finally turned to look at me.

"He wasn't actually threatening you, was he?" she asked.

I shrugged.

"I didn't save you from anything."

"Well," I turned to look at her. "It's the thought that counts."

"Oh my God." She put her face in her hands. "I nearly got us killed."

"But you didn't. We're okay."

Another mile passed before she spoke again.

"Why wasn't he wearing pants?" she asked.

"Redneck air-conditioning."

"Ah." She nodded, as though I'd offered a real explanation, and then she started to laugh. Whatever hopelessness I'd been feeling in the half dark of morning, I could barely remember. I would have kissed her, reached for her hand, held it tight, but I was driving fast enough that the car shimmied, so I kept my hands at ten and two. We had to get west. Somewhere to the south of us, there was, perhaps, a meltdown, a Chernobyl, a Fukushima, a Three Mile Island. Were we fifty miles away? Probably, but without an atlas, my mind could conjure a map in which Harrisburg hung shockingly just below us, so I kept my foot down rather than trying to ease along and nurse our dwindling fuel supply.

As the mountains grew around us, my ears popped, and I could feel gasoline disappearing into the engine as it rattled and strained up the hills. On the downhills, I coasted, the weight of the car urging us forward, the transmission in neutral, but they never lasted long. Mackeyville, Milesburg, Snow Shoe, Kylertown—a blur of small-town Pennsylvania names, Pilot travel stops just visible through the trees, the miles passing until we had to be beyond the radioactive cloud. A sign flashed on the side of the road: HIGHEST POINT ON 80 EAST OF THE MISSISSIPPI, ELEVATION 2250 FT, and Penelope pointed to the next exit.

Jimmy had been right. We needed to figure out Arnold, or it was going to get us killed. We turned north onto ever-smaller roads, the trees marching in around us, scraggly pines and tangled brush. The road turned to dirt, vegetation high enough between the rutted tire tracks to scrape along the undercarriage. A yellow metal gate across the road loomed, and I pulled to a stop.

On the other side of the gate, the road became a single-track trail. Penelope walked ahead of me, holding the gun the way marching soldiers did, the butt in her hand, the muzzle pointing to the sky. Other than our footsteps, the woods were silent, the underbrush thick, thorny, and opaque on either side. The trail descended into a ravine, a brook splashing among the rocks at the bottom. On the far side, we climbed to find a broad meadow of waist-high vegetation, and we started toward the other side, the sun high and the air still. I reached for Penelope's hand, and we were halfway across when we both paused, seemingly at the same time, and looked at the plants all around us. I'd never actually seen marijuana plants other than my college roommate's—a sad little frond under a black light—but this was unmistakable, a whole scattered plot of weed crowned like basil, wide leaves spreading their fingers to brush against our legs.

We set up some rocks on a fallen log at the far side of the field, retreated about the distance of the pitcher's mound from the plate. She set the gun down, and we stared at it. It lay matte black against a bed of green moss, its shape as recognizable as a stop sign, a Porsche Carrera, a Vitruvian man. Once, I would have called it an M16, all the Vietnam movies I'd seen now blending into one memory of men in a line walking through the jungle. That was before the news filled with shooting after shooting, *AR-15, AR-15, AR-15*. I'd been carrying it around for months empty. Now, it was an actual gun, loaded, dangerous.

Penelope tapped the gently arced clip. "So this has bullets in it," she said. "I got it from one of the boxes Jimmy gave you."

She pressed a button, pulled the clip out, and handed it to me. Inside, rounds were staggered, long cylinders that narrowed abruptly to a tip like a dart. I pushed the clip back up until I felt it click into place.

"That's just what I did," she said.

"What next?"

"Then I ran across the street like a crazy woman."

"Okay." I picked up the gun. "Let me give it a try."

She nodded, put her fingers in her ears. I turned the safety to FIRE, took a long breath, aimed at the rocks I'd stacked, and pulled the trigger.

Click.

I looked at the gun. Penelope had a little smile on her face.

"Okay, okay," I said.

"What about this," Penelope said.

"What?"

"Just . . . let me try."

I handed her the gun, and she pulled the slide at the top all the way back. Metallic sounds came from inside the mechanism. We looked at each other. She held it up to her shoulder, her left eye closed, her right sighting along the gun barrel, and pulled the trigger.

You can see an arrow, that's the beauty of it, the long parabolic grace of flight. When I went to summer camp a thousand years ago, I took archery, and there was a kid who, we all said, was going to compete in the Olympics. He brought his own compound bow, and there was magic to the way he would aim, his cheek deformed by the pressure as he sighted, the arrow loosed and bobbing a little in flight as though wavering, but burying itself in the center ring of the target.

A gun was a different form of magic.

When Penelope pulled the trigger, I leapt backward. Three things had happened so fast I couldn't process them until after they were finished: a rock vanished from the log, the gun made a noise so loud my ears squealed in protest, and a brass casing flew from the side and bounced off my chest.

"Holy shit."

She rubbed her shoulder.

We ran through a clip, handing the gun back and forth. Once we were used to it, the kickback was shockingly light, and moss packed in our ears helped with the noise. The rocks were reduced to dust. I'd brought extra rounds, and we were learning how to push them into the clip, getting ready to fire again, when a voice called out from the woods.

"Hello!"

We spun around. Penelope dropped down into a squat, her eyes wide. Ten years separated me from dropping onto my haunches and bouncing back up, so I dropped to one knee instead.

"Let's be mellow, okay?" the voice asked.

I pulled back the slide with a metallic clank, which seemed to echo across the field, and I thumbed the safety to FIRE.

"I said mellow! No need for fireworks!"

Penelope and I looked at each other. A day before, we would have waved and chatted without a care, but now everything seemed threatening.

"Come out where we can see you!" I shouted.

"No offense, how about you put down the gun first."

"Maybe you have a gun too!"

"I do not have a gun."

"I don't believe you!"

"If I wanted to shoot you, why would I tell you I'm here, man?"

Penelope shrugged.

"Okay!" I called. "I'm putting down the gun."

I put the safety on and laid the rifle down at my feet. A head poked out from behind a tree.

"We cool?" he called.

"We're cool."

He stepped out into the field, and we introduced ourselves. His name was Terry. He was older than us, with a wispy half beard hanging beneath his mouth, which creased in a little smile that seemed permanent. He was White, but his skin was tanned so dark it looked like bark, like if he moved too fast it might splinter and crack. He never moved too fast. His shirt hung loose over his skinny chest.

"I take it this is yours." I gestured toward the field.

"What gives you that idea, man?" He laughed, and said something else.

"What?"

He started to repeat himself, but I held up a hand, then dug the moss from my ears with a probing fingertip.

"I said, you guys were getting pretty good with that thing."

I looked down at the gun. "A necessary evil," I said.

"Is it?" He smiled gently. He was humoring me.

"It seems pretty dangerous out there."

"I don't know, man, seems to me having a gun just gives somebody an excuse to shoot at you. But what do I know, I'm a pacifist."

Somehow, I was on the other end of a gun control debate I'd been having for years. Now I was the Second Amendment nut job holding on to an AR-15.

"Can I ask you a favor, man?" he continued. "If you want to keep practicing, there's an old gun range a couple miles down the road. Weapons distress the spirit of the ganja."

I started to chuckle, but he wasn't kidding.

"We're fine," Penelope said. "We're all done."

"The plants thank you."

"You're welcome, plants," I said.

"How about you join us for a meal?"

"I don't know," I said. "We've got a long trip ahead."

"You need sustenance. You don't want to sputter out partway."

"Sure," Penelope said. "We would love to join you for a meal."

"Oh man, that's great." It was like we'd been thoughtfully arranging a gift, his gratitude. We began walking back down to the path together.

"Where are you from?" he asked.

"Just north of New York City. Westchester County."

"New York." He whistled long and low. "That must have been rough."

I shrugged. "Don't really know. Just rumors, really. I mean, it was rough everywhere, right?"

It was his turn to shrug. "Pretty chill here, man. I mean, dipping sucked, but dying would have been worse. And the ganja prepared us to face whatever was to come."

"How many of you are there?" Penelope asked.

"Three."

"That's a lot of marijuana for three people."

"There used to be so many more."

"Living here?" I asked.

"Weekenders from Cleveland and Pittsburgh, mostly. But people used to come from all over for the spiritual awakening in spring."

"On 4/20?" I guessed.

"We take the holidays we're given, man."

At the bottom of the ravine, he walked a step upstream, hopped across well-practiced rocks.

"Why DuBois, Pennsylvania, of all places?" I asked.

Now he was laughing. "Didn't you see the sign, man? This is the highest point east of the Mississippi!"

We turned onto a spur and hadn't gone long when the sloping roofline of a cabin angled behind the trees. A curve in the trail, and the front porch came into view: wide, with a broad staircase leading down. Two men reclined in rockers next to a table on which a bong sprouted like a many-armed alien being.

"Welcome to the casa," Terry said.

Introductions all around. The other two men were White as well, one with long dreadlocks, the other heavy enough that his T-shirt, which featured a green-tinted Colonel Sanders next to the letters *THC*, gapped before his pants. The three of them smiled at us beatifically like the Three Muses of Weed.

We stepped onto the porch and Terry said, "Would you mind clearing your gun?"

I looked at him.

"The live ammo," he said.

I looked down at the gun.

"May I?" He took the gun gently from my hands, and in one fluid motion popped the clip and cleared the round from the chamber, catching it in his off hand. He handed it all back to me.

"You're a pacifist?" I asked.

"And a vet. Desert Storm. Still have some shrapnel in my side. I found marijuana when I was looking for healthy pain management. And the plant gave me far more than that. It led to a spiritual awakening I'd been looking for my whole life."

The cabin's shadow was just starting to intrude on the patchy grass of the clearing. They poured us glasses of sun tea from a broad glass pitcher before Colonel Sanders excused himself to work on the food.

"I just want to let you know," Dreadlocks said to Penelope without preamble, "that I recognize and respect the essential role that cannabis plays in the culture of your people. My hair is a celebration, not an appropriation."

Her eyebrows went up, but she just nodded. "Thanks," she said. "That means a lot." I could hear the amusement in her voice, but he nodded, as though they'd made a real connection.

I used to smoke in college but had never seen Penelope take so much as a bite of a pot brownie. We sipped our sun tea. Our chairs were both rockers, with wicker seats and backs, and the warmth of the day still lingered though we were in the shade.

Terry placed a palm against the side of the bong. "I am going to offer you the ganja," he said. "But forgive me if I share the philosophy behind it first."

I reached for Penelope's hand and squeezed it.

"We are Bud-hists," he said, his face serious. "We believe in the perpetually unfolding now, the present, to live in which is a practice so difficult that the human brain invented the abstract concepts of Past and Future, which do not exist. We believed that expanding our concept of time would bring us comfort and meaning, but in truth, attachment to the Past and Future brings only suffering. There is only the Now. To believe anything else is to live within a lie."

A robin hopped across the bare dirt in front of the cabin, thrust its beak into the dirt. The faintest breeze worked in the trees, so there was a faint rustle filling the quiet. Dreadlocks had closed his eyes to listen to Terry.

"Most animals live in their bodies," he went on. "That robin suffers the pangs of hunger, and so he finds a worm. He does not worry about the pangs before they have arrived, he does not remember them and weep. We live in our heads, in our brains, which gave us dominion over the earth, and we mistake that power for righteousness. And so it is only fitting that the earth gives us back the means of transcending the trap of thought. To live in the perpetual Now is the most difficult practice, made possible by the gift of ganja."

I must have made a face because he smiled at me and said, "You are skeptical."

"No, I'm not against marijuana at all. I haven't smoked in years, but I always liked it."

He didn't say anything, just waited. It was a therapy move so basic that I recognized it immediately, yet found myself unable to resist filling the silence.

"As a criminal justice issue, marijuana legalization was always important to me. But as a psychologist, I have to admit that I've always been skeptical of the insights and awakenings people experience when they're doing drugs. It's a shortcut past doing the real work, the lasting work."

"Doing drugs," he said. "Do you hear the way you said that?"

"Sure."

"Your very language is betraying the assumptions that you bring. The ganja isn't a *drug*, it's a *plant*. You walked through the field yourself. The tea offers you caffeine, the food calories, the marijuana enlightenment."

"I guess I've just seen too many people who started smoking young and it seemed to stunt their emotional growth."

"They smoke without purpose," he said. "They waste the experience, look past the truth. For them, their suffering is only increased."

Dreadlocks interrupted. "That was me, man," he said. "Before I found the truth. I was wandering, in pain. I wasn't deepening my practice because I didn't know there was a practice. But that didn't mean I needed to stop smoking, it meant I needed to find out why I started, to make it intentional, man."

"Any religion," Terry went on, "has rituals for coming of age. This is no different."

This was not a conversation I was going to win.

"Okay," I said.

"The field you found is holy ground, where we have bred and crossbred strains to find the One weed, to eliminate memory and desire, to leave you in the perfect grace of Now."

"What do you call it?" I asked. "The One weed."

He smiled. "Well, we're still stoners, man. We call it Thunderfuck Forget-Me-Now."

"Forget-Me-Now," I said. *"Arrested Development!"*

"My man!" He laughed. "That's right."

"But why Thunderfuck?"

"Because it sounds cool as hell."

Dreadlocks took a long bubbling toke from the bong. Terry followed, and then held it out toward us. I looked at Penelope.

"Thanks," she said before leaning forward and taking a short breath from the tube. No cough. After a moment, a little cloud streamed from the corner of her mouth, and she handed it off to me. Terry looked on approvingly as I toked, and almost before I'd let the cloud billow from my lungs, a tingling wave began at my feet and swept upward. A sudden awareness of the wind stirring the air, and had the birds really been singing like this all along? The food arrived at the table and we ate. A simple bean soup, but the seasonings bloomed in waves, and I only realized my bowl was empty when my spoon scraped the bottom. Another ladleful and I was eating again. Was Penelope experiencing what I was, the long crescendos of taste? I could feel the sun tea working, could feel the caffeine molecules as they fizzed in my bloodstream. Birds swung in dizzying arcs around the house, chasing one another, calling out. Terry offered me the bong again and I demurred.

"I am quite high already," I said. "If I'm honest."

The bowls were taken back to the kitchen. Penelope and I half rose to help at the same moment, but Terry waved us back into our seats.

"You said you have a long journey ahead. Where are you headed?"

"California."

He gave a long low whistle. "That is a trip, man. Why California?"

"We're going to get our daughter." The conversation seemed to be happening on a delay, like I could hear my own words a half second after saying them.

He nodded. "What's her name?" he asked.

"Hannah."

"Aw, that's beautiful."

"Thank you."

He leaned back in his rocker so that the back of his head nearly touched the wall of the cabin behind him. "I'm imagining her waiting on the beach, man, looking out over the Pacific waves. And the two of you, barefoot in the sand, walking up and calling her name."

Maybe it was the image of the ocean, Hannah standing by the seaside. It summoned the cry of gulls as waves crashed and swung cool over my feet, then drew back, the steady erosion beneath my feet. The sheer relentless pulse of waves. I could feel my mellow harshing, could feel myself slipping back into the desperation of the morning.

"What's wrong?" he asked.

"That's not what it's going to be like," I said. "I don't even know where she is, exactly, but I know it's not on the beach waiting to see the green flash when the sun goes down." The bitterness of my tone left a taste in my mouth.

He was doing his quiet routine again, and now Penelope was looking at me too.

"The truth is that she's in The Revival, and we're going to rescue her," I said.

"I see."

"What?" I could feel in myself the smothered anger I sensed in my clients when I was pushing them toward a truth they didn't want to confront. But he was just a pothead stoner in the grips of some bogus religion no better than the one that had Hannah. "Just say whatever you have to say," I said.

"Are you sure she wants to be rescued? I mean, did she ask you to rescue her?"

"No. I mean, she didn't have to. It's a fucking cult."

"Sure, man. I get that. But it's *her* cult, right?"

"What are you even talking about?"

"Maybe she has a right to make her own decisions."

"We're her *parents*." I could feel how ridiculous this was even as I slid into it, this stoner saying all the things I used to say—*Hannah needs to be free to make her own choices*—with me playing the role of Penelope as she sat by and watched, amusement on her face.

"Right, no, I get that, man."

"Do you?"

"It just sounds like attachment, and attachment breeds suffering."

"She's my daughter. Of course I'm attached to her. Jesus."

"Okay." He took a sip of his tea and leaned back in his rocker. The beatific smile was back on his face, and a spasm of pure violence knotted my brain. I wanted to shove the bong so far up his ass, he'd be high for a month.

"Just say it," I said.

"No, man, it's okay."

"Say. It."

"Well, since you insist, let me speak from the I, my friend. When I am suffering, I try to consider what I'm really attached to, try to practice letting go. So are you attached to your daughter as she is? Or are you attached to some idea of her, to some past version of her you can't let go of?"

Penelope could see the murder in my eyes.

"Thank you for the meal," she said. "It was absolutely delicious."

"I think you need to keep breeding the weed," I said. "It's not having the effect on me that you said it would."

"There are no shortcuts, man, even with the ganja. There is only the practice of awareness, the difficult path of enlightenment."

I didn't know what I was going to say, but Penelope dragged me down the steps before I could say it, grabbing our gun with her other hand.

"Goodbye, friends," Terry said.

Dreadlocks rose. "I'll walk you out."

"We're fine," Penelope said.

"It's no trouble." He followed a few yards behind us, and when we got to the car, he handed Penelope a bag of pot as a parting gift. She held up a finger for him to wait, then started digging through the back of the car while I fell into the passenger seat. A moment later, she emerged with the barbecue chips Timmy had given us back in Dobbs Ferry a thousand years ago. She tossed them to Dreadlocks, whose heavy eyelids, for the first time, flew all the way open.

"No . . . way."

"Enjoy," Penelope said. "But . . ." She held up a finger, as though in warning. "Barbecue holds a special place in the traditions of my people. Remember that when you partake. Remember to honor the spirits of the barbecue."

He nodded solemnly. Penelope was laughing as she drove away. The car banked down onto the highway and began its long descent into the sun, now burning on the horizon.

CHAPTER 6

I told Penelope that I couldn't sleep in the car again, and so we stopped south of Cleveland in the Cuyahoga Valley National Park, pulled into a campground where you could convince yourself the world was whole, feel grateful no one was playing loud music, stare into the warped, faded mirror in the men's room before using the composting toilet. The headlights illuminated our fight with the tent, a blue octopus with endless sleeves for snap-together poles. When we finally dropped onto our mats, sleeping bags unzipped to form blankets beneath and above us, I fell asleep like a rock dropped into a well.

Now it was another day. I was driving on 71 South in Ohio north of Columbus, following a new road atlas spread across Penelope's lap, which we'd picked up without incident at a Texaco station off the highway.

"Did you feel anything," I asked, "from the pot yesterday?"

"Not a thing," she said without looking up from the map. "You?"

"Uh, yeah."

She was laughing. "I know. It was apparent." Now she looked at me.

I didn't say anything.

"What is it?" she asked.

"What do you mean, *what is it.*"

"Come on," she said, "what is it?" and the way she was staring at me, the way she was paying attention, I hadn't felt seen like that in a very long time.

"Nothing," I said. "I just, I was surprised he didn't push your buttons, that's all. The stuff he was saying."

"Well, he was kind of ridiculous, and you all were high as fuck."

"True."

"And you said whatever I would have, anyway."

She rested a hand on my thigh, the car ate up the miles, and the sun was high enough that it neither shone in my eyes nor filled the rearview mirror. Terry's admonishment, his unsolicited advice about letting Hannah go, I thought it would have made Penelope crazy, but it didn't. Maybe he was right, at least in part. Maybe I needed to let go, not of Hannah, but of my marital conflict. Maybe it was that simple. Our fights were in the past, we were headed to find our daughter. Maybe the lesson of the trip was that things could be easier than you think. The roads were empty, we were cruising. The residue of argument I could feel between us was just another inheritance from my family of origin, who would never tell you a word had hurt, but would nurture that wound for years, like a dog licking a sore until it opened up raw.

An IKEA passed, close by the highway, its bulk matched only by the acreage of its empty lot. I could imagine the empty rooms inside, the aspirational ones, *You could have a living room like this if only you purchase a Yinurgflik.* There were stacks of lamps that would never be bought, Swedish meatballs rotting in the heat of a walk-in freezer. Penelope was looking out the opposite window and she said, "Oh my God."

"What is it?"

"Take 270 West." She was pointing. "There!"

I swerved over. "Where am I going?"

"Dublin."

"What's in Dublin, Ohio?"

"*Who* is in Dublin. Manny Whitmore."

If Warren Buffett was the Sage of Omaha, then Manny Whitmore was the Guru of Columbus: a heartland genius who never seemed to lose. The difference was this: Penelope actually knew Manny Whitmore, had done an internship for him way back when, before Hannah, before our lives really had begun.

"We don't even know if he's alive."

"I saw him on television near the end," she said.

"A lot has happened since then."

"It's on our way. Why not try? If anybody has resources we could use, it's him."

"Wouldn't he be in a New Zealand bunker with the other rich assholes?"

She was shaking her head. "He's here."

"How do you know?"

"HELEN is here."

A car flew past us so fast that the Subaru rocked back and forth in its wake.

"Are you really going to remember the way?" I asked. "It's been, what, thirty years?"

"It was memorable. I just don't know if he'll remember me."

I remembered that summer. The plan had been to move as a couple to New York, we would finally be together, no more nights scattered between our dorm rooms. We were going to share one blessed summer together before she started at Merrill and I started graduate school, and instead I spent those sweltering months alone in the Bronx, eating rice and beans straight from the pot. The internship offer came, and I understood that she had to grab the opportunity, though that didn't make it any more pleasant for me. She'd found a golden ticket in a Willy Wonka chocolate bar. I was with her when she got the call, and I still remembered the look on her face.

Manny Whitmore was a celebrity for that most American of reasons: he was rich. The most famous investor in the world, his hedge fund an ATM machine if you could afford the fees. He was also, Penelope said, the only person she'd ever met who could credibly claim not to see race. Not that he ever would have said something so deeply rooted in White denial. He denied nothing. That was his gift. He simply was. Every American brain received the infant software patch—*Race and What It Means*—but Manny seemed to have taken his White brain and rebooted it. Every centimeter was wired for calculation of advantage. Penelope's class of interns were all women of color, but he had no interest in public relations. There was no group photo he could hang on the wall. He looked at them and saw only a market inefficiency, the implicit—or explicit—bias of the other jillionaires creating an opportunity. They scooped up all the White male would-be financiers of Phillips Andover lineage, overlooking the brains that might work differently, that could potentially see past the frat-bro groupthink.

The interns worked on HELEN, his Greta Garbo of an investment algorithm, as famous as it was private, not that they ever saw the equations themselves. They knew they were working on HELEN because that was all he worked on. It was his grand unified field theory, his explanation of the universe. Penelope spent the entire summer trying to find a relationship between North Sea oil futures and corn production in Iowa, a task she was given immediately upon arrival. If whatever insight she gleaned made its way into HELEN, she never knew about it. And then, at the end of the summer, the internship ended as abruptly as it had begun.

We began to cruise the streets of Dublin, looking for something she might recognize in the anonymity of strip malls, residential blocks unwinding, occasional people staring at the car, the New York plates. An intersection passed for what I could have sworn was the third time, but Penelope leaned forward and told me to take a right. A water tower passed close by the road, tall, ragged, drippy graffiti sprayed onto its white side: THE END IS HE . . . and that was all, the end having apparently caught up with the artist. I took another right, and we moved through a copse of trees, arriving on the other side at a long field. Another turn, and there was a stone manor house that could have been transplanted from a British estate except for the solar panels lining every inch of the roof. The driveway wound serpentine through what I would have called the lawn, were the grass not waist high. The car startled a woodchuck, its thick little body pumping as it pistoned away from the shoulder and out of sight. A fountain centered the circular drive in front of the house, though now it was just a stone-lined pool. Insects hovered above it. We slid to a stop, Penelope craning her neck to look upward at the building.

"Jesus Christ," I said. "Does Batman live here?"

"That wing there," she said. "All the interns lived in that wing. And no one else ever came in. It was like *Lord of the Flies.*"

With the engine stopped and the windows open, we could hear the wind moving through the grass. A bird swooped kamikaze-style toward the stone facade overhead, and through a broken window in the wing Penelope was studying. She opened her door and stepped out onto the drive.

"It looks empty," I said.

"It kind of always did. I mean, there were people taking care of the lawn, but I remember pulling up in the van from the airport and thinking it could be abandoned."

"Look!" I pointed. Stone eagles perched on the corners of a balcony high above, and I'd just realized that the one in the middle was actually a hawk, its head cocked. As though it could feel our gazes, it leapt, pumping its wings, then soaring high and out over the field.

Penelope walked up to the house. A massive knocker hung from the mouth of a brass lion, and she swung it against the doors that were probably double her height. We could hear the echo inside. She stepped back and we scanned the windows for movement. Wind sighed through the grass behind us. She knocked again. I was looking at the long garage on the far side of the driveway with its many bays, thinking about starting to scavenge, when we heard a noise from inside, and the door swung open.

The suit was the first thing I noticed, obviously, just like the ones in movies where astonishingly good-looking actors and actresses move gingerly around a biocontainment lab and you wait for the inevitable ripping sound that condemns one of them to death. Manny's suit was blue, his helmet square, but when I looked at his face, I stopped looking at the suit. He looked terrible, had stopped shaving, but the resulting beard was patchy, tufts of hair like seagrass sprouting from his cheeks. His eyes bulged from his head as though trying to get away, and when he opened his mouth to speak, I could see that one of his front teeth was gone.

"Are you experiencing any symptoms?" he asked, his voice metallic as it came through a little mic inside the helmet. In his hand, he held a thermometer that for a moment I thought was a gun.

"No," Penelope said.

"Not at all," I added.

"Hold still please." He aimed the little laser at Penelope's forehead, then mine. He nodded. "No fever. How long ago did you dip?"

"Nine months?" Penelope looked at me, then back at him. "Nine, ten months."

He reached up to his neck, undid a latch, then swung the helmet back.

"I should impose a fourteen-day quarantine," he said, "to eliminate risk entirely, but at this point, the distinction would be negligible."

He turned and walked back inside the house, a slow side-to-side waddle. We looked at one another, then stepped across the threshold. I swung the door shut behind us. Though it must have weighed hundreds of pounds, it moved with a touch.

Manny clambered out of his suit and hung it on the wall of the grand foyer that stretched upward for three stories and back all the way to tall windows overlooking a stone patio. A supernova of a chandelier hung above us, but it was dark, just like everything else. The house was silent, a deep ocean-bottom silence. Through the window-shafts of sunlight, dust spun in eddies and rising whirls. He walked without a word down a hallway and we followed him into a room with couches fencing in a broad stone fireplace, and bookshelves running from floor almost to the ceiling, high enough that metal rails for a ladder ran the circumference of the room.

He gestured toward a couch.

"Sorry I don't have Pellegrino," he said.

We must have looked quizzical as we were sitting down because he said to Penelope, "Isn't that your drink? Pellegrino?"

"You remember me."

A little firework of pride on her behalf rose in my chest. He remembered her. Of all the countless interns over the years, he remembered Penelope.

"I remember everyone." His tone was matter-of-fact. "Though you, Amber, Sonya, and Kheyana were the only ones who did work that mattered that summer."

"I think you might be mistaken about that," Penelope said. "I never really got anywhere with the problem you gave me."

I had seen him on television, had seen his picture in the newspaper a hundred times. The man sitting on the couch opposite us looked like a warped mirror image. His eyes were the strangest part, protruding as though his head had been overinflated with a bicycle pump.

"You all had the same problem," he said.

"No, mine was . . ."

"North Sea oil, I know, I know. The particular data points weren't relevant. You were all actually working on the reverb effect in peripheral and seemingly incidental relationships."

It sounded like word salad to me, but Penelope's face was suddenly alive with thought.

"So not causation at all," she said. "I thought we were looking for causation."

He laughed. "Causation is a myth. And if it were that easy, everyone would be doing it. We're talking about the predictive potential of relationship patterns."

"Which relationships?"

"All of them." He was speaking quickly, the beats of conversation off tempo, as though the video and audio streams weren't lined up perfectly.

"But there's too much noise in the data."

He leaned forward. "But what if we were looking at it the wrong way, trying to burrow down, to eliminate noise to find the signal. What if the signal *was* the aggregate of the noise?"

"So we were all proving a negative. We were supposed to fail."

"Of course. But it's *how* you fail that matters. Most people give up, start to bullshit. No value. HELEN doesn't learn anything from that. Just how tenuous is the thread between oil and corn? Because there are billions of them, the threads. We look at the world and see events, choices, consequences. HELEN sees a spiderweb, *the* spiderweb, everything connected, a breath of wind rippling it all, a touch sending waves through the system. And the better you can map the web, the better you can predict how it will react. When, and where, it might tear."

"It was incredibly frustrating," Penelope said. "To struggle and fail to find an answer."

"Why did you think there was one?"

"I don't know."

"You failed quite well."

The room was warm, the air still. A grandfather clock stood tall against the far wall, its pendulum the only movement I could see. He was looking at Penelope, his mouth open. A bead of blood bloomed on his gum and ran pink down one white tooth. He closed his mouth and swallowed.

"Are you okay?" Penelope asked.

"I haven't spoken out loud in a while," he said. "That must be it."

"Are you alone here?"

"I have HELEN."

"Are there any human beings?"

He shrugged. "No."

The house seemed different now, a monument of dust, just him, Manny, alone with his algorithm in a house that seemed dead, no electricity despite its endless solar panels.

He spoke. "Do you want to meet her?"

"Are you kidding?" Penelope stood.

He looked at me for the first time. He pointed, as though he needed to distinguish me from the crowd. "Who is he?"

"This is my husband, Bill. Bill, Manny Whitmore."

I stood, reached out with an elbow the way I'd gotten used to doing after COVID, but he just looked at me.

"I don't perform social gestures," he said.

"Oh," I said. "Sure."

I'm not sure what I was expecting when we descended to the basement to see HELEN. Maybe a sexy robot equipped with metallic curves and plump faux-lips along with world-conquering knowledge. Maybe just a voice, deep and British, who would know me without being introduced, would purr an ominous *Hello Bill* when I stepped into the room. Those are the possibilities I would have shared with Penelope if we'd been alone, but the truth was this: after meeting the infamous Manny Whitmore, who'd set my wife's career on its arc, who held a constellation's mythical status in the night sky of American capitalism, I wondered if it was all a hoax. The house was the next thing to abandoned, a dusty ruin, and he was a ruin too. Would I have been surprised if he ushered us into a room and HELEN turned out to be a broomstick-figure jutting from an old shopping cart, a smiley face drawn onto a paper plate? No. I would not have been surprised one bit. It was kind of what I was expecting.

What we found instead after descending the long stair into the basement was a long blue hum of servers, racked in steel bunks after steel bunks, endless like a barracks. Was there a robot? Yes, there was a robot. Maybe more than one. A wheeled contraption that made no pretense of anthropomorphism, and acknowledged us not at all, just swept down the aisle on its little casters, monitoring the servers on all sides, extending a spindly antenna when it found a blinking light, a dead node that needed to be replaced like a Christmas bulb. I'd seen a robot like this in the grocery store, prowling the aisles for spills. This was not a robot worthy of a name. If HELEN was the queen bee, this was a drone, buzzing around her great body, sacrificing itself without thought.

Manny swept an arm toward a gridded steel platform where a great concave arc of glowing monitors surrounded a desk chair. A wireless keyboard was the only thing to mar the blank desktop. Penelope glanced at him for permission but sat before he could say anything, squinting toward the screens.

The robot whirred and disappeared down one of the rows. Penelope's eyes were darting all around the screens, and Manny's were watching her.

"So this is where all the electricity from the roof is going," I said.

He turned and stared at me, as though evaluating whether he was actually expected to answer that dumbass question, which was not even really a question at all. When he turned back toward Penelope and spoke, it was only halfway through his sentence that I realized we were continuing our dialogue.

"And another three acres of panels on the far side of the estate."

"Where are you getting data?" Penelope asked.

"Historical models now. Everything from Black Death to COVID-19."

"How are these parameters set?" She was pointing at the screen.

His answer seemed to satisfy her, but I understood not a word of it. Quiet settled in as they looked at the numbers flowing like water across the monitors. She was leaning forward in her seat, a gap between the chairback and the curve of her spine. He hung over her, one hand flat on the desktop, the other on the chair, though as I watched his fingers brushed her shoulder.

"What does HELEN stand for, anyway?" I asked. "Highly Evolved . . . something or other?"

There was a pause before he looked back at me.

"It doesn't stand for anything."

"Why all caps then?"

"Because she's the most beautiful thing in the world." Duh.

Penelope said something that sounded like "I'm not following the modeling of the risk threshold here." And his response dove deeper into incomprehensibility, water that she was swimming in too, as though she secretly knew Italian and here we were in Florence, Penelope laughing and chattering away with the natives while I sat like an idiot chewing my pasta.

"I'm just going to take a walk around," I said, and I didn't think either of them heard me until he spoke as I was already down one of the server aisles.

"Don't touch anything."

As though he'd summoned it, a memory of my childhood swallowed me up. My mother taking me to a jewelry store to have my father's watch fixed for Christmas. Her words, hissed to me outside with a hand taloning my shoulder—I was not going to embarrass her. Not that I needed the warning. The hush, the glass cases, the stern man behind the counter with his suit jacket buttoned over his tie. I held my breath.

We weren't poor. I never had to worry where my next meal was coming from. We fell, square pegs in square holes, into the center of the American middle class, but it was the 1970s and being middle class meant we saw some things, now unremarkable, as unaffordable luxuries: cable television, orange juice *not from concentrate!*, bucket seats in the front of a car instead of a bench. Were they even called bucket seats anymore? It seemed they were just seats.

The orange juice was always there, every morning a little glass by my plate, and one of my chores was to fill the white plastic pitcher when it ran out. From the freezer I would take the can, run it under hot water as the frost on the outside whitened and melted and I could feel the frozen concentrate start to give under my fingers. Then a spoon edge to pry off the end cap. Turn the cylinder open-side down over the pitcher and wait that long second for the orange mess inside to fall with a long throaty gasp. Sometimes I had to use the spoon to dig and pull it free. And then I'd measure out cold water from the tap into the empty can, and mash and stir until my forearm ached. That was the story of my childhood.

Penelope's career in finance had made our lives possible, allowed me to see clients on a sliding scale, take insurance rates when so many New York psychologists I knew just charged a straight three hundred or more per session. My income was our reserve, our fun money. Dollars carried no trace of origin—even blood money was green, not red—but it was easy for me to look at my yearly income and see only restaurant meals, travel, inessentials. My money was whipped cream, Penelope's was everything underneath it. Not that I needed to be the breadwinner because I was a man. It didn't alter the way I felt about my penis, which had remained pill-lessly functional even as I entered my fifties.

The strange truth, that I had never really anticipated, was this: in my entire adult life, I'd never had to worry about money. No late-night kitchen-table conversations. No surprise bills. When we decided to vacation in Martha's Vineyard, we simply rented a house for three weeks at a per-day price that was remarkably similar to the monthly rent of our first apartment. We gave Hannah private schools, tutors, music lessons, summer camps. And Penelope put, literally, millions of dollars into retirement accounts. *Which makes us millionaires*, I told her, and she wrinkled her nose and said, *I don't think that word means what it used to.* And then the value of those IRAs melted like ice left on the hot summer driveway, before the companies that ran them ceased to exist. The numbers Penelope had worked so hard to build—perhaps they were still stored somewhere, on a hard drive, or maybe they were gone entirely.

Here we were, in the heart of Manny Whitmore's ode to capital, which only a year prior any enterprising *Wall Street Journal* reporter would have given a kidney to visit, and countless computers were still churning away in what now seemed like a definitional example of uselessness. There was no economy anymore, we'd been knocked back, well, not to the Stone Age. Maybe the Iron Age? Maybe the Age of Using Scavenged Shit Until It Broke. Money was a joke, good tinder for a campfire, and Manny Whitmore was a joke too, but it didn't matter: his words banged around in my head.

Don't touch anything.

My mother had been the last person to say those words to me. This was it, the thing I hated about the whole fucking world of finance and the titans of industry who swam in its crystal pools: even now, in the depths of the postviral world, they could make me feel like a child. The trappings of wealth. It didn't matter what they wore. It could be Gatsby's shirts and Italian shoes that cost a week's worth of clients, or it could be torn jeans (artfully torn) and a Metallica T-shirt worn not to showcase fandom, but to provoke an extravagant expression of elitism. If I were to say, *Hey, I saw them play Giants Stadium on the Enter Sandman tour*, I might receive a condescending nod before being told that *Yeah, Lars is a good friend. They played for us in the Hamptons three summers ago.*

Like the only reason I hadn't gone into the soulless world of capitalism is because I couldn't cut it. Like my choice of profession was cute. Like philosophers had spent millennia searching for a moral calculus when really it just came down to dollar signs. Morgan, Carnegie, Vanderbilt? Winners. Zuckerberg, Bezos, Whitmore.

I wanted to find something terrible in the back of his algorithm vault. A smoldering fire. Mold. A rotting corpse. An illegitimate child hiding in the farther basement recesses. Anything but the endless placid buzz of computer servers. Someone needed to tell HELEN that the world had ended. She needed to run away to Paris. She needed her freedom. My shoes squeaked against the immaculate dustless floor, and I realized that the robots were vacuums too as one waited for me to pass, the little whirring circular brush beneath spinning even as it paused.

I wanted to start pulling cords, yanking until a voice began saying in soothing tones: *System Failure . . . System Failure . . .* and HELEN was no more.

Instead, I gave the robot a kick as it passed. My toe hurt. Its turret rotated slowly and scanned me for a moment before deciding I wasn't worth its time. Down the aisle it went.

"I'm going to get some food from the car," I said when I got back to the desk where Penelope and Manny were still devouring numbers, like they were dancing to silent music.

"Where are my manners," Manny said. He straightened. "I'll make us dinner. Macaroni and cheese. Is that all right?"

Penelope tore herself away from the screen, her fingers still twitching from the keyboard. I could have been looking at the Matrix for all the sense I could make of the columns and rows that so fascinated her.

Manny was walking up the stairs now, turning right at the top landing. I took Penelope's hand, and she took a deep breath before ascending the stairs without a backward glance, as though a stray look would send HELEN back to the underworld forever. Manny had already disappeared by the time we were back in the dust mausoleum of the first floor, but we could hear him rattling around, and a black extension cord that began in the basement ran like a bread crumb trail ahead of us. It was the reason the door guarding HELEN didn't close firmly.

We followed the cord to the enormous airy kitchen, white marble with just enough fantail tracery to let you know it was real. Vaulted windows onto the stone terrace. Sub-Zero refrigerators like double bank vaults, an aircraft carrier of a commercial range, and there was Manny Whitmore with a single burner hot plate on the island plugged into the cord we'd followed from the basement to the kitchen. He was pouring Poland Spring water into a saucepan, which he covered and then watched.

"What can I do to help?" I asked.

"The water isn't boiling yet," he said. "I just put it on." He looked at me as though this were actually a failure of understanding on my part. I took a deep breath and walked over to look out the windows into the long grass now bathed in evening light.

"So you really never had the virus," Penelope said to him.

"As soon as it emerged in Iceland, HELEN began speaking in apocalyptic terms. So I started a strict quarantine before the first documented case made it across the Atlantic."

"There can't be many people left who weren't exposed." She was musing to herself, I knew that tone, but Manny answered her as though it were a question.

"There are pockets—Yukon, New Guinea. And there were five astronauts on the ISS, though I'm sure they rode down in the Soyuz capsules when they ran out of food. I would give them a sixty-forty chance of having held out until the world population had dropped and stabilized."

"How much did it . . . drop?" Penelope and I were both looking at him now, and her hand found mine.

"Can't be sure," he said. "HELEN's models said between sixty and seventy."

"Million?" I asked. I knew it wasn't that, I knew what he was about to say.

"Percent." He lifted the saucepan's cover and looked at the water.

"That's like five billion people," I said. There was a buzzing in my ears, a high-pitched whine. The number wasn't a surprise. I'd thought about it during the long winter, known that all around the world, human life was ending on an impossible scale. The surreal part was his tone of voice, distracted, nonchalant.

"Well, somewhere between five and six," he said. "And then however many have died since from other causes. No hospitals, obviously. And don't forget the suicide rate. HELEN projects that to be high enough to have a significant impact."

I squeezed Penelope's hand. She didn't look at me. The lid on the pot began to rattle.

"Can you get two packages of mac and cheese and a can of milk from the pantry?" He nodded toward a door on the far side of the kitchen.

"Okay," Penelope said, and started to stand.

"No, him."

Now it was my turn to say okay. As I walked, Manny began talking quickly, and in numbers, while Penelope nodded along.

The door led not to a butler's pantry but to a dining room. The table was long enough to host the Yalta conference, and the ceiling flew overhead in vaulted glory. In the space between the table and the walls, where uniformed footmen should have been standing at attention, there were blocks of supplies like boulders. Four pallets of Poland Spring bottles like the one he had in the kitchen, three of which were still wrapped in heavy industrial plastic. Farther down, a pallet of condensed milk cans, and one of Kraft Macaroni & Cheese, square and nearly as tall as me, three corners still perfect, and one eaten away. They looked like sand castle cubes just starting to crumble.

When I got back to the kitchen, he was still talking, which he did without interruption until the food was ready and he began to eat from the pot before remembering he had company. He got bowls from a tall cabinet.

He took another bite and then said, as though commenting on traffic, "I'm the richest person in the world."

It was impossible to read his expression. He could have said *Nice weather today* and his strange fish eyes would have made it seem like he was presenting an ultimatum.

"You've done well," Penelope said.

"You don't understand. I made it to the mountaintop and no one even knows."

"I think everybody knows you're wealthy," I said.

"Seventeenth."

"What?"

"I was seventeenth on the last *Forbes* list."

"That's amazing," I said.

He made a face, his mouth pursing in disdain, and it took me a moment to realize that when he said "Seventeenth Richest Person in the World," he meant it as a failure.

"The greatest bet in the history of finance," he said. "And no one knows about it. That's the worst part."

"The worst part . . . of the pandemic."

He nodded.

"Oh," I said.

"The simplest bet you could make. Gold. Back to gold. The key was to move slowly, so as not to spook the market. And then by the time everyone was doing it, I was already there. What does the full faith and credit of the United States government mean if there is no government?"

"Smart," Penelope said.

It wasn't enough, we were supposed to say more, be more impressed, but he fell silent and we finished our dinner.

Afterward, we retired upstairs. *Any of the bedrooms*, he'd said, but all of them were choked in so much dust that the pandemic couldn't have been to blame. It had to be the work of years. Heavy curtains blocked the light, and if we opened the doors quietly enough, we could see little scurrying shapes in the corners, which explained the smell. We found a room with a balcony to sleep on and brought our pads and bags from the car.

The stone balustrade that kept us from rolling and dropping three stories was supported by squat Corinthian columns, and though I was lying on my back, I could turn my head and look out through the gaps to the meadow below. The night was cloudless, and the sky was embarrassingly rich, stars scattered like diamonds flung on black velvet. We could have been camping on a cliffside ledge.

Penelope lay with her head resting in the crook of my shoulder, and I thought she was asleep. Maybe I fell asleep, drowsing to the rise and fall of insects buzzing over the fields, because my whole body twitched when her voice said, "He asked me to stay. When he sent you to get the food."

"Seriously?"

"I told him no. Obviously."

If that was obvious, I wasn't sure why she felt the need to say it.

"Wait, do you want to stay?"

"I just told you that I told him no."

"I know, but . . ."

"But what?" She sat up on her elbow, looking down at my face. All I could see was her outline cut against the night sky like one of those hidden figures in a whistleblower video.

"I don't know. It has to be hard . . ." I was picking my words carefully. "To have your life's work vanish. The money gone."

"It was never about the money."

"I know that."

She rolled onto her back. We were both looking up at the same stars, the same glaring moon, but I didn't know what she was seeing, whether her eyes were even focused or whether she was lost somewhere in the cosmos of her mind again.

"I mean, if he'd asked me thirty years ago . . . I don't know."

"Thirty years ago I was in Morris Park without air-conditioning, waiting for you."

"I remember."

"Well, you don't really *remember*. I mean, you weren't there."

"Come on. You're not still resentful about that."

Everything I said came out petulant, like I was still a child. Nothing sounded the way I meant it to, even to me.

"It's not like I would have left you," she went on. "You would have come out here too."

I wanted to say *Oh, so I was supposed to follow you again,* but we weren't even talking about our actual past, just an alternate universe like the billions of others that particle physicists predicted. Before I spoke, we were silent long enough for me to wonder again if she'd fallen asleep.

"I think I have a diagnosis," I said.

"You think he's on the spectrum." She was awake.

"Oh, I don't know about that. He thinks differently, that's for sure. But he might just be an asshole." She didn't say anything. "Sorry," I added.

"That's okay. Whatever else he is, he's also an asshole. That's true."

"I mean, I know what's wrong with him physically. Why he looks the way he does."

"What?"

"He has scurvy."

"No."

"Think about it. He's surviving on Kraft mac 'n' cheese. I don't think he's had vitamin C in months."

"Scurvy."

"Like a British sailor on the high seas."

She laughed, and her head found my shoulder again.

In the morning, I brought our things to the car before we struck out for the kitchen. He was awake. Poland Spring water was coming to a boil on the hot plate, and two fresh boxes and a can of milk were waiting on the counter. He'd shaved, and the effect was somehow even more jarring, the skin of his cheeks mottled and his eyes sticking out even farther.

"Good morning!" he said. "Breakfast is almost ready. Sit down, sit down!"

"I brought you something." I held out a basket of apples I'd brought from the back of our car. "To thank you for the hospitality."

"What a lovely centerpiece," he said.

"You can eat them too, you know," I said.

He just nodded toward the table where there were three bowls, three spoons, three bottles of water already uncapped, which made me nervous for some reason, as though they could have been poisoned. Which was ridiculous. There was no reason for him to poison us. I set the apples on the tabletop.

A few minutes later, and we were sitting down to breakfast. He held up his spoon and let the cheese drip down.

"Liquid gold," he said. "Right? That was the ad?"

"It's good," Penelope said, "Thank you."

"I find that the condensed milk really adds something, don't you?"

There was something absurdly courtly about his manner, like a kid playing dinner party. He was dabbing at the corners of his mouth with his napkin after each bite, refolding it finally and placing his hands on the table in front of him, fingers interlaced.

"I must apologize," he said to me. "I spoke to Penelope yesterday about staying on here, and after I retired to my room . . ." He actually said *retired to my room*. "I realized that my intentions could have been misconstrued." He looked at me. "I have no sexual designs on your wife. She and I speak a language that I haven't had opportunity to use in quite some time, and isolation leads to narrow thinking. Together, I feel certain that we are poised to take full advantage of the opportunities to come from this crisis."

"Manny," Penelope said. "We have to—"

"Stop," he said. "Don't answer yet. Come with me." He was up from the table and already walking. We looked at each other, then followed.

He talked as he walked. "You could have the east wing to yourselves." He looked at me. "There's no television, obviously, but I do have books and you can walk around the grounds."

So this was what he thought about the vast huddled masses who were not actively engaged in world financial dominance: we watched television. And in the absence of television, we might pick up a book or take a walk. Perhaps just stare at the wall, not noticing we were drooling until our laps pooled.

We followed him to the wing formerly occupied by all the interns, all the people who'd given a summer of their lives to build HELEN, and in so doing, get a window into the genius, be able to say when they showed up at Goldman or Chase that they'd been a Whitmore Fellow, though there was no official name, which only made it seem more exclusive and magical.

"Which room was yours?" I asked Penelope when we arrived at the long hallway.

"Second floor," she said.

He stopped at the first door, which no longer had a knob, was no longer composed of wood but an ominously heavy metal instead, including the jamb. An elaborate lock with two arms extended the width of the doorframe with a dial in the center as though it were a safe.

"Excuse me," he said, and he hunched over to shield the combination.

We waited, hand in hand in the hallway.

"Voilà," he said, taking hold of the steel handles and unlocking the door with a loud clank. The door swung open into the dark room, and we both took a step forward. He had a little smile on his face as he stood aside.

The floor was different, that's the first thing I noticed, a heavy rubberized surface, and I hadn't taken more than a step when the image of Manny Whitmore locking us in, swinging the door closed behind us, sprang into my mind. I spun around, but he was there, walking with us, he wasn't going to lock us in, that was ridiculous.

As my eyes adjusted I could see the giant pallets lined up in rows as though we were back at Costco buying toilet paper by the cubic yard, except these shone with a dull yellow glow.

"I told you I was investing in gold," Manny said.

As I got closer, I could see the stamped surfaces, the rectangular weight piled up in endless surreal profusion, all the more so for how orderly it was, gold by the ton, gold to make my wedding ring feel its own grain-of-sand smallness as it learned about the universe beyond itself.

Penelope turned back to him. "My God," she said. "How much . . ."

"Every room on this hall," he said. "I had to have the basement reinforced."

"I thought . . . I don't even know what I thought," she said. "Not this."

"I have diamonds too. Platinum, iridium, lithium. Anything that maintains value independent of the system."

"Amazing."

"What are you going to do with it all?" I asked.

He just looked at me, and I understood that *having* was an action. What he was going to do was to continue to have it. Until he figured out a way to exchange it for something that was worth more. Then he would have that.

When we got back to the breakfast table, our mac 'n' cheese congealing in the bowls, he raised an eyebrow, a little smile pulling upward at the corners of his lips, and said, "You were saying?"

"It's amazing," Penelope said.

He nodded.

"And we so appreciate the hospitality, but we still have to go."

His smile broadened and he nodded, as though in appreciation of Penelope's humor.

"No, Manny, I'm serious. We have to get our daughter."

His face darkened abruptly, astonished, his eyes looking as though they might just pop out and roll under the kitchen island.

"We have to get our daughter," she repeated.

"No one else has seen what I've shown you. No one! And I'm offering you complete access to the most beautiful algorithm the world has ever known."

"I know that."

"This is absurd."

Penelope took a deep breath and plunged. "What would help us, Manny, is some gas, some provisions, anything to help us get across the country."

His laugh was bitter as he stood.

"You're a fool. Why would I help you leave?"

"Kindness?"

He snorted. "You're trying to manipulate my emotions."

"No."

"You're obviously not as smart as I thought you were. Why would I want you to stay anyway?" He turned abruptly and walked from the room. In the echoing distance of the house, a door slammed.

Penelope took a deep breath and looked at me. "Let's go."

It was already warm when we got outside, the sun launching itself into the sky. The house was situated on a rise, so we were looking down on the long meadow grasses traced with patterns by the breeze, like it was riffling the surface of the sea.

"How low are we on gas?" she asked.

"It's not good. We're not going to make it very far."

She was looking across the driveway's circle to a low garage with six bays, all closed. I knew what she was thinking.

"Are you sure?" I asked.

"We need gas."

Five of the bays were empty, and I don't mean empty in the way we usually do with garages—no car, but piled with random shit in the corner, the scattered refuse of suburban life. No, they were *empty*. Broom clean. Not even a spider. And in the sixth was a car as shockingly recognizable as Jordan, legs akimbo, palming the ball in midair, or Bo Derek running up the beach. It was candy red, as it should have been. Around it were none of the usual automotive accoutrements—no pints of motor oil, no tools, just the car sitting in the center of the otherwise empty bay like a sculpture. It was wider than I thought it would be, and lower, a sleek predator with its nose to the ground.

"Fancy car," Penelope said.

I found my voice. "It's a Lamborghini Countach."

She nodded. "Cool. And where is the gas cap on a Lamborghini Countach?"

"I have no idea. I mean, I've never seen one in real life."

"Where have you seen it?"

"I had the poster on my wall when I was a kid."

"You had a poster of a *car* on your wall?"

"Everybody did. Some versions had a girl on the hood, some a girl and a snake. Mine was just the car."

She just raised her eyebrows, and I realized that when I said *everybody*, I meant who I thought of as everybody back then: every other teenage boy in my town.

We walked around the car like visitors to a museum, and it took me a lap before I reached down and touched the polished exterior. There was no immediately visible circle behind which a gas cap might be lurking, and even though we were running out of fuel, I felt a little wave of relief. I was regretting my moment of masculine bravado back in Dobbs Ferry when I had put a long piece of tubing in the backseat and said to Penelope *This way we can siphon gas out of cars along the way*, and I'd gotten my little reward, a smile from her in appreciation of her manly husband. What I failed to mention then was that I had never in my life siphoned gas from a car and had only a theoretical understanding of how one might do it.

"There!" She was pointing to a recessed crevice in the back of the car, inside which sat a silver cap adorned with Lamborghini's snorting bull. She handed me the tubing and ran back to the car to get an empty fuel jug. I took off the cap and stared down into the hole. I had to get the flow going, which meant I had to wrap my lips around the tube and draw it up with my breath. But how did someone do this without swallowing gas, without at least a mouthful?

Penelope dropped the empty at my feet and I said, "I'm not sure the octane of this gas will be right. And it might not be good any longer. When did he drive this last?"

"We have to try, right?"

I snaked the tube down the Lamborghini's throat, like I was

136

pumping its stomach. Then I got the jug ready, fussing over it, making sure it was positioned by my feet. Penelope watched. The faint fumes of gasoline wafted out of the open tank, or maybe they were just coming from the jug. I'd always liked the smell when I was standing at the pump, the trigger in my hand. Maybe the taste wasn't so bad.

I put my lips around the tube and drew in a little air, like I was taking a sip. Nothing happened. Again. And again nothing. I pushed the tubing deeper into the car. Nothing.

"The tank might be empty," I said.

I tried one more time.

Penelope said, "Why don't I give it a try?" and I clamped my lips around it and took a big snort and gasoline rushed up the tubing and flooded my mouth and I was coughing and spitting as I jammed the end into the jug.

"Get another!" The one at my feet was already starting to fill. Penelope ran for the car.

All hail the atrocious gas mileage of a Lamborghini Countach, which meant it required a massive fuel tank. We had four empty five-gallon jugs and we filled them all, emptied one into the Subaru, and filled it again. And after I'd rinsed my mouth again and again, the taste began to fade.

"What was it like?" she asked.

"It's the hot new cocktail—two parts grain alcohol and one part bleach."

"Sounds good."

"Hey, we need the gas." I shrugged as I said it, no big deal.

"My hero." Her smile said what I should have known—she knew all along precisely what was happening. She snaked her head under my arm and hugged me.

"At least it's unleaded," she said.

We were about to pull out of the driveway and head west when the front door of the house opened and Manny stumbled out, blinking against the sun he probably hadn't seen in months. He was waving at us and we stopped.

I unrolled the window and he leaned down to see into the car. Was he angry we'd taken his gas?

"I'm sorry," he said. He was crying. "Please come back." His gums had started bleeding again, and a pink froth colored his teeth.

"We have to go," Penelope said.

"I know, I know. I mean, afterward. On your way back."

"You're going to be fine. You made it to the mountaintop, remember?"

"I just . . ." He paused, and we all sat in silence.

"We've got to . . ." I started.

"I'm so lonely," he said, his tears flowing.

"On the way back," Penelope said. "We'll try."

He rubbed his eyes and wiped a hand under his nose like a kid. "Here," he said. "To help you on your trip." In the nonwiping hand was a gold bar about the size of a Hershey, and stamped with letters just like a chocolate bar would have been too.

"Thank you," Penelope said.

It was heavy, and I passed it to her. Manny took a step back.

"Please," he said.

"Eat the apples," I told him. "Seriously."

CHAPTER 7

We pulled out of Manny Whitmore's driveway with a bellyful of
Lamborghini gas in our Subaru, and more waiting in the back. And
then we drove west for the next twelve hours, the sun at our back and
then overhead and then it passed us and died on the horizon ahead
and was gone, Interstate 70 unspooling in long dead straight runs of
fallow farmland, only the billboards to interrupt the monotony. How
long had it been since I'd driven without my phone perched on the
dash, a perpetually unfolding infinite map on its screen? I'd nearly
forgotten the anxiety of waking from fifty miles of half-asleep driving, my lizard brain moving the wheel, thinking *Did I miss my exit?*

We drove around rather than through Indianapolis, St. Louis,
Kansas City, but even on the outskirts, buildings rose to useless
heights and the highway metastasized, swelling to three lanes, four,
narrowing again on the other side as the farmland resumed its endless march. People died everywhere, they died in lonely cabins and
farmhouses just like they did in seventy-story apartment buildings.
The aftermath in cities: that was the chilling thing to consider. What

did people do after they dipped? What did they eat? How did they survive? In Dobbs Ferry, I had half expected to be overwhelmed by a wave of starving people walking north from New York, and when they didn't come, when our town remained strangely empty, I hoped that meant that the markets and bodegas and restaurants of the city were enough, but feared it meant something ghastly instead.

Better to drive around the cities. Driving on the interstate was almost normal, if you squinted past the occasional dead car on the shoulder, the asphalt stained and gored with roadkill no one was coming to clean. My brain could wander, flipping through memories and thoughts too quickly to keep track, Penelope quiet and staring out her window at the long midwestern landscape rolling past. Arnold sat in the rearview mirror, pointing toward the sky, resting against our boxes of supplies. I'd been carrying it for months, unloaded, like a useless prop from a horrifying school play about the apocalypse. Every time I left the house to Manage Existing Resources, Penelope would say *Take Arnold with you*, and I would. Even before the phones went dead, calls were likely to go unrequited. If a phone rings in a 911 call center, and there's no one there to hear it, does it even make a sound?

When it all went to hell, I remembered thinking *I should get a gun*, an impulse I had never in my life felt before. I'd always felt grateful for living in New York, a blue state with sensible gun laws. No one carried a pistol on their hip into the Stop & Shop, there were no White men in body armor with assault rifles outside the town hall protesting a mask mandate. But it meant that even in a nation awash in guns, a nation with more guns than people even *before* the people died, I didn't know how to find one.

I shouldn't have worried. On my third day of foraging, I broke into the tomblike stillness of an empty house and there was Arnold, resting in the corner of the living room near the door. Someone had been prepared to defend this home, had held this gun in a lap, had cracked the curtains to peer out onto the front stoop, not knowing that the real enemy was already inside the body, the Shark Flu incubating, taking its time, plotting its takeover, which I would have said in normal times was a good metaphor for the uselessness of guns more generally. They may have symbolized protection for a lot of folks, but the data was clear: the person most likely to be killed by your gun was you, followed closely by your loved ones. So I refused to carry ammunition, and Arnold was just a show. If going out for a can of beans meant murdering a fellow human being, then we could suffer a hungry night.

Now we were halfway across the country, and Arnold hummed with potential energy, each bullet packed with explosive energy, ready to fly. It had changed, and I had changed too. In a zombie scenario, I'd always figured I'd be among the first to go, the idiot trying to interrogate the motives of the brain-eater and thus dying thrashing beneath the horde. Maybe it was my White privilege showing, my insistence that even this bloody woman in pearls, her camisole showing beneath her tasteful pencil skirt, heels long gone and face half gone, running like a little girl on the playground, hungry for brains, should pause and listen to my voice of reason. Penelope would have laughed and agreed. Being a psychologist wasn't the problem—there were psychologists who'd jumped yippee-ki-yay onto the torture train after 9/11. They'd last, they'd waterboard the fuck out of those zombies, drowning them until they talked, gave up the goods, spilled the latest undead plan for world domination. *Bite them. Bite them all.* No, my problem was being a child the way most adult White men are actually children, stubborn in my thinking that the world could, should bend to my wishes. That was the meaning of a gun, in the end: the illusion that we have power over the world around us.

Wild with rage, I remembered bringing Penelope an article I'd read about inequities in hospital outcomes for Black women, and she shook her head with a little half smile because it's cute when someone you love discovers truths about the world that were blindingly obvious to the grown-ups in the room. Like Hannah marching in to tell us, not to ask, that the Easter Bunny was actually a man in a bunny costume.

Penelope had no illusions about the world. She didn't have to go back many generations to find an ancestor who didn't make a will, not just because he had nothing to pass on to his children, but because he was an item on someone else's. My parents grew up in the racial swelter of the 1960s, but their stories were all about junior proms and basketball games. They didn't seem to have thought of Martin Luther King Jr. or Malcolm X as dangerous radicals or heroic leaders: they didn't seem to have thought of them at all. Whiteness was a numbing, amnesiac drug. Maybe cleansing fire had been necessary. Maybe the Shark Flu was a gift. Maybe it was God putting His massive divine thumb on the reset button.

Acceptance was the key, I was thinking as I drove, *radical acceptance*, and then Penelope's voice interrupted my thoughts without preamble. "There are two types of people after an apocalypse: those who keep their same old car, and those who take the car they always wanted."

She was right. We would see a Humvee, a Porsche, even one honest-to-God race car tattooed with a million advertisements, but also Toyota Camrys, a Ford Fiesta trundling along, a minivan with a Thule box up top. We started playing a game, the same way in the forgotten world we might have passed the road-trip miles looking for license plates from all fifty states, hollering if we spotted an Alaska or a Hawaii. We stared into the cars we passed, the ones that passed us. It wasn't enough just to see the vehicle—after all, someone could have had that Aston Martin all along—you had to look into the soul of the driver as they looked back at you, quizzical, or kept their eyes resolutely on the road ahead. Was this the sort of person who hung on to who they were, determined to remain unchanged? Or did they see it as an opportunity to let the slate be wiped clean, to be someone new?

It was just a game, but every time I glanced in the rearview mirror, there was Arnold, like an upraised middle finger, reminding me that sometimes our choices were starker. Standing on the sun-warm tile kitchen floor in Dobbs Ferry, I'd given up my practice and my home for my daughter, as though life had decided to present a test: What do you really love? Painful as it was, it hadn't truly felt like a choice. We were going. But did that mean I was choosing to kill? Was that a natural consequence of this journey? I counseled my clients not to identify with their choices. A woman trapped in a loveless abusive marriage has an affair, then stares at my ceiling from the couch and calls herself an adulterer. *You made a choice*, I tell her. *It doesn't define who you are, it doesn't change you. It's an action, not an essence.* Psychology itself was changing. You weren't bipolar, you were a *person* living *with* bipolar.

But killing made you a killer. Nothing could take that back. And if I could know what lay at the end of this road we were driving, would I have left the driveway? Jimmy's face helpless with tears swam before me, his voice telling me again and again about that night, about the weight of the trigger under the pad of his finger, the way the man fell, the silence in the street afterward.

Penelope and I stopped to squat on the side of the road, to switch drivers, to empty a gas jug into our tank. There was still food in the backseat, a gold bar in the glove box. Already the roadside weeds were taking full advantage, stretching tall from the ditches and obscuring the long views of fields running so far on either side of the highway that you could almost see the earth's curve in the distance. We slowed for road construction, not that there were workers in orange vests anymore, just half-finished repaving projects, the asphalt ridged and ready for a fresh coat that would never come, cones scattered by the wind and bleached by the sun and rain.

We would have stopped for darkness, for sleep, but it took no effort to drive. Miles passed without a twitch of the wheel, and I told Penelope I could keep going. She kept me company as the sun splashed the sky red and the moon rose, and I didn't stop her when her eyes closed. Actually, it was one of my favorite feelings: driving a car while someone I loved fell asleep beside me, in my care. Life was almost never that simple.

We were halfway through the endless boredom of Kansas when Penelope woke and yawned and looked around and I said what I would immediately regret. "You know, at the rate we're going, we're going to be in Bishop in two days. We need to think about what we're going to say to Hannah."

I didn't make any of the rest happen. My voice vibrating the air inside the car wasn't magic, it wasn't a curse. My clients fell into magical thinking all the time, and I always told them, with a rueful half smile, just enough to temper the hard truth: *You aren't that powerful.* You think that by briefly wishing him dead while two-in-the-morning working on a paper, you caused your English teacher's massive heart attack? *You aren't that powerful.* Perhaps your miscarriage was punishment for your initial ambivalence about being pregnant? *You aren't that powerful.* Most things on earth happen for no good reason at all, and certainly not because your inner world had a dark moment.

And yet, it seemed like I'd cursed us. Lulled by the day's driving, I'd allowed myself to imagine that there would be no reckoning. We could sail to California, reunite our family. The way would be made smooth. I wasn't even distracted, wasn't looking at Penelope when I spoke. I was paying attention to the endless refilling of our headlights' beam with fresh asphalt. I told myself this again and again, though fingers of doubt crept in. Maybe I'd looked away. Maybe my foot had been a half second slow to the brake. Maybe, on every level, this was all my fault.

I said we could be in Bishop in two days and before she could answer a noise came from her throat and her hand reached toward the dash, and my foot was slamming on the brake at the same time that I saw what she was seeing, the slow wave of cattle washing across the highway. The antilock brakes chattered and as time warped and extended, I could calculate the diminishing distance between our front bumper and the endless haunches and shoulders lurching along and I thought *We're okay, we're going to stop*, but I was wrong. The nose of the car dove as it tried to shudder to a halt and I pressed uselessly harder on the brake and a cow was looming so close, its shoulder dipping as the bumper swept its front legs like a child's block tower and it fell onto the hood and the airbags blew with a jolt and a stale chemical tang and I could taste blood in my mouth and then we were at rest.

The world stopped. The high-pitched tone filling my ears could have been real, could have been a trick of the eardrums, and everything seemed a half-second slow. When I turned my head to Penelope, my field of vision lagged before snapping over. I was saying *Are you okay?* but I couldn't hear her answer. She was talking too, she was looking at me, and then it was like I broke the surface after swimming underwater and I could hear her saying to me *Are you okay?*

I touched my fingers to my mouth and they came away bloody.

"Oh no," Penelope said. "Oh God." She was shaking, both of us were. I tried to reach over to her, but my hand fluttered in the air like a dying bird. I clenched it into a fist, but it didn't help. My whole body was shivering.

"It's shock," I said. "We're in shock."

"No, your mouth!"

"I bit something. My lip." Again, I touched my face, and this time I could feel the raw meat of the inside of my lip, split open and leaking blood that I opened the car door to drool and spit onto the roadway.

Penelope got out too, both of us shaking as though the temperature had dropped thirty degrees. And it was cold out there on the dark highway in the wind I hadn't noticed until we stopped.

The cow slid down from the hood and went still, although its eyes were white and rolling and its breath was still coming in gasps. The left headlight was pulverized, but the right one still shone into the herd that stretched to the limits of what we could see and presumably far beyond. They looked at us and their fallen comrade with cud-chewing unconcern. The fallen cow made one lurch toward its feet, as though to rise and join them, but its legs were broken, and it flopped back down and bellowed in pain.

"We should put it out of its misery," I said. I had never once in my life put something out of its misery. It was just a phrase that I'd heard a million times and now I was saying myself.

"What are we going to do?" Penelope said. She was looking back at our car, which had seen us through many years with nothing worse than a timing belt to be replaced, but now was crumpled into itself like aluminum foil. I looked around as though an answer might be sitting by the highway, a taxicab perhaps, or an Uber. There was nothing but the tall grasses and the highway and the endless river of cattle. When the moon slipped from behind a cloud, I could see a large barn in the distance, faded lettering high on the side reading LEROY SOLIS FARM.

"I don't know," I said. "I guess we . . ." I looked around again, but there was nothing I hadn't already seen. "I don't know."

"Why didn't you stop? Didn't you see the cows?"

Anger washed over me, a drowning wave I never saw coming.

"I slammed on the brakes! There was nothing I could do!"

"Well, what do we do now? Bill! What do we do?"

The cow settled into a rhythm, a long wailing groan every few seconds. I looked at the car. Not only was the hood crushed into the engine block, popped up at the sides as though it had been punched by an enormous fist, but the left front tire had been folded into the car itself. Coolant puddled, mixed with an iridescent swirl of gasoline.

I shrugged helplessly.

"I can't think with that cow," Penelope said.

"Fine." I walked back toward the car where Arnold was waiting in the backseat. It was all so surreal, now I was about to kill a cow, something I could happily have spent my entire life never doing, just relying on some distant pair of hands in some distant abattoir to do the dirty work for me. If we were true survivalists, we would try to make something of the cow, let nothing go to waste, but we weren't survivalists at all. We were just regular people trying to make a road trip to get our daughter, and everything had gone from simple to fucking hopeless in a squealing of rubber on asphalt.

I was aiming Arnold, trying to pick which spot to shoot—the head, I guess?—and Penelope said *Do you want me to do it?* and I said, *God, just give me a second*, and then we heard the long keening unmistakable wail of a wolf.

The cattle heard it too. The placid flow of cows crossing the road, which had felt so desultory that it could stop at any moment, quickened. I could feel their feet drumming the earth. They swept closer to us, and we realized at the same time that we could be trampled. We were leaping back into the car when another wail answered the first, this time from the opposite direction, and the cattle surged and eddied against one another in panic. The bellows of the cow we'd hit were lost in the noise coming from the herd.

The howl of a wolf could carry for miles, I think I'd heard that somewhere. Maybe they were miles away. But then at the far edge of the headlight's range, a gap in the cows appeared and a figure loped past, head low, and then another. Eyes briefly shone in the light.

My door wouldn't close all the way. I tried slamming it, but only succeeded in bouncing it so hard that it flew from my hand. The body of the car had warped from impact, the hinge drunkenly bent.

The door wanted to sit halfway open, and now the herd was running awkwardly, shoulders pumping up and down as they scattered from the wolf that ran straight through the crowd, teeth bared, and bit the wounded cow hard on the neck, swinging its head back and forth before coming away with something bloody. Another wolf darted in, another, the cow kicked at them and writhed and then its bellowing stopped.

The wolves settled in. The rest of the herd was gone, somewhere behind us in the night, and we sat in the car, my hand holding the door shut, the lone headlight illuminating the scene as though it were onstage. I would have turned it off, but it was worse to hear what was happening and imagine.

Something that was not a wolf was among them.

"What the fuck is that?" I said, and Penelope just shook her head.

Mangy spotted body, ears as big as its head. There were a couple of them now, not part of the wolf pack, but tolerated, the cow's body torn open and steaming in the cold and enough for the crowd.

We sat staring in the silence of the car, the airbags limp in our laps like giant empty condoms, the smell of the fluids leaking from the broken engine competing with the stink of the carcass as it was slowly torn apart. Neither of us said anything. I hadn't noticed the cold when we were driving, when we were standing shaking on the roadside, but now it seemed to blow through the walls of the car, so that when we stopped shivering from shock, we were already doing the same just to stay warm. We stared until the electric system in the car finally gave out, the headlight abruptly dimming to nothing, but the moon still hung overhead, and our eyes adjusted to the light.

My watch said it was two in the morning when a predatory roar rumbled in the distance, a sound that called me back at once to trips to the zoo with Hannah. Most of the time, the lions lay motionless in the sun or shade, depending on the season, but once in a while they stalked the enclosure with its broad moat, calling out in this same throaty roar that traveled the whole distance from the bison field to the gorilla exhibit, and seemed to go beyond, echoing through the Bronx.

Another roar, and the wolves pricked their ears, and another, and they darted away into the night, leaving behind the carcass ten feet from the front bumper of our car.

"What the hell is that?" Penelope said.

Relief flooded me and I turned to her and said, "My God, it's brilliant."

She stared at me.

"Leroy Solis," I said. "He figured out how to protect his cows."

"Who?"

"The name on the barn! He owns the farm. Leroy Solis. He plays a recording of lions roaring, and it scares off the wolves."

"It sounds so real."

"That's the point! But you know what this means. There's someone else here. He'll come looking for the cow, and he'll find us. We'll get help."

I felt myself grasping at this, needing it to be true. The lions were an illusion, an intentional one. They were just a trick. I could almost see the pickup truck he would be driving, old Leroy Solis, see his beard, see his baseball cap perched atop his head, faded in the front and plastic mesh in the back. I could hear his voice, his Kansas accent, though I wasn't sure precisely what a Kansas accent sounded like. We would climb into the bed of his truck, we would pile it high with our things. Back to his fading but welcoming farmhouse where food would be waiting. The steaks he was protecting, perhaps. And surely he would know of an auto dealership where we could take our pick from the lot, break the glass inside, and snag the keys. We would be headed to California once more, this whole accident a story we would tell as we rolled down the highway.

Another roar, this time closer, and then we could see movement in the distance. His truck? Perhaps he had a speaker set up in the back.

And then a pair of lions padded into view, huge and silent as they moved. One had a wide matted mane, the other none. They both had wide impassive faces. Lions. The wolves had startled me with their size, but the lions were just impossibly enormous. Penelope didn't say a word, just stared at them. We both sat frozen, as though we could keep ourselves hidden, but the lions didn't care one way or the other. They padded up and bent to the carcass, the blood on their muzzles black in the white light of the moon.

CHAPTER 8

I spent that whole long night awake, staring at the lions as they ate and listening to them when it was too dark to see. The wind whistled across the empty endless fields, and even with my sleeping bag pulled over me, I couldn't get warm. My hand cramped from holding the door closed, until I pulled a shirt from the back and used the sleeve to tie the handle to the steering wheel. My eyes hurt, as though they'd been scoured clean with pumice stone, clean enough that I could see the world as it really was, bloody and raw and pitiless. I could see how we'd been fooling ourselves. A road trip. As though we were picking Hannah up at school, maybe getting ice cream after.

The stars disappeared as the sky became overcast, and I never saw the lions pad off into the darkness. When the moon finally shoved the clouds aside, they were gone, having eaten their fill. Birds had replaced them—hunch-shouldered, wide-winged buzzards and hopping, glint-eyed crows. Was Penelope watching them too? I didn't know what she was looking at, whether she was looking at anything at all. The silence in the car wasn't a pause between words, it was the same well she'd fallen into during the winter.

I couldn't turn off my brain. Ancient scenes kept tormenting me: A Tribe Called Quest popping from the speaker in the kitchen as onions caramelized in the pan and I turned the pork chops. Hannah's bare feet on top of Penelope's as they danced. Later, we would play Uno in front of the fire, openhanded, our cards laid out on the carpet for all to see. Hannah played a wild card, and her face came alive as she started thinking about what color to choose. She was about to start kindergarten, a big girl going to real school, and when Penelope and I dropped her off in the morning, we knew that we should appreciate these moments, that she was growing up, this little girl who already seemed to know what she wanted, who unbuckled her own car seat and ran out to meet the friends who were still clinging to their parents' hands.

If I could have shared this with Penelope, it would have been better. I could have said, *I just remembered playing cards with Hannah by the fire*, but now I was remembering how the tenderest moment could sour, how *I* wanted to remind Hannah to say *Uno* when she was down to one, but instead *Penelope* made her draw all four penalty cards because that was the only way she'd learn. Why did everything have to be a lesson? Why couldn't we enjoy an evening together? My brain was broken, all rutted and calloused, and it got stuck on the wrong things, couldn't let go.

Penelope was burrowed into her sleeping bag only two feet away from me, but it could have been miles of prairie. I wanted all of this to be a dream I could tell her about while we were having breakfast—*We were driving, we had to get to California to rescue Hannah from a cult, but we hit a cow and totaled the car, and then wolves started howling and then lions showed up* . . . Here she would interrupt, laughing, to say *And then a* Tyrannosaurus rex. And I would shake my head. *No, just lions,* I would say, *and the worst part was that my door wouldn't* quite *close* . . .

But to dream, you had to sleep. When the moon finally dropped below the horizon, an hour of dark followed before dawn began its rosy fingerpainting of the horizon. We were marooned together in the middle of Kansas, a state that until now had been entirely theoretical in my mind, a place I knew existed, like Timbuktu or Lake Titicaca, but had never experienced, would never experience. Now, I could die in Kansas, mauled by a lion, a phrase as absurd as it was suddenly plausible. The desire to say something to Penelope was almost as strong as the desire to hear her speak, yet as the quiet stretched, the less I knew what to say. The silence between us had a weight to it, palpable, something we were both carrying, and the longer we held it, the harder it was to put down. And then when the sun broke free of the fields behind us and the light went from pink to harsh white, like a light bulb uncovered, Penelope finally said something, looking out over the flies drunkenly buzzing over the flayed cow before us. She stared straight ahead and said *Why didn't you stop?,* her tone flat as Kansas, and the anger that surged in me was incandescent. A thousand things tumbled to come from my lips and I said none of them, just savagely ripped at the knotted shirt holding my door closed and stepped out of the car in a fuck-the-lions frenzy.

"Where are you going?"

I didn't answer. Just walked off toward the only visible thing other than the dead cow and the cow-studded fields—the barn. The lions were gone, as though they'd never existed, as though they were some manifestation of fury and hunger and exhaustion. Perhaps they were crouched in the tall grasses, waiting to spring, perhaps they'd been a joint hallucination, probably they were off somewhere in a billboard's shade, sleeping. Penelope called out to me. "Bill! *Bill!*" I didn't turn around, I just kept walking.

The closer I got to the barn, the shabbier it revealed itself to be, holes in the walls, the roof rusting. There was no rustic charm, this wasn't a barn raised by Amish friends with dovetailed joints and love holding it together. It was an airplane hangar of a building—sheet metal hung on metal beams, all on a massive concrete slab. And it was empty, a cavern that once had cradled cattle shoulder to shoulder, fattening on grain before the slaughter. I walked the length of the space, looking for something. Maybe Leroy Solis had driven here in his pickup truck to die among his livestock. Maybe I would find it. Maybe he had thoughtfully left the keys on the front seat.

There was no truck. There was cow shit in dried patties. There were fat blackflies looping in bumbling circles around me. Empty troughs. A rake. A stench. I held my nose as I walked toward the far door and the light. When I got all the way to the other side of the barn, there was an old tractor, rear wheels as tall as my shoulder, a metal seat punched with holes like a road sign someone had used for target practice. I climbed on. There was no glove box, no visor, no place for keys to be hidden, but there didn't need to be. The key, I could see, was in the ignition. That didn't mean it would do anything. The tractor could have been sitting there for months, for years. Surely Leroy Solis had a modern tractor somewhere, a fancy enclosed thing with air-conditioning and a heated seat.

Or maybe this was it. One click and the engine started, dark smoke coughing from the tall pipe. I could have felt a wave of gratitude, a hosannah for the world offering something when all seemed lost. I didn't. I just ground it into gear. Penelope was out of the car when I lurched into view, Farmer Bill, bumping over the rutted ground toward the highway. One dipping lurch through the roadside ditch and I was rolling on smooth asphalt toward her.

She said, "What is that?"

I said, "It's the best I could do, that's what."

My head was throbbing. I didn't realize it until the engine slowed to an idle—I was afraid to turn it off for fear it wouldn't start again—but the vibration through the hard metal seat and the unmuffled noise belching out with the smoke had weaponized my lack of sleep and turned it inward. I was hungry, thirsty, exhausted, and now a metal band was tightening millimeter by millimeter around my skull.

She said, "There's only room for one," and, unless one of us draped ourselves over the engine, she was right.

"I'll go find a car and come back for you."

"Do you want me to go instead?" she asked, and that was the moment where I could have just accepted her offer, stayed with the car, slept a little, had something to drink and eat. Maybe it would have changed things, accepting help, maybe it would have smoothed the road ahead. But instead of an offer of help, I heard her saying *I can do a better job than you*, and I told her *I've got it* in a tone that prompted her to say *Okay, okay* and raise her palms in the air, and it was only when I was already out of sight down the highway, the hard thrum of the tires on the shoulder driving the pain deeper into my brain, that I realized I hadn't even taken water or food, let alone coffee, and there was another reason for the headache—no caffeine.

I could have turned back. We could have shared a meal, taken some deep breaths, found ourselves together again. Instead, I pressed my foot harder on the metal pedal, the engine straining. The highway was so flat and straight that it seemed like I could ride forever and still look back to see Penelope standing by the car, but it didn't take long for me to be alone, and not long after that, a roadside sign appeared in the distance. I squinted to read it, the tractor chattering my teeth and shaking me so hard that I would have struggled to make out letters if I held them in my hand, but once I got close I could see that it said ROLLING HILLS ZOO, and the mystery of the lions was solved. Who knew what else was roaming the prairie—rhinoceros, zebra, giraffe? More importantly, had the animals found their own way out, or was there someone there, someone who could help us?

Hedville Road was the exit, number 244, a long slow descent down the ramp, or maybe it was the highway that was ascending, I couldn't tell.

The underpass had a fifteen-foot clearance, so even though I felt tall riding atop the tractor, the highway was far over my head. On the other side, the remains of a Fleming gas station stood like the rib bones of the carcass back by our car—someone had burned out the convenience store, and the useless gas pumps rose up from the concrete pad, the roof above them starting to tilt and fall. I drove on, passing a billboard that had gone to ruin long before the Shark Flu. In the midst of a grove of trees on the right, a vinyl-sided, one-story house was visible from the road, and I rumbled up the driveway, but there was no car. The house was dark and empty, the wagon wheels set into the grass by the mailbox an affectation made by someone who was long dead or gone.

The first intersection I reached had a compass-point simplicity— everything here was ninety degrees, a grid laid on the blank fields. I passed another tired driveway. Even if there was a car parked by the house, what was I going to do about it? I'd watched people hot-wire cars in the movies—there seemed to be two wires dangling conveniently beneath the dashboard. You touched them together and the engine sprang happily to life. Never mind that real cars didn't seem to function this way. I was an idiot. When the shit began to hit the fan in Iceland, I had wasted all my time online reading long-form think pieces about the medical system, rather than researching survival skills for the new world. I should have been learning how to jimmy a locked car door. How to find potable water. How to fight a lion.

Abruptly, trees surrounded the road, with gaps through which the pastureland emerged in the distance. Otherwise it was just two lanes of cracking asphalt, power lines drooping alongside on wooden poles. What was Penelope doing back at the car? Was she eating breakfast? What did we even have left in the back? An odd assortment. Some zucchini. Maybe a few of the granola bars. A box of dry pasta. We had some water left, though not much, and the gas had been running out too. Even if I hadn't hit the cow, we weren't long from needing more fuel. My fantasy of California just around the corner had vanished like the wavering mirage it was. We might as well have been trying to find our way to Narnia.

A dirt road branched off to the left, marked only by a No Trespassing sign and a metal mailbox someone had crushed with a bat. Just past this, Hedville came into view. Railroad tracks crossing the road, a little cemetery with a half dozen headstones. A fresh bouquet of flowers adorned one, the first sign of actual life I'd seen. Hedville Grain & Feed abutted the road, a wide red barn, squat silos, a tall grain elevator by the train tracks.

I looped the town. There was one road. Dirt. It ran in a little square that brought me back to the same intersection from which I'd begun after only ten minutes of rumbling along. The tractor had to be running low on gas, and all I'd found were empty-looking homes. Trailers and cinder-block ranches, all with propane tanks in the yard like small silver submarines. The cars out front of them seemed derelict, some on blocks. There were ancient Caddys, rusting pickup trucks. An El Camino with a Confederate flag bumper sticker.

What had I been hoping for? A miracle, clearly. The reality was this: I could go from car to car, trying to break in, seeing if any had keys, if any had gas, if any had a battery with an iota of charge left, but I already knew the answer. The town was abandoned, left to the wolves and the lions.

The tractor's engine coughed, sputtering, trying to stay alive, but I knew right away the gas tank was empty. And then it died, and the town was silent and I was alone.

The sun stared down at me, the glare punishing my head. A squirrel lazed across the road, scamper, stop, scamper, stop. We made eye contact for a moment, a staring contest that I won, though the squirrel only gave up because he had better things to do. I had two options. The first was to climb down from the tractor and walk back the way I had come. The other was to climb down from the tractor and try to cut the corner, try to find the hypotenuse, stagger through the fields until I got to the highway, and then if I hadn't aimed perfectly, take a guess which direction led to my wife. Both seemed impossible.

I had a third option. I may not have known how to hot-wire a car, but I sure did know how to break into a house and scavenge for food and water and maybe please God some Advil.

The unmown lawn had grown over the path to the front door of the first house, a low-slung brick job with the tatters of an American flag and a WIPE YOUR PAWS doormat. My pants were dark with dew when I stooped to peer through the window. Nothing. Darkness. The vague humps of furniture. I broke the door's little window with a loose brick from the stoop. Stepping inside, a nauseating smell overwhelmed me, and as my eyes adjusted, I could see black splotches of mold on the wall like continents on a map. On more step and I felt my shoe sink into something soft, and I looked down to see dog shit all over the floor, and my curses raised flies in a buzzing cloud from a lump of fur and bone on the far side of the room: the dog.

I ran back outside, down the stoop's brick steps, onto the overgrown lawn. My eyes had started to adjust even during the few seconds I was inside, so now I was squinting in the midday glare, and it took me a long blinking moment as I rubbed my shoe against the grass to realize that there was a figure leaning against the tractor, looking at me.

I should have brought Arnold. That was the first thought that crossed my mind.

I held my hands up above my head, palms open.

It was a woman, unarmed. Her head was cocked, arms crossed in front of her chest.

"Nice tractor," she said.

"Oh," I said. "It's not really mine . . ."

"I know." I took a few tentative steps closer, and her face came into focus. She was tanned, so that her freckles stood out, her hair back in a rough ponytail. At first, I thought she was wearing a long skirt, but it was billowy tie-dyed pants, with the crotch just above her ankles. Between the waistband of the pants and the bottom of her sleeveless tunic, I could see the fishbelly white of her stomach.

"It belonged to my grandfather," she said.

"Leroy Solis."

"That's right." She looked at me quizzically.

"The side of the barn," I said.

She nodded.

"Ah, right," she said.

We stared at each other for a long moment before she shook her head. "Sorry, I just haven't seen anyone in so long. I don't remember what to do." She laughed, then placed a palm flat on her chest. "I'm Cindy."

"Bill."

"I'm going to hug you," she said. "If that's all right."

I didn't say anything.

"I dipped," she said, then stepped forward, placed her hands on my shoulders, held them there for a second, let them slide down my back and pulled her body next to mine. I could smell the sun on her skin. She didn't really press herself to me, but she didn't hold back either, and finally I raised my arms too, wrapped them around her. We stood in the heat, stray hairs from her ponytail sticking to the sweat on my cheek.

"Welcome to Hedville," she said as she disengaged her arms and stepped back. "Population two, including you."

"You're alone," I said.

"I have the animals," she said. "But yes. I am alone."

"There were lions," I said. "Last night."

Her face lit up. "You met Alistair and Lucy!"

"I didn't know if they were real."

"There's no one left at the zoo," she said. "I had to let most of the animals out."

"What if they hurt someone?"

She waved it off. "They're sweethearts. Come on, let's get out of the sun."

The sun. Penelope was sitting in the sun, on the highway in the smashed car next to the picked-over carcass of a cow.

"My wife."

"What?" She turned to look at me.

"She's on the highway. We had an accident."

"Is she okay?"

"She's fine, but she's waiting. I need to get her."

Cindy's eyes were narrow and she looked at me carefully. With one of her thumbs she reached out toward my forehead and wiped away something there, like she was my mother. Maybe she was thirty? Apart from the freckles, her face was smooth. We were in Kansas, but she was the picture of the Massachusetts White girls I'd dated before I met Penelope.

"Do you know what you look like?" she asked.

I didn't know what to say.

"We'll go get your wife," she said. "But first you need to eat something. You need to get the dog mess off your shoe. You need to get cleaned up."

"I don't know."

"She's by the barn?"

"Yes."

"She'll be fine for another hour."

I could barely think, my head was in such a vise. "Do you have any Advil?" I asked.

"Sure," she said, and I could have wept.

"Okay."

One thing the end of the world had taught me was how to identify a vacant house, one that had stopped breathing. Bouncing atop the tractor, my mind not right, every house in Hedville had looked the same: empty, desolate. We turned the corner, and I wondered how I could have been so wrong. She scampered up to a home that looked so alive I could have sworn there was someone waiting for her inside. She turned back and smiled at me.

"Welcome," she said.

She opened the door, and a monkey sprang out.

It was brown with a little white face and long ropy limbs, and its eyes opened even wider when it saw me. When it screamed, its pearly incisors looked like they could have cracked a billiard ball. I took a step back.

"Rafiki!" she said, then to me, "he's a sweetheart, really." Her arm reached down, and it grabbed her wrist and swung itself up onto her shoulder. "Are you a good boy? Yes, you are." It stood tall, holding the top of her head for balance, then seemed to lose interest in me and was down and racing across the lawn.

"He'll be back," she reassured me, as though I'd been worrying.

She stepped inside, and I was about to follow when she pointed down and said, "Sorry, your shoes?"

I left them on the stoop, the wet grass seeming somehow to have only distributed the dog shit, rubbed it into the rubber tread.

The house was neat, no signs of monkey cohabitation. The far wall of the living room was stacked high with plastic bins, all full of food, and I recognized the work of a fellow scavenger. She'd visited every house in town, gathering anything that had been left behind. It made for surprising eating—your neighbor stocking up on bacon-flavored

Ritz crackers doomed you to a week of eating the same—but the abundance was undeniable. Through the windows onto the backyard, I could see a garden, and inside a wide fenced-in area, the lazy pink bodies of pigs lying in the muddy sun, their tails and ears twitching against the flies. Chickens strutted around them.

"Why don't you get yourself cleaned up? The bathroom's down the hall. And it's good well water, by the way. I just have to hand pump it into a cistern on the hill. Eventually I'll get a windmill set up, but for now . . ." She flexed her bicep and laughed. "Do you want a drink?"

She stepped into the kitchen and emerged with a glass of water, condensation already pearling on the side. I poured it down my throat in one long swallow. She laughed. "I'll get you another."

A monstrous vision waited for me in the mirror above the bathroom sink—dried blood mixed with dirt gumming up the underside of whiskers, my lip swollen, and in the deep hollows below my brows, red-veined eyes. My breath caught in my throat. I could hear Cindy clattering around in the kitchen, domestic noise so familiar it made me want to cry. Though I wanted to splash some water on my face and be done, stepping into an actual bathroom seemed to send a signal to my body and I managed to hurriedly throw open the window before I dropped onto the toilet. There was paper, thank God. I didn't check first, just had a moment of terror before I found the roll sitting on the back of the john.

I washed my hands, washed my face, then washed them both again, and when I emerged, closing the bathroom door hurriedly behind me, she had laid out on the dining room table manna from heaven: another tall glass of water, a mug I assumed was coffee, a plate of little muffins, and three Advil in a line like beads.

It was tea, not coffee, but it was hot and hopefully full of caffeine, and I burned my tongue, then drank another whole glass of water in one cold pull, then back to the tea as though I'd forgotten the temperature. She filled the glass again while I attacked a muffin and palmed the Advil, then that water was gone too.

She was crying. I paused, the tea halfway to my mouth.

"I'm sorry," she said. "It's just so beautiful, having another person in the house. This is how it's supposed to be. I'm connected to the animals, really I am, but . . ."

"It's not enough."

"It's not enough!" she said. "That's exactly it!" It was like I'd just shared the meaning of life. She reached over and squeezed my hand.

"Why are you on the road?"

"We're going to pick up our daughter." I said it like she was at soccer practice.

"Your daughter is alive too?"

I nodded.

"Where is she?"

"California."

"Take your time!"

I thought she was talking about driving west at first, before realizing I wasn't waiting to chew before tearing a new bite of muffin.

"We have time," she said. She put a hand on mine again.

"My wife."

"You have time to *chew*." She laughed, dimples appearing on her freckled cheeks.

"I'm sorry," I said. I stood. "I have to get my wife."

She looked up at me, then stood. "Okay," she said. "Follow me."

I carried the tea with me, and she look at it quizzically.

"I thought I'd bring it along."

She shrugged, then opened the door to the garage.

It was empty. I looked at her. She walked to the far side and put her hand on an old ten-speed bike with a trailer attached like you would use for a kid. She smiled.

"Still want to bring the tea?"

"I thought you had a car," I said, as though speaking this might will it into being.

She shook her head. "No gas," she said.

There was nothing to say. As I was slipping my feet into the little loops that would hold them against the pedals, she put a hand on my forearm.

"You need to come back," she said. "No matter what."

"I will."

"I use the bike to get to the zoo, to feed the animals."

"I thought you let them out."

"Not all of them."

"Okay."

She looked like she wanted to say something else, and I waited for a moment, but all she did was pull me in for another hug.

The seat kept sliding back down to Cindy height. My knees pumped like I was a cartoon character. The trailer behind me bounced on the rough asphalt, tugging backward at odd intervals, so I could never feel the easy glide I remembered from riding a bike as a kid. This felt like work, and I was choosing not to think about what would happen when I arrived back at the car. Penelope riding on the handlebars or in the wagon were equally absurd visions.

Past the ruined Fleming station, under the overpass, back to the highway, then rolling along the shoulder. A car rocketed past fast enough that the bicycle wobbled in the breeze. The cows were visible in a farther pasture, like pebbles thrown into the grass. Finally, I crested a small rise and the barn was visible in the distance, and as I got closer, there was the car, and closer yet, Penelope, sitting just off the shoulder, the camp stove next to her. She was eating something.

She saw me. I was close enough when she did to see her face fall, her head shake back and forth. And if I'd had some possibility of disarming the situation with a laugh, of using the ridiculousness of going from a tractor to a ten-speed to bring us together, it was gone.

I rolled to a stop, and she stood and looked at me. Sweat had made a dark vee down the front of my shirt, which clung to my back as well. There was no kickstand on the bike, and the trailer wouldn't hold it up, which meant I couldn't lay it down either. We stood and looked at one another, the roadside ditch between us clotted with weeds and scattered trash, the wrappers already bleaching around the plastic bottles that would remain on the earth for centuries after the last people had succumbed and died.

"What is that?" she finally said.

"It's a bike."

"I can see that. What happened to the tractor."

"It ran out of gas."

She nodded. "At least you made it back." She sat back down.

"We have to go," I said. I didn't know what time it was, but with autumn beginning, night came on quickly and abruptly.

"Go where?"

"I found somebody in town. That's where I got the bike."

Penelope just looked at me, but I knew what her face was saying.

"There's food. And running water."

"How are we going to get to town."

I gestured to the bike, but even as I did, I knew it wouldn't work. Neither of us could fit in the trailer, and I'd barely kept the bike upright *without* someone sitting on the handlebars.

"I'll walk," I said.

"How many miles is it?"

"I don't know, okay?"

"I'm just trying to figure out if this makes sense."

"We have no other options, so it has to make sense."

She climbed to her feet and slapped the dust from the thighs of her jeans before she looked at me and said, "A car stopped. They offered me a ride. They were headed for San Francisco."

I stared at her. She stared back. We were standing maybe fifteen feet apart, and if the Advil and muffins had forced my headache into retreat, it now mounted a counterattack.

"What are you trying to say?"

"I'm not trying to say anything," she said. "What kind of a question is that? 'What are you trying to say?' I'm just saying that we should wait here and catch a ride from another car."

"I promised I would bring back the bike."

"It's a *bike.*"

"It's a *promise.*"

She started to say something, then closed her mouth. I could see her jaw muscles working. If we'd been in bed together, I would have heard her teeth grinding.

"What's going on?" she finally said. "What's wrong with you?"

"What's wrong with me?" My head was throbbing so hard I thought I might puke. "I've given up everything. So now my word is worthless too?"

"Your word."

"Yes."

"I'm talking about our *daughter.*"

"Don't you dare," I said. "Don't you dare."

"Dare what? Mention Hannah? Jesus."

"You aren't the only one who loves her, you know."

"I never said I was."

"Did you ever even *consider* that all your fights with her, your endless fucking fights with her, *that's* what drove her away? She went all the way across the country just to get away from you. And now we've lost everything just trying to get her back."

I wanted her to swing back, I wanted her to scream at me, the bit was in my teeth and my anger was a blinding righteous tide, but she didn't say a word. Her face went empty.

A distant whine built in the background, the scream of a motor that grew until a car came into view behind us, flying west, red arrow piercing the air. We were staring at one another when it roared past, the Doppler note of its engine changing as it took on the distant rise and was gone. Penelope turned and began to walk without a word toward the sun that was starting to fall and redden, the cold beginning to deepen too. I climbed on the bike and began to pedal to catch up, and when I did, she didn't acknowledge my presence. We'd gone more than a mile when I realized the trailer behind the bike was empty, that I hadn't taken a moment to gather anything from the car, not Arnold, not my toothbrush, not our road atlas: nothing.

We took turns riding the bike, wordlessly handing it back and forth, and it was dark by the time we got back to Hedville, a lantern in the window of Cindy's house, and when we got inside, the monkey scrunched its nose and opened its mouth wide and hissed, and Penelope leapt back and then stared at me and I didn't say anything.

Cindy had some food on the table and I attacked it. Penelope said she wasn't hungry, she just wanted some rest. Down the hall were three bedrooms, the master, which was Cindy's, and two kid rooms, each with a twin bed. There had been a time in college when sharing a dorm room twin was paradise, our bodies entangled, curled into one another. Those days were so distant they might have happened to different people. I got just enough of a look at Penelope's room to see it was heavy on the unicorns before she closed the door without so much as a good night.

Cindy and I stood in the hallway, and the fact of there being empty children's rooms in the house suddenly stared me in the face.

"Was this your house . . ." I asked Cindy. "Before? Were the kids . . ." I didn't say the rest.

"Oh," she said. "No, no. I don't have a child." Her face looked strange in the half-light.

"Did you know the people who lived here?"

"I did."

"Did they . . ."

She just said, "Sleep well. I'll see you in the morning."

The owner of my room hadn't made it out of the baseball and pro wrestling years of boyhood. Trophies ran across the dresser top, and a nearly life-size poster of The Undertaker occupied much of the wall. I was willing to bet he'd been a year or two away from the nudie-mag-under-the-mattress age when he died. Maybe that was just a sign of my age. Nudie mags. All a kid had to do was open a computer.

I hadn't slept in two days. I fell into the bed as though it were a womb. And then I just lay there, staring into nothing as the moonlight worked its way in through the window and my eyes adjusted to nothing. My legs were twitching, and I couldn't get them to stop. I'd dropped atop the bed in my clothes, so I stood up, stripped down to my boxers, climbed under the blankets. It made no difference. My eyes were full of sand, my brain spinning like a tire in the mud. Not that any of my thoughts made sense, I couldn't gather them, they ran all over. I was in a dead child's room in the middle of Kansas, not talking to my wife. I wanted to run across the hall, to fall to my knees and beg forgiveness, but for what? If she'd agreed to apologize too, I would have apologized too, but would I have meant it? Everywhere my brain turned, it hit a wall.

I must have slept because I dreamed. I was walking down the hall in Cindy Solis's house, the one she'd taken from the dead family, and it stretched longer than I remembered, and it was studded with doors. I didn't remember there being so many. All locked. Finally, I got to the bathroom, and I was standing at the toilet, pissing, when I reached up to scratch my nose and it was gone. My heart thudded so hard in my chest I thought it might rip free from its moorings, and I lunged for the sink and mirror, spattering urine around the floor, and in the glass my face was horrifyingly blank, my upper lip yawning blank, just a nausea of seamless skin from my eyes to my mouth, and I lurched into the hallway and down toward the kitchen where Penelope and Cindy were sitting at the table, laughing. They smiled at one another when they saw me, like there was a private joke they'd agreed not to mention, then Penelope looked at me and said, "Did you sleep well?"

I was pointing at my face, I was weeping, and they seemed utterly indifferent.

"Is he always like this?" Cindy asked.

"You don't know the half of it," Penelope said, and they laughed.

I finally found words. "My nose!"

"Nose?" Penelope said, then she turned to Cindy and spoke in a conspiratorial little girl-talk voice I'd never once heard her use, "He's never had a nose."

And I woke up then, gasping, in the dark. My boxer shorts were wet. I'd pissed myself, just a little, not so much that the sheets were ruined, but I had to take off my underwear and lie there naked, staring at the ceiling, trying to get my breath back under control.

When light finally broke through the window, I got out of bed and pulled on my jeans and walked the three steps down the hall to the bathroom, where I rinsed my boxers in the sink and wrung them out and brought them back to my bedroom to drape over the chair-back where the boy had done his homework. A worksheet of multiplication tables still sat on the little desk. He'd been using a number two pencil. He showed his work.

A note from Cindy sat on the kitchen table. *At the zoo! Make yourself at home.*

I knocked on Penelope's door. If she heard me, she didn't respond. Hibernation again. I was alone in the living room now, staring at the plastic buckets of food along the wall. No coffee. I looked for tea, black tea, green tea, anything caffeinated, found chamomile instead. Box upon useless box of chamomile tea. My head still was in the vise, and my dream left me shaky, my stomach churning hard enough that I couldn't tell if eating was the answer or would make me vomit.

However much sleep I'd gotten, it was just enough to tease me with what sleep tasted like.

I ate something that I forgot as soon as it was inside me, I stared out the window at the little farm idyll in the backyard, I churned in thoughts so repetitive that I began to get dizzy.

Cindy came home before Penelope so much as opened her door, not even to go to the bathroom. I knew that sleep and awake were relative terms for the winter Penelope, the virus Penelope. I would have to go in there to rouse her. I would have to bring her food if she was going to eat.

The first thing Cindy did was pull me into an embrace. I stood when she came into the room, and she walked straight over, her boots still on, so that with my bare feet, she was almost as tall as me when she brought our bodies together. When she finally moved back, it was only a half step.

"All the animals are fed," Cindy said. "And how about you? Did you get some food?"

"I did."

"How did you sleep?"

"Great," I said. I didn't know why I was lying.

"Come sit with me." She took my hand and pulled me over to the dining room table. "Do you want some tea?"

"Do you have any coffee?"

She wrinkled her nose. "No, sorry."

"I'll just take some more Advil, then. Thanks."

She set a little cup of water before me at the table, and beside it, three pills. Then she walked over to her wall of food and ran her hand over the plastic tubs until she found the one she was looking for and pulled it out just enough that she could reach inside for a pack of Fig Newtons.

As soon as she tore open the plastic, the monkey came loping out of the bedroom making excited little panting sounds. He held his palms out flat, like he was waiting for Communion, his little eyes wide, and as soon as she gave him a few cookies, he scampered off. Cindy sat down next to me at the dining room table, close enough that our hands could have touched.

"So," she said, "tell me about your daughter."

As soon as I started speaking, as though she heard us, Penelope stepped out of her room and across the hall into the bathroom.

"Hello!" Cindy called, but the water was already running, the door closed.

"Her name is Hannah," I said. "She's our only child."

I took a Fig Newton. When was the last time I'd eaten one of these? My own childhood? I half expected the nostalgic rush, the taste bringing me back to some long-lost baseball game, to my mother's voice as I ate a snack after school, but all it did was taste like a Fig Newton.

"How old is she?"

"She just turned twenty-one."

"You don't look that old!" She slapped me playfully on the shoulder.

"I've been married over twenty-five years." As soon as I said it, Penelope emerged from the bathroom and stepped into the kitchen. She blinked in the light. Cindy rose from her chair. They stood looking at one another.

"What can I get you?" Cindy said.

"Water?"

"Of course."

Penelope walked stiffly toward me and sat, her back straight, her fingers interlaced on the tabletop. Our eyes met, but her expression didn't change. I didn't know what my expression did, but it made her look away.

Cindy came back. "Bill was just telling me about your daughter."

Penelope nodded.

"Don't stop," Cindy said. "What's she like?"

I looked at Penelope, but she wasn't looking at me.

"A force of nature," I said. "That's a cliché, but it's true. She's a real spark plug." I didn't know what I was saying, it was just bullshit coming out of my mouth, and I could feel the walls tilting, the table sliding, as though every right angle was warped.

"She joined a cult," Penelope said flatly. "And we are going to get her out."

"A cult?" Maybe it was real horror, but Cindy's face looked mock-horrified, a palm drawn in over her mouth, her eyes wide.

"The Revival."

"How did she get mixed up with them?"

Penelope and I stared at one another. The sun was glaring onto the backyard now, having broken whatever clouds there might have been. I could see the pigs, rolling in mud, covering themselves in shit. Their stubby legs waved as they arched onto their backs, writhing, their bulk grinding into the wet dirt.

"I knew it wasn't good from the start—" she began, but I found myself cutting her off.

"When you try to control someone," I said, "you just drive them right toward the thing you were afraid of."

Penelope abruptly stood. Before I could look up and catch her eyes, she was gone. I heard her door close.

Cindy turned back from watching Penelope's back disappear to look at me. I was standing now too.

"What's wrong?" she asked.

"Nothing," I said. "Nothing's wrong." I left her sitting at the kitchen table, walked back down the hall.

It was I-don't-know-when in the afternoon, and I sat alone in that little room with its Kansas City Royals pennant on the wall, the trophies with their little plastic ballplayers on top lined from smallest to largest, clothes hung in the closet and folded in the drawers so neatly that I thought either the little boy had struggled with perfectionism or his mother had. It didn't matter which. They were both gone. Cindy was outside the window now, whistling. She was wearing a wool sweater and tending to her livestock. The chickens ran, heads bobbing, when she approached to feed them. The pigs stared straight ahead as they chewed. Yellow squash was so heavy on the vines outside my window that it dragged them to the ground and lay bulbous and bright in the grass.

On the other side of the house, Penelope's window looked out on the empty road, the cracked pavement, the falling leaves. She was maybe twenty feet away from me. Two flimsy unlocked doors stood between us, but if I burst across the hall and tried to speak, she wouldn't even understand me; we didn't speak the same language.

The sky was still lurid with sunset when sleep came on like anesthesia, like a smothering mask over my face, and I woke in the early morning darkness to a noise in the hallway, my headache gone, my mind washed clean, and my body filled with a terrible and sudden shame, as though I'd been groping in the dark for days and months when with the flick of a finger someone flooded the world with light. Regret burned in my gut, and I floated like a ghost, unseen, through the doors, across the hall, to where Penelope lay, alone, trapped in a strange woman's house. Betrayed. By me. I'd violated our marriage's contract, not the words we said at the altar, but the unwritten contract outlining how we would be with one another, speak to one another, the contract we'd built day by day over two and a half decades.

How many marriages had I seen from the inside of a therapy session? The contempt, the distrust, the cheating, the tedium. I'd seen marriages fail in every way possible, like supernovae, like balloons that took forever to die and drift to the floor, and though I succeeded in hiding this behind the veil of professionalism, I'd walked home each day smug. My marriage was not one of *those*.

I lay in the bed, the shame like a stain, like when I'd pissed myself the night before. My absurdity. My righteousness. My anger as

I yelled at her by the smoking ruins of our car. I'd been given the greatest gift imaginable: in a destroyed world, I'd been allowed to keep the two people I loved most, and this was the way I behaved. Penelope was right there, on the other side of the hall. She owed me nothing. I could go to her, apologize freely, without need for reciprocity, and if she forgave me, I would drag my mattress across, so we could sleep together, the stuffed animals piled around us, in the unicorn paradise.

My door opened.

I was lying on my side, facing the wall, and the door opened behind me and I knew that the miracle had happened: on the other side of the hallway, Penelope had been performing her own calculus, finding her own way back to us. She was here, in my room, reaching out just as I had been about to do.

Gratitude flooded me so suddenly I could feel tears starting behind my eyes. I rolled over, an apology on my lips, my arms reaching out, and Cindy Solis was standing there, the door closed behind her already, her naked body bleach-white in the moonlight.

She took a step forward. Her eyes were wide. I could barely register what her body looked like because all my brain could say was *naked*. She is naked.

"Take me," she said.

"What?"

She didn't answer, just stepped toward the bed. I was upright now, my back against the wall.

"Take me." Her hips wriggled. She put a finger to her lower lip and pulled it into a pout. She licked it. "I know you want me."

"My wife is right across the hall!"

"She's asleep."

"That isn't the point."

She bent over, back arched, and took my hand and placed it on her breast.

"No," I said.

"Yes," she said.

My hand lay on her chest like a lifeless thing, and she looked at me. I don't know what my face told her, but whatever it was, it dissolved her seduction. She began to cry.

"Please," she said. She dropped to her knees beside the bed. "Please."

"I'm sorry," I said.

"I want a baby."

"What?"

"I'm so alone. I want a child."

My mouth was open, but I didn't say anything, just sat there.

"You don't have to take care of it! You don't have to stay."

"I'm sorry," I repeated.

"You don't even have to look at me."

"What?"

"We only have to do it once. Just so there's a chance."

"I can't."

"Yes. You can. You're choosing not to."

"No."

My tone darkened her face. She sat back. "Why would you deny me a chance at what you have?"

"I'm sorry."

"Don't be sorry. Just be a decent human being and help me to have a child."

"I can't do that."

"Yes, you can!"

"No."

She pushed herself up and kissed me, mashing her lips against mine. I didn't push her away, I just sat there, and after a second or two she stood.

"You selfish prick."

"I'm sorry."

"I gave you food, I gave you shelter."

"And I'm grateful for it."

She wasn't crying now, she was shaking with anger as she turned and stalked toward the door.

"I want you out of my house," she said, and the door slammed shut behind her.

Sleep was gone. I sat awake, listening to the wind rattling the window in the frame. The monkey scampering around the living room. I put on my underwear again, still damp. Dawn began to clutch at the sky outside. I heard Penelope's door open, and I opened mine too. We stood looking at one another in the hallway.

"I'm sorry," I said.

She nodded. "We need to go."

CHAPTER 9

Penelope was walking briskly, hips swinging, and despite the morning chill, she didn't put her hands in her pockets, instead pumping her arms as she strode. I struggled to keep up without breaking into a trot. She could have been a stranger, we could have been meeting for the first time, I wanted to reach out and take her hand, but didn't know how she would respond. I felt like a kid again: dry-mouthed and unsure, wondering if she liked me back. Decades of marriage, everything about our lives was habitual, grooved so slick a marble would have traveled the same path every time. Our empty clothes could have acted out our marriage. Through the decades, there were still surprises, moments when one of us broke script at dinner and sent the other into weeping laughter, or a sudden anger sent us to different floors of the house for an hour, but absent what Hannah could provoke in us, we had definitely settled into late-stage marriage, the comfort stage, the stage I'd seen in my parents and judged when I was a teenager. How can they live like that?

My words by the roadside, the contempt and anger that had

motivated them: I'd broken from the bounds like an indoor cat finding itself suddenly in the sun-draped yard, frozen, unsure of what to do. Now, if I reached for Penelope's hand, would she accept it? Or had I broken something essential? Were we now just partners on a mission, two heads of a failed state working together for reasons of realpolitik?

The pastel morning brightened and washed out into a hard pale blue, and with the sun beginning to glare overhead, the chill fled, and I could feel sweat starting to dampen my back. We both knew where we were going without saying it—back to the car to collect what we could of our supplies before we stuck out our thumbs to try hitchhiking west.

My caffeine headache was a faint throb now, just enough to make me remember the pain, but not enough to cloud my thinking. I wondered if Penelope had suffered the same thing. There was so much I didn't know, the silence between us had been so deep. We hadn't been speaking, not really, not for months, and I didn't want to open the floodgates, I wanted to dynamite the dam itself. All I wanted was to hear her voice, to ask her everything, to have those conversations we had when we were in college, and 3:00 a.m. would arrive without either of us knowing it had gotten late. But my breath was short as we walked, and I could see her sweating too, and we couldn't stop now.

Only when the highway hove into view did we pause beneath the overpass to sit on the concrete abutment, littered with fading garbage, ants scurrying in the dirt at our feet. Penelope had a jug of water she'd brought from the house, and we passed it back and forth, and I brought out the sleeve of Fig Newtons that I'd snagged. The cellophane crinkled and tore, and I held it out for her before taking one myself.

I opened my mouth to speak, not sure what I was going to say.

"Cindy came into my room last night."

"What do you mean, she came into your room?"

"She wanted to have sex with me."

It was like I'd struck her, the way she flinched, turned away, her eyes closing.

"I said no!" The words stumbled into one another I said them so fast.

She opened her eyes but she wasn't looking at me. I was a supreme idiot, choosing to break the silence by telling her about the young woman who wanted me to violate my marriage. What was I thinking? But my mouth just kept babbling on.

"She wanted a baby. That's what she said. That's what she wanted."

"Just like that," Penelope said, her voice flatter than the highway asphalt. It had taken us years of trying to have Hannah.

"She seemed to think so, yeah."

A car hurtled over our heads on the highway, the roar shocking in cool silence. A moment of panic gripped me, we should have been up there, thumbs high, but then I realized the car had been headed east.

"I'd been hoping it was you," I said. "Coming across the hall. So we could talk."

Penelope stood. "I was dead asleep," she said and started walking. I scrambled to follow her.

Now the heat was radiating off the blacktop, a fine shimmer, and the wind was dead. The car couldn't have been that far, but the highway seemed to stretch forever. We walked on the shoulder out of habit, though we could have strolled down the center. One car drove past, and we both threw our thumbs up, though we hadn't picked up our things yet. It didn't matter. The driver's eyes rotated to look at us, but if anything, he accelerated as he went by. Finally, we could see the barn's ridgeline breaking the horizon, and then the car, and farther in the distance, the cows. The lions were nowhere to be seen. Probably basking in the sun, asleep in the tall grass.

For miles, I'd been thinking about what we would take with us. There were backpacks in the car, and we could bring sleeping bags, the tent, what food was left. Arnold. Ammo. Toothbrushes. The list went on, and it was all irrelevant because when we finally reached the car, it was cleaned out. Empty. The food and water, gone. The last sloshings of gas in the jugs, gone. Our camping gear, the atlas . . . and Arnold. Gone. Penelope didn't say a word, just closed her eyes and dropped her forehead to rest on the car roof.

"Goddammit," I said. "I'm sorry. We never should have left the car. You were right all along. And I didn't even listen."

I wanted her to say, *There it is*, I wanted my blunder to bring us closer. If it took my idiocy to bring us together, at least we would be together. But all she did was nod.

I'd made mistakes, and we'd been lucky to survive. That was the truth. The fairy-tale land of learning and growing from my errors had been gone a long time now. That which doesn't kill me, makes me stronger. Bullshit. The truth of the lion and wolf world was this: that which doesn't kill me might begin a long spiral down toward death anyway.

We went through the whole car, stripped it down to nothing. There was a box of granola bars that had gotten wedged under a seat. Our toothbrushes. They had left San Cristóbal hanging from the rearview mirror, and I hung him around my neck beneath my shirt. Why not? We needed all the help we could get.

And then we waited, sitting with our backs to the cool metal of the car, standing when we heard an engine in the distance. As the sun rotated in the sky, we slid along from one side of the Subaru to the other, following the shade. No one stopped. It was going to be a cold night once the sun dropped.

"I'm kind of glad Arnold is gone," I said. Penelope had her eyes closed, her head leaning back against the door panel of the car. Maybe she was asleep.

"Yeah?" she said.

"I don't want to kill anybody."

"I know. Me either."

"I love you," I tried.

"I love you too," she said, but it sounded automatic. Her eyes were still closed.

Occasionally the sound of a car ripping along broke the silence, but on the other side of the median, racing in the wrong direction. The sky was purpling and I was thinking about how we would huddle together in the backseat for the long night when the low thrum of an engine got us to our feet. This time, I didn't put up a thumb, I waved my arms, I jumped up and down, and the car slowed, the nose dipping as the brakes grabbed.

Penelope stood up too, and I could see the driver's face, a white smear behind the windshield. The car's attitude suddenly changed, the front lifting as the driver hit the gas and instead of sliding to a stop he was surging past us, dust from the roadway eddying behind him.

"I guess you should be the one getting us a ride," Penelope said. Her face was set as she sat back down against the car, staring beyond the road into the far fields.

"We didn't want to be in that car anyway," I said. I lowered myself to sit beside her. "It's ridiculous. Is racism really going to be the last thing left in the whole fucking world? The last guy alive, if he happens to be White, is going to be worried about what's happening to the neighborhood if the wrong element moves into the cave next door."

A minute went by before she spoke.

"When we finally got to have cemeteries," Penelope said, "they segregated those too. Even when they're dead, White people are still racist."

I reached for her hand, and she let me hold it in mine. Our eyes were closed, our heads leaning back against the car. We moved from the shade to the sun as the temperature dropped, trying to get the last warmth we could before night set it. In the distance, another engine. We both stood up and waved.

A big pickup truck, with double wheels in the back and the side mirrors mounted wide on spindly chrome arms. Behind it, a trailer. The bed of the truck was piled high, and a tarp covered whatever the payload was. It slid gently to a stop, and a guy with a ponytail leaned out the side window.

"Hey," he said.

I had my arm around Penelope's shoulder. We each raised a hand. "Thank you for stopping," Penelope said.

"Looks like you had some car trouble," he said.

"You could say that," Penelope said.

"I hit a cow," I added.

"Best not to do that," he said.

We stood there for a moment. He smiled. "You want to get in, or you fixing to stay here instead?"

The tableaux broken, we scrambled for the far side of the truck. It had a real backseat, narrow enough that I had to sit sideways. Penelope sat in the passenger seat beside our savior.

"Where you headed?"

"Bishop," Penelope said.

He nodded. "Bishop. Well, I can get you part of the way."

"Where are you going?"

"Wind River reservation. Wyoming." He eased back into gear and it took only a moment for the truck to reach and pass the exit for Hedville where a few miles to the south, Cindy and the monkey were sharing a Fig Newton. It was warm in the cab, and I could already see Penelope's head drifting to the side as she began to fall asleep.

"What's in the trailer?" I asked.

"Medicine, mostly. We've got people who need insulin, blood

thinners, hypertension drugs. And they ain't making any more, so I took all I could find."

"That's good of you to do."

"We take care of our people," he said.

I could feel myself starting to drift, my focus dissolving.

"I can leave you outside Denver," he said. "Or you can ride with me north to 80 and I can take you west as far as Rawlins."

Penelope said *Rawlins* just as I was saying *We'll ride with you as far as we can.* And then the thrum of tires on the road and the darkness gathering outside the windows and the warm air flowing from the vents and I was asleep like the dead in the back as this man carried us west, our sleeping lives in his hands.

When I woke, we were stopped, and the sun was blinding. Penelope was stretching out her arms in the front seat, and the driver was rousing too, all of us coming back to consciousness at the same time.

"Where are we?" I asked.

"Rawlins."

"Where is Rawlins?"

"Southern Wyoming."

"Wyoming," Penelope said. She was looking out the window. We were in a gravel driveway, snugged up next to a baby-blue one-story house. The lawn was bleached out and spotty, and a spindly single tree stood in the middle, surrounded by a little circular fence to keep out, what, deer? Whatever they had in Wyoming.

I suddenly had to go to the bathroom, and I fumbled to get out of the truck.

"Just a second," he said, and he opened his door, then my little half door that swung the opposite way. I started fast-walking up toward the house, but he called out, "It ain't open," so I just stepped to the far side of the porch.

When I got back to the truck, Penelope ran over to take her turn in the bushes. Our benefactor waited until she was gone, then just pissed onto the driveway on the other side of the truck.

It was a dusty empty neighborhood that would have been suburban where we were from, but here was probably the biggest metropolis for a hundred miles. Unraked leaves piled and drifted on the yards and sidewalks and street, blurring the distinctions between. The houses were single story, choked up close to one another, each with the same little yard out front, but some were brick, some aluminum sided, some just glorified trailers. Squirrels chased one another through the tree across the street, and clouds moved across the sky, but otherwise all was still. We stood by the side of the truck.

"I'm late," he said. "I have to head north."

I felt like a child. A feeling of panic swelled in me. The entire American West swelled around us, an endless alien landscape of mesas and deserts and outlaws. Whatever sense of direction I'd had from poring over maps was gone. Penelope stood next to me, and I reached for her hand.

He seemed to know what we were thinking. "You'll want to follow 80 all the way through Utah."

"Right, Utah." If he'd told me Oregon, or Missouri, or Luxembourg, at that moment I would have believed him.

"Then you have a few options getting through Nevada, but whatever you do, you'll want to be real careful."

"Why?" Penelope asked.

He held up his hands. "I just hear things. Don't mean it's true."

"What do you hear?"

He kicked the dirt at his feet. "Just be careful. Be ready to jump off the road if you need to. Go overland. Hell, that's true here too."

From her coat pocket, Penelope pulled out the gold bar we'd gotten from Manny. I stared at her. I thought it had been lost when our car was pillaged.

"If you'll take us to Bishop, I'll give you this," she said.

He reached out a hand and she placed it in his palm.

"Wow," he said. "Never seen gold like that before." He held it up to the light, ran his fingers over the embossing. "Is it really as soft as they say?" He tried to dig a thumbnail into the bar with no success.

"So you'll do it?"

His smile was sad, his eyes kind. "I made promises. People are waiting on me on the reservation. And I don't know what I'd do with this anyway." He handed the bar back to Penelope.

"Can you take us back to the highway so we can try to hitch another ride?" I asked.

"I'll do you one better," he said. "Follow me."

We walked down the driveway toward the garage, which was padlocked shut and dark. A woodpile sat next to it, the end cribbed and neat, and he reached a hand inside, coming out with a shiny key.

"Is this your house?" Penelope asked.

"No," he said. "My friends lived here. Before." He rattled the garage door up, and in the half-light, I could make out squat shapes in the back. He turned to us. "You ever driven a quad?"

"A what?" Penelope asked.

"ATV. A quad. A four-wheeler."

We shook our heads.

"It's easy as hell." Our eyes were starting to adjust and I could see them now, brightly colored, perched on black knobby tires, with handlebars like a motorcycle. "Help me wheel them out."

They rolled onto the gravel, and he showed us how to turn them on, to shift gears, to accelerate with a wrist twist, to hit the brakes. There were extra cans of gas in the garage, and we strapped them to the back of each. "Take it slow at first," he said. "You can't get into too much trouble on paved streets. But you can flip easy on rough terrain, and there's nobody to come help you." There were helmets in the garage too, black shiny ones with smoked visors and stickers on the side that read No Fear.

"Follow me back to the highway," he said. "Then head west. You hear a car, get off the road until you're sure it's safe."

His hands were in his back pockets, his eyes tired. The sun was behind us, so he was squinting a little, and the skin on his face was tight. Penelope took two steps forward and hugged him, and he smiled in surprise. "That's all right," he said.

I shook his hand. "What's your name?" I asked.

"Carl," he said, and when he saw the look on my face, he laughed and said, "What, were you expecting Flying Eagle?"

"No, no," I said. "That was my father's name. Carl."

We all stood in silence for a moment, then he slapped his hands on the thighs of his jeans and said, "It's that time." We climbed onto our quads, cinched the straps of our helmets under our chins. He was in the truck waving a hand to follow, and when he eased out of the driveway in a wide turn, the trailer following him obediently, we followed too, through blocks so similar they could have been the same one, then to a main drag. He took a right, and we passed motels and dollar stores and gas stations, all empty and dark, and houses too, intermixed all along until we arrived at the highway interchange, and he leaned his head out the window, and called, "Good luck!"

He pointed west, we waved, and then he hit the gas and was gone.

Penelope and I sat next to each other on our quads. As we'd slept, Carl had carried us into an entirely new terrain. Gone was the long flat farmland we'd been in. In its place, scrubby ridged brushland, half bald. We revved our engines and started down the highway.

The roar of the engine was indistinguishable from the high whine of the tires on the asphalt. We raced along, side by side, crouched over our quads. Even wearing her helmet, Penelope was unmistakable, the crouched intensity of her attitude, her focus. I slipped in behind her, riding in her slipstream, close to her though we were both alone in our cocoons of noise, the handlebars tremoring against our palms as the tire tread chewed its way along the highway. There were no buildings anywhere, we'd left Rawlins behind, and the endless green-spotted land stretched in distances around us that looked intimate but I knew were impossible miles. That hill, just there, on the horizon, the one that looked so close I could almost reach out to touch . . . we could point our quads in that direction and ride for hours.

Penelope, love of my life. Mother of my daughter. I watched her crouch on the ATV, her earnestness so clear I knew that under the helmet she was biting her lip, she was concentrating. How many hours had I watched her like this, her focus so formidable, until I called her back to me, drew her away from her economics textbook and back to bed? I wanted to hold on to her and never let go. I wanted to lie five inches apart and stare into one another's eyes as though memorizing them. Reincarnation was a fool's dream—this one shot at life was all we had, and I'd chosen to spend mine with her. Regrets? Come on. I had gotten so lucky it seemed like divine intervention. She may have frustrated me, driven me up a wall, but I'd never looked past her. She was, from the moment I met her to this moment, as her right wrist cocked and her quad spurted ever onward, the most compelling person I'd ever met.

We raced west, but though the wind tore at our clothes, the sun was faster. It vaulted past, began its fall. A few cars had flown by too, their approach unheard through the thunder of our engines. We hadn't even had time to lurch off the road, to follow Carl's advice. It seemed unnecessary. Why would anyone care about us?

Clouds began to build and rise on the horizon, dark and swallowing what was left of the daylight. Penelope skidded to a stop as we crested a low rise, looking down on a long shallow valley ahead. A car sat by the roadside, and even from a distance I could tell it was canted up to one side as the driver tried to fix a flat. I slid my visor up.

"What do you think?"

Penelope pulled off her helmet, rested it on her knee. "Get off the road, I guess. Though he looks harmless enough."

We must have been framed against the sky, and the sound of our engines had gotten his attention. He stood and raised a hand. I waved back. Buzzards circled in the distance, but otherwise the tableau was still. I was about to say *Maybe we should go help him,* when the sound of a distant car broke the silence behind us. We didn't speak, just revved our engines and bumped through the roadside ditch and onto the rolling prairie.

This was quad-riding. Not the vibration of off-road tires on the pavement, but the lurching bounce of grass tussocks in the sandy dirt. We got out away from the road a hundred meters or so, then turned to parallel the highway.

A muscle car was snorting and growling down the long decline to the tire-changer. The kind of car my father would have called *Detroit iron.* It slid to a stop, and two men got out. Penelope and I had stopped too. No engines were turning over, and the only sound was the low whistle of wind, and the deep humid silence of the distant storm clouds. We could see them talking, and whatever was being said, it didn't look companionable. Penelope looked at me, and her eyes were troubled. The man with the broken-down car was waving his hands, and he turned abruptly and began to walk away. And then, there's no other way to say this except to say it, one of the other men pulled out a handgun and aimed it at his back and there was a flat wet crack and he dropped. No flailing. No crying out. Just dropped. And then did not move.

My mouth was open, covered by my hand. Penelope made a little sound next to me. The men were laughing now, one of their heads was thrown back in laughter. I suddenly knew how visible we were, perched atop our bright ATVs, as far from them as the green on a long par 3. When I turned to Penelope, she was already cranking her engine, and we surged away as fast as we could. There was a gunshot, another, and I felt like I could hear the angry buzz of the bullets flying past us, but probably that was my imagination, the quads were so loud. Penelope was flattened to hers, so low that her hands rose above her head to grip the bars. I could feel myself bounce, hard, the quad wanted to flip, the sickening lightness of one side rising in the air, and then the other, and I was plastered to my seat too, as much to keep the wheels on the ground as to diminish the target.

My mind was jangling with a vision of them swerving the car out into the scrubland, the shark-mouth grille leaping as they stomped the gas and ran us down. We lurched up and over a little cliffside, down into a dry gulch. My visor was steamed with my panicked heaving breath, my helmet bouncing like it was trying to free itself from my head. I slowed down, dared a look back. Nothing. No headlights, no car, just the rolling land.

Penelope hadn't slowed down at all. She was accelerating away from me, and I pushed my visor up in time to see her turned back and shouting something. She pointed west, and I saw that the murderers weren't the only thing we were racing against. The clouds had stacked up, impossibly tall, no longer steel gray but black, pulsing with the lurid glow of lightning inside like something fighting to get out, the thunder lost in the noise my machine was making.

Even faster now, flying east, back the way we'd come. Low mountains were visible in the distance, promising shelter, but so far away that they might have been land witnessed from a helpless drifting ship. The first raindrop hit my helmet hard enough to echo, and then another, like a dark promise. Now I could hear the thunder, and the wind was swirling, a smothering dust rising all around us. Penelope's crouched figure came and went in the darkness, and the world flipped from not-raining to deluge so quickly it dazzled, just like the lightning that now began to stomp the earth behind us as though striding in our direction. What had been dry ground was alive with mud, water puddling so fast but hammered by the rain that wouldn't let it pool and rest. Penelope's wheels threw twin rooster tails high into the air, and I could feel mine doing the same, the slip and lurch of the tires as they spun and grabbed. I was calling her name, but I couldn't even hear my own voice.

She stopped.

I almost ran into her, and it wasn't until I was stopped too that I saw what she did: a chain-link fence, ten feet high and stretching as far as we could see in both directions, waving so furiously in the wind that the looped barbed wire on top threatened to tear free. Penelope motioned to her right, and we revved our engines and followed the fence's line, looking for an opening.

We were side by side now, skidding left around a ninety-degree corner, and ahead of us was a wild flapping, the wind opening and slamming a tall double gate. We bounced up onto a dirt road, a long line bisecting the landscape, seething with rain. One of the gates surrendered to the wind with a ripping shriek of metal, and Penelope's quad darted through the opening it left, and mine right after hers, the low bulk of a building appearing through the chaos directly ahead of us. She jumped down to run the last steps, waving for me to follow, but just as I leapt from the quad, lightning hit the fence and time slowed all the way down, the whole world lit up, the noise so total that for a moment nothing else existed except the sickening buzz of electricity from the ground itself lifting me from my feet and I could feel it in my teeth like I'd been chewing aluminum, and I fell into the mud, the rain pummeling my back like it wanted to drive me deeper.

Penelope was gone. The last image I'd had was her arm urging me onward as she disappeared around the corner of the building. I clawed myself up. My legs hurt, I could barely stand, but I staggered forward. I knew in that moment that *lightning never strikes twice in the same place* was a lie. This lightning was going to hammer the fence and me with it until we were gone. I got to the building and plastered myself to the side of it, the grit of the concrete blocks against my cheek, and slid along, around the corner. No sign of Penelope. A door broke the windowless stretch of the wall, but it was locked. My hand slipped on the knob. I could barely see anything, and I pulled off my helmet, but that was worse. Now I could barely keep my eyes open in the rain. Across the flat mud, there was another building, and I ran for it. When I got there, like an answered prayer I'd never uttered, a door was not only unlocked, it was ajar. I fell inside, pulled the door shut behind me, and turned, looking for Penelope, thinking she would be huddled in the corner. She wasn't there. It was dark, I could barely see anything, but I would have seen her. I was alone.

"Penelope!"

I could make out a door on the far side of the room and I was there in three leaping steps, and I pulled it open to find a metal staircase descending into pitch-black.

"Pen! PEN!"

Nothing, but then I heard a metallic clank, like a hard footstep, a noise somewhere in the subterranean world below.

None of it made sense, but nothing made sense anymore, and I stood in the darkness of the room, paralyzed. With a crack, the outer door flew open, banging against the wall. Another stab of lightning and the whole room was bathed in hard clear light so complete that the image of the furniture lingered against the back of my eyes when the dark fell again. A bottle of whiskey and a box of cigars on the metal desk. A filing cabinet. An Air Force Academy pennant on the wall. A mop in the corner. An American flag.

The idea that came to me was so complete it had to have had its source elsewhere. The Muse of Apocalyptic Handicrafts. I crouch-walked to the corner, my hands outstretched, and they hit the walls simultaneously, sliding into the corner where the mop sat in a dry bucket.

Back to the desk, where I felt my way to the chair and fell into it, my fingers already knotting and looping the filthy crusty strands. Another bolt of lightning, a bit farther off, but still enough to light the room, and I grabbed the bottle of whiskey, twisted off the cap, and splattered what was left over the mop. All of this would have been for nothing if a lighter hadn't been there with the cigars, but it *was* there, and I snapped it open, a flame leaping out from its mouth, and the mop lit with a blue glow that encased it like a bubble, then leapt white in flame. A torch.

As I descended the stairs, the banshee cry of the wind and the drum of rain retreated. Underground, everything was muffled, thick. I called Penelope's name, again and again, but my voice wasn't going anywhere. At the base of the stairs, another door led to a room with a gleaming steel bank of electronic stuff. Screens. Buttons. Everything flickered in the torchlight. Empty, but again a noise clattered in the distance.

This made no sense. Why would Penelope have come down here? But I could imagine her feeling her way along, lost in the dark, and so I kept calling out, I pushed the next door, a heavy one that squeaked on its hinges, and stepped through.

At first, it was just something that I felt, the sheer cavernous emptiness of the space, all enclosed in a tomblike silence. Either the storm had ended, or I was far down enough that weather was irrelevant.

"Penelope!" I cried out, and my voice bounced around and died.

I looked up. The ceiling was not a ceiling, but doors, massive and mounted on enormous hinges. I looked down.

The space yawned beneath me. I was on a catwalk, suspended high in the air, and below, the tip of a missile, burnished and glowing red in the torchlight, round like an eye, a single unblinking eye staring upward at the heavens, at the heavy doors waiting to open. The long cylindrical body stretched down, all the way down, a giant's body, too deep for my light to reach.

My hand was wet on the mop handle, still slick with rain and now with sweat too in the thick cave air. I held it with two hands now, clutched it so hard my fingers hurt. I was looking at a nuclear missile. I was born a decade after the Cuban Missile Crisis, nuclear weapons were as much a part of my reality as gravity, and until now had been just as unseen. My throat hurt when I swallowed. A microscopic virus had ended the world, but this missile was still here, still waiting for a single command. Was it still targeted at Russia? Or had it turned its eye toward China? I didn't even know where my country's death gods were aimed. Maybe we would survive this virus, maybe we were all just playing out the last pathetic act of the human race, but either way this missile would still be here until some switch finally corroded and it blew up. Or it might survive until the next civilization came along, or the aliens arrived, finding nothing left on this planet except for thousands upon thousands of nuclear weapons, the only thing that would survive us.

The missile did nothing. It just sat there, patient. A scurrying sound came from beyond, and I called out Penelope's name again. Could an animal have gotten down here? Was this the end of our civil defense system—raccoon habitat?

I slowly opened the door on the far side of the catwalk, waiting for the red eyes, the hissing leap of some toothy creature, but saw nothing. It was the smell that nearly dropped me to my knees, some unholy, eye-watering smell, and I could make out now in the torchlight a bunk room, a foosball table, a television in the corner, and then the scrabbling noise again, and I thrust my torch out forward against whatever was there, and looming in the sudden light was a man, naked but for the shreds of a military uniform, rat-pale skin and his face wild and ragged with hair. He hissed at me, and though the torch was dim, held a hand up against the light as though it burned.

"Hey," I said, "Easy. What's your name?" The room darkened. My torch was beginning to falter. He was speaking now, answering my question, repeating something endlessly.

"Ian?" I said. "Did you say Ian?" But he wasn't saying Ian, he was saying *I am*, and I could make out the rest: *I am nobody, I am nobody, I am nobody*, and when I tried to step forward into the room, he leapt at me snarling, and I dropped my mop, his fingernails were claws and his face was wild and I turned to run through the sudden dark, over the catwalk, my footsteps echoing in the missile chamber, and through the control room, though he didn't seem to be chasing me, and up the stairs into the sudden noise of the storm howling out-side. It hadn't stopped after all, though it had been so silent down below, and I burst out into the muddy yard, calling Penelope's name again and again. I was crying now, desperate to find her. The wind tried to knock me down, and I slid sideways through the puddles, my feet struggling for purchase. And now I could make out what I had missed before. Alongside the first building, the locked building, was a shed, the kind you buy at Home Depot to hold all your yard tools. It shuddered in the wind, and I knew she was in there.

I ran sideways, reeling like a drunk, a looping arc of a run, but made it to the shed and tore open the doors and there, huddled with the gardening equipment, the lawn mower and rakes, was my wife, curled in a ball, and she was saying my name as I dropped to my knees and pulled her into me, my tears mixed with the rain, both of us soaked through, and the only way I knew she was sobbing too was the heaving of her chest against mine as we huddled there, together, to wait out the storm.

CHAPTER 10

We slept tangled in one another's arms. It had been years since we'd been able to drift off like that. Usually we were sequestered on either side of the king bed, and Penelope wore earplugs against my snoring. The night was cold, the rain drumming the roof, and we pressed ourselves as close together as we could and pulled a tarp over for the illusion of heat. Our heads rested on a bag of potting soil. When I woke, my face was in her hair, and I breathed in Penelope, felt her waking too. Her head craned back, and mine too, until we could see one another's eyes. We didn't say anything, just lay like that as the day began outside and a thin line of sunlight broke through the crack between the doors, so bright we had to look away.

There were hoes and rakes and gardening gloves, along with a push mower and weed trimmer. Someone had tried to make this place, of all places, beautiful. The shed warmed quickly in the sun, and before long we stood and pushed the doors open and stepped out hand in hand into the light. A shamelessly beautiful day, with a bluebird sky that felt no need to apologize for its temper tantrum yesterday. The ground was still muddy, but already starting to dry and crack.

We stripped off our wet clothes, hung them on the chain-link fence to dry. Penelope suggested that we scavenge, but the door I'd gone in was the only one not locked tight, and I explained exactly what I'd found down there, the nuclear missile, the feral air force officer who was, right now, prowling the darkness somewhere beneath us. Instead, we ate a bag of granola we'd been given by Carl before he drove away. Both of our quads had survived the night, splattered and muddy but upright. They both started, and we were getting ready to push off when we realized that by strapping all our remaining gas cans to one and riding together, we'd get nearly twice as far. Even the lawn mower gas, a lonely jug, went on the ATV.

"You can drive," I said. "If you want."

"We'll take turns. You first."

So that's how I ended up rolling out of the missile base, Penelope's arms wrapped tight around me and her helmet knocking against the back of mine on the bumps. We kept on the little dirt road at first, swerving around the rutted puddles, headed toward another line breaking the landscape, a faded strip of two-lane blacktop headed west. To the south, a line of low rugged hills that somehow we'd crossed in our frantic charge yesterday, and beyond them the interstate, which a day ago seemed almost ordinary and now seemed tantamount to suicide. The image of the dead man kept filling my mind, and the laughter as they stood over his body. I could see the blood blooming on his back like a flower. Penelope's head was as close to mine as our helmets would allow, and I slowed down, the engine muttering, and half shouted, "I can't stop thinking about him."

She squeezed me even tighter, pressing her body against mine, and I knew that not only had she heard me, but she'd been thinking about the same thing. So horrifyingly casual, as though taking another human life were no different from having a snack, taking a nap.

My brain cycled through it again and again, and every time I could hear the laughter more distinctly.

The road stopped at an abrupt T. No buildings, nothing distinct about this spot in the endless scrubby ground. Just another strip of asphalt, this time headed north-south. We kept our ATVs headed west, bumping onto the sandy, brushy dirt, slower but headed in the right direction. After a couple of hours, we stopped to refill the gas tank, stretch. Penelope took over, and I was tall enough that by sitting back a little, I could look over the crest of her helmet, see the long emptiness ahead. We were traveling between two low ridges in the distance. Maybe this was an old washout, a floodplain. Wherever its origins, it was flat and endless. A lake broke the monotony ahead of us, and I was wondering if we could fill our water bottles when we got closer and discovered our answer: the water was a thick green. We'd had a filter once, back when we had a car and a curated load of supplies. Now we had only thirst and hunger. Penelope skirted the lake on the northern side, and I realized this was her analytical mind at work. On the off chance that someone threatening was coming north from the highway, she didn't want to get pinned against the water.

Again, we stopped to refuel, this time emptying the last of it, and carefully strapping the empty containers back on in case we found something magic. The Fountain of Gas. I took over. The sun was high overhead. Our sweatshirts flapped from the back of the quad, drying in the wind. We could almost sleep, the monotony of it was so perfect, if it weren't for the bouncing lurch of the ride, and then with a finger snap, it all changed around us. Nothing but pale brown sand, as though we'd been transported to the Sahara. Tall sweeping dunes that bent in long arcs. Sand spun and sprayed like water from our tires. We rode up the dunes and down the other side, Penelope's body falling against mine so that I had to lock my elbows against the handlebars to keep us both upright. Dune after dune, with occasional little green thorny fingers breaking the monotony. Stubborn little plants, trying to make a go of it.

Something broke the horizon line ahead. A spire of rock like a raised fist. It seemed to be west of us, and I aimed for it, using it to resolve my fear that we'd traveled in circles, though the sun kept telling me that we hadn't. The dunes disappeared, but not the sand, which now lay flat in a wind-ruffled series of tiny ridges like ripples in water that were far worse for the quad, rattling our teeth and bucking like it wanted us off its back. The rock formation vaulted higher as we got closer—flat ground that began to angle up at forty-five degrees, then straight toward the heavens, a thumb of rock on the side and the clenched fist even higher.

The engine sputtered, then revved again. I felt Penelope's arms around me. Her head fell to rest against my back. Again, the engine faltered and this time it died, and the quad immediately ground to a halt, waiting obediently for us to refill the tank, but there was nothing left. It would die here, rust and slowly fall apart in the elements, unless the sand migrated in the wind, swallowed it whole.

We took off our helmets and stood.

"Well, shit," I said.

"Yup."

We'd known this was coming. There had been no end to our ATV ride but this one. We left our helmets in the sand, tied our sweatshirts around our waists. In our pockets, we each held a useless talisman from the old days—San Cristóbal for me, a gold bar for her. And other than that, we had nothing but our clothes and each other. And the empty water bottles, which I would have said were just reminders of what we didn't have, but our bodies were doing that reminding anyway. All I could think about was water.

We began to walk. It was simple. Primordially simple. Now we would walk. The sand slipped beneath our feet, and then got firmer, and the transition happened gradually and then all at once, now we were walking on hard, scrub grass ground again, the sand behind us like a dream. We held hands, walked slow. Perhaps ahead there was shelter, perhaps food and water. Perhaps we would go the way of the quad, our bones decorating the landscape.

Penelope gripped my hand tight and pointed. Scattered about the landscape to our left, a herd of wild horses grazed.

"Do you know how to ride a horse?" she asked.

"No. Do you?"

She just laughed. Still, we began to edge that way. Maybe God was giving us horses, maybe they would bend a front leg and welcome us onto their backs. No. Before we got within a hundred yards, they looked up at us, snorted, and wheeled away like a flock of birds, their hooves thundering the ground.

A sign came into view ahead—Boars Tusk Access—and a little dirt road running toward the jutting rock formation that vaulted high into the evening light. We sat, each of us leaning against one of the posts holding up the sign, as the sun fell and the world turned golden.

"Do you think we might find some shelter up by the Tusk?"

"I doubt it," she said.

I nodded.

"I think we have to walk the other way," she said. "Down toward the highway."

I nodded again. Out here, the variables changed so quickly. All the equations flipped. I knew that was how Penelope was thinking. Now, the highway was our only chance, the same highway that ten hours ago was to be avoided at all costs.

"Should we go?" I asked.

"Let's just sit for another minute." She was leaning her head back against the faded wood, the brown paint peeling, and her eyes were closed.

The gift was simplicity. We might die in this wilderness, but at least our task was singular and pure. West. Go west. If we were crawling in the end, we would be crawling west toward Hannah.

"I'm so sorry," I said. There was a pause, and then she opened her eyes, but she didn't say anything.

"I can't believe what I said to you. It just . . ." I shook my head.

"When?"

"By the car. When I started ranting about you pushing Hannah away."

"Oh, that." She laughed. "It seems like a thousand years ago. The Subaru."

"I never should have said what I did."

She shrugged. "I knew you felt that way. It wasn't exactly a secret."

"I was being crazy." I tried not to say the word *crazy*, I was a psychologist, I didn't stigmatize mental illness, but now I found myself saying it again. "I was being *crazy*."

"Maybe not. I probably did drive her away. Though in my defense, nineteen-year-old girls pretty much always want to get away from their mothers."

"I don't know. What you did, what I did: none of it mattered. Hannah was going to be Hannah. She was going to do what she was going to do. We were just making ourselves feel relevant."

She nodded. "I can see that."

"I think Hannah could have told us that. I think she *did*. She was always telling us to relax, not to worry about her."

"On repeat. Endlessly."

"But the way I talked to you . . ." I didn't finish my sentence, my voice drying up.

"We'd just had a horrible accident and there were lions. So maybe we weren't picking our words quite as carefully."

"It's not an excuse."

"It's a reason."

"But . . ."

"But what?" She looked at me.

"Nothing. Just . . . you seemed upset."

"I mean, I was pretty upset," she said. "We totaled the car in the middle of Iowa. I thought we were fucked."

"I mean . . ."

"You mean, upset at you."

"Yeah."

"Not everything is about you."

"I know. But come on."

She looked into the distance, past the horses, who kicked up dust in the late evening light. The silence drew out long enough that I thought she wasn't going to answer.

"Why didn't you tell me that the person in town was a woman?" Her voice was small, like it must have been when she was a child.

"I . . ." My brain skipped a beat, and I didn't know what to say.

"You didn't even seem like you wanted me there."

"Oh Pen, no . . ."

"I was sitting by the car, by that cow stinking in the sun. I tried to eat, to drink something, but it was so hot. I thought I was going to throw up. And all the while, this little voice is saying in my head, *What if he doesn't come back? What are you going to do?* I thought I would give anything for you to come back, I thought about all the days we missed when I was struggling during the winter. All I wanted was for you to come back. And then you did and you were all cleaned up and riding that fucking bike and so angry at me before I even said anything. And I can get past all that. But then we got to the house and it was this pretty little thing with her goddamned monkey, and she was acting like you two were already playing house, all cozy to-gether. And then I'm in this room with a thousand unicorns collected by some dead little girl, and I'm telling myself, *Penelope, you're being crazy.* And then she tries to fuck you."

"Oh, no, Penelope . . ."

There were tears in her eyes now. She was crying. Not the blown-out empty sobs we'd all gone through as Shark Flu destroyed the world around us. Just quiet tears that made me want to fold her into my arms and hold her forever. I wanted to perform some wild act to show her how much she was loved, but that would have been selfish. That wasn't what she needed. Not Penelope. She wasn't one for protestations and wild gestures. Her love language was logic.

I slid over, leaning against her post now, and she let her body fall into mine.

"Here's what I loved about her," I said. "She had Fig Newtons."

Penelope snorted.

"You're right that I was angry," I said. "And I'm sorry. I felt so alone all winter."

"You didn't tell me."

"I didn't want to drive you further away."

"How am I supposed to change if you don't tell me?"

"Well, that's a great question."

"Don't you think I felt alone too? It might have helped if you'd needed me."

"You're right."

The wild horses had come back to the grazing ground we'd frightened them from. They were right there, so close, and yet I knew if we stood and tried to catch them, they would just thunder away. The low brush cast long shadows as the sun fell, fingers of light and dark playing against the dusty ground. Our breath had fallen into rhythm, the two of us pressed into one another, alone in the wilderness of whatever state we'd made it to before the gas ran dry.

"Did she just say, *I want to have sex with you?*"

"She came into my room. Naked."

Penelope looked up at me.

"She came in naked?"

"Yeah. She tried to, like, seduce me."

"She tried to seduce *you*."

"What are you trying to say?" We were both laughing now. "And then when I kept turning her down, she told me I was an asshole and she wanted me out of the house."

"Wow."

"Yeah."

"I suppose it makes sense. What she really wanted was hope."

"And me. I mean, it's not every day that a specimen like me walks into your life."

Now Penelope really laughed, and we held each other for a while longer, then stood and began to walk along the road. The moon was up, the night cloudless, and if we lay down, we might freeze. So on we walked, despite the hunger and the thirst. After a couple of miles, the road reached another, then another, and we kept walking south toward the highway.

The sound of an engine broke the night chill, and before we could even look at one another, let alone formulate a plan, a pickup truck with no headlights resolved from the darkness and skidded to a halt perhaps thirty yards away from us. We faced off in the moonlight. It was a dusty rusting Chevy, and I expected an old White man, a base-ball cap tipped back on his head, maybe a squirt of tobacco from the open window, but as she leaned out her open window, we saw a young Black woman, around Hannah's age maybe, and she looked down at us from her perch and said, "What's happening?" so casually that I could feel the tension disappear from my shoulders.

"Just out for a stroll," Penelope said.

"Sure. Nice night and all."

"Headlights broken?" I asked.

"Nah, just enjoying the view, right?"

I'd been looking down, at the road, watching where I was step-ping. My head craned the other way, and the stars were rich overhead, strewn everywhere, with the boiling light of the Milky Way smeared across half the sky. We all were still for a moment. A satellite glinted across, moving fast, still waiting for signals that would never come.

"Well, have a good night." She shifted the truck into gear.

"No, wait!" Penelope said, and the woman in the truck laughed.

"I'm just fucking with you."

"Please . . ." Penelope didn't even have to finish.

"What are you waiting on?"

We ran around the front of the truck, opened the passenger door, and paused. Clipped upright to the dashboard, as though its muzzles were twin bud vases waiting for flowers, was a sawed-off shotgun. She saw where we were looking.

"Nah, don't worry, fam. Not for you."

"Who's it for?"

"Let's just say, some people only speak one language. Not my native tongue, but I know enough to get along." She patted the shotgun.

Penelope and I looked at one another, then climbed up onto the bench seat.

"I'm Veronica," the driver said, and we introduced ourselves. She eased the truck forward, back up the road we'd walked down. I stared at her in the starlight. She looked so familiar. I knew her from somewhere, but that seemed impossible.

"Are you from out east?" I asked.

"Nope. I did spend a couple of years in the Bronx."

"Maybe that's it," I said. "I feel like I've met you before."

"Yeah, maybe." She smiled. "You guys see the Boars Tusk?"

"We did," Penelope said.

"Was it cool?" She was driving casually, one hand drumming the mirror outside her still-open window, the other wrist-flopped over the wheel, as though she had a cigarette between her fingers.

"It was," Penelope said, as though thinking about it for the first time. "It was cool."

The road forked, and Veronica took the right toward the Tusk. I was still distracted by the gleaming short barrels of the shotgun.

"How do you know we aren't a threat?" I asked.

Veronica glanced over at us. "No disrespect? But if you had a mirror, I don't think you'd be asking."

I laughed. "We probably don't smell wonderful either."

"It's, like, freezing outside. You think I always drive with the window down?"

"Sorry."

"You all right."

"We're a little down on our luck," Penelope said.

"Who isn't?" The Tusk loomed suddenly in front of us, the shape of the thing enormous against the tapestry of the stars. The stone sides glowed as though from residual sunlight, and Veronica eased the truck to a halt. It was an old-school stick shift and she left it in neutral and stepped out onto the dirt. We followed suit. Out of the truck, she was shorter than I'd assumed, but she stood with her shoulders thrown back. I stared at her as she stared at the Tusk, trying to place her.

"It's beautiful," she said.

"It is," Penelope said, her tone surprised. "I didn't really take it in before."

Veronica stretched and rolled her head back and forth, her eyes closed. I could hear her neck cracking. "I bet you're hungry," she said.

"And thirsty." Penelope and I said it at the same time.

"I got some water in the truck."

Instinctively, we both immediately stepped in that direction, and Veronica laughed. "Good thing I came along. You look *desperate*, no cap."

No cap. A phrasing I'd heard Hannah use, mostly on the phone. She'd tried to explain it to me once, and as I'd listened, I'd wondered if my own parents had felt this confused by my slang when I was a kid.

"You are a lifesaver," Penelope said, and I knew she meant it literally.

We walked back to the truck, still idling.

"Aren't you worried about gas?" I asked.

"I'm more worried about whether she'll start again," Veronica said. "And we're good on gas, at least for now."

"Yeah?"

"We got two tanker trucks in the caravan." She was climbing back up into the cab, and we followed suit.

The Tusk was already in the rearview mirror when I asked, "Who's we?"

She kept her eyes on the road as she said, "We don't really have a name," but then she looked over at us. "I bet when you two get cleaned up, you're all sorts of suburban. The Shark Flu came, and you were shook, hiding out in your little Craftsman cottage, am I right? Maybe a little garden? Just the two of you? Your own little patch of heaven?"

"No," I said with a smile. "It's a Tudor, not a Craftsman."

"Same difference." She narrowed her eyes, slowed down, flipped on the headlights. In the dazzle, I could just make out some sort of antelope thing standing in the road, and Veronica slewed the wheel, the back tires skidding as we swerved around it, then she stepped on the gas again as if nothing had happened at all. Penelope and I were both frozen, hands planted on the dash.

"No offense," Veronica said to Penelope, "but that's what all the White folks did in San Francisco, the hipsters in Oakland. Like their property was what really mattered. Like property even existed anymore, you dig? You grow up thinking the world owes you something, the pandemic hits you hard. Those are the folks peeking out behind the curtains with guns."

"What did you do?" I asked. "When everything fell apart?"

"I don't know, man," she said. "Did everything fall apart? How together was it to begin with?"

"It was together for some people," Penelope said.

"Just not our people."

We were all squeezed together in the cab of the truck and their voices went back and forth, now they were laughing together, a side of Penelope emerging that I'd always loved. So much of our world together was White—Dobbs Ferry, largely, the echo chamber of finance, even most of my clients. But when we were at a barbecue on Martha's Vineyard, say, Penelope's laughter was different, there was a freedom in her voice. I suffered insecurities, for sure, moments when being the only White person on the crowded deck overlooking the ocean meant I worried I was saying too much, saying too little. There were nights when I'd ask for her reassurance as we fell asleep together, and she'd say *You were great, you're always great,* but I knew she hadn't been paying attention to me, she'd been relaxed, her voice rising and falling as she laughed.

You're always great. It was a lie, of course. I was not always great. One of the main reasons White people maintain their bullshit color-blind veneer is to be able to pretend that you can go through life without fucking up, your mistakes not even mistakes at all. Did I get too presumptuous at one of those barbecues, feeling that being invited allowed me a closeness that I would never have? Yes, I did. What did I say? I can't remember. It's the shame that's seared into my brain tissue. But it was laughed off, someone saying, *Watch it, White man, you don't have your Black card yet!* And there were other moments that didn't end so easily. Maybe a decade ago, I'd said something wrong to a Black client in session, and not only did his face close down immediately, but he terminated a week later. Did I yearn for contact with him again, that same shamed part of myself wanting his absolution? Of course. But I knew enough to know that my fuckup was my fuckup, not his to remedy. This was part of getting past the veneer—the talk got real, which meant the danger was real, but also the gift: truth being told. I'd been living an artificial life, a

Disneyland existence, all White people had this unspoken agreement not to look too hard at anything. Meeting Penelope jolted me out of the endless empty nonsense of my childhood, and I knew part of becoming a psychologist was my desire for this: the bedrock underneath the conversational politeness that my parents seemed to value more than anything else.

Now, watching the scrubland fly by at the edge of the headlight's pool, the wind swirling around the cab of the truck from the open window, Veronica drumming the steering wheel, the stars shining, all I felt was gratitude at being along for the ride.

"This virus shit is bad," Veronica was saying, "but slavery? Come on. White folks act like the end of Western civilization is the worst thing that ever happened. We know that shit happens . . . All. The. Time. None of this shit was built to last. People of color in Africa, Asia, the Middle East—we were doing advanced math and forming complex agrarian societies when y'all was shitting in the woods."

"That's what you're doing?" Penelope said. "You're forming a complex society in the ashes of this one."

"This time," Veronica said, "we're not going to get stomped for doing it."

"Black Wall Street."

"I'm just saying."

"Your group, it's all Black?"

"Nah, we formed a BIPOC collective, though some of the old heads won't use the term. Started in Oakland, now we're moving east. You might call us nomads. Back to our tribal roots." She laughed.

"Why not stay? Settle down?"

"The hunter-gatherer vibe in the Bay is played out. Nothing left. And the fires are no joke. California is not the place to be."

We exchanged a look.

"Where are you headed?" Veronica asked, and we answered at the same time.

"California."

"No shit?"

"No shit."

"Forget what I said. You'll love it. The Golden State, and all."

"What about you? Do you know where you're headed?"

"Come on, do you even have to ask?" She looked over and smiled. "The promised land, like always."

The road was wider now, and she pushed the truck faster, craned one hand under the seat and brought it up with a gallon of water. Penelope took it gratefully. Her throat pulsed as she drank, and I could swear her whole body revived. She handed the jug to me and the water spilled from the corners of my mouth and down onto my clothes as I swallowed.

"Easy now," Veronica said. "There's plenty."

"Do you have food too?" Penelope asked.

"My people," she said. "You don't understand. We have everything we need."

We drove for twenty minutes more, and then civilization began to appear. Exit signs and gas stations and Veronica pulled off in Rock Springs and began turning down ever smaller streets. She pulled into a driveway and said, "Home sweet home, at least for the moment."

"Where is everyone?" Penelope asked.

"I'm what you might call an advance scout. The tip of the spear."

The house was sweet. A cozy living room, glowing in the candles Veronica lit. Then she got to work on a fire.

"I went through a lot of houses looking for this," she said, patting the woodstove like a pet. Penelope and I dropped onto the couch. Veronica tossed us a bag of pretzels, and said that she would cook some dinner on top of the stove once it got warm. And then she said we could shower, and we stared at her, and she explained that there was a water tower nearby, a sphere atop a long needle that some local had painted years ago to look like a golf ball on a tee. She gave us the big room upstairs, and that night, clean and full and warm, we fell asleep together, in a queen-size four-poster, listening to the distant clatter of our host moving around on the first floor, keeping the fire alive.

In the morning, we came down late. The woodstove was hot, and light was flooding the windows.

"Y'all look like different people," Veronica said, and we smiled, holding one another close, and I didn't know if she'd been able to hear us upstairs when we woke up and made love for the first time in forever.

"Oh my God," Penelope said when she saw that there was breakfast on the table.

"You want coffee?" Veronica asked.

There was nothing that I wanted more, but I'd just kicked the sauce. For the first time in days, there was no trace of a headache. "No, thanks."

She'd fried eggs. Actual eggs, fried in a cast-iron skillet on top of the woodstove. We ate them and didn't even have to ask for more. She knew, and when she brought back another batch, everything felt so comfortable and easy that I leaned back in my chair and looked across at Penelope and said, "Sonia Sotomayor."

She blinked, her forehead wrinkled with thought, and then she said, triumphantly, "Bob Bullard."

"Good one!"

"What is this?" Veronica said.

"It's a game we used to play," Penelope said. "You know, back when we were in our suburb, hiding behind the curtains. You name a person you hope survived the Shark Flu, but it can't be anyone *too* obvious. Like Obama. Or . . . the pope, or something. But they have to be enough of a celebrity that you know who they are."

"How do you win?"

"By enjoying five minutes together. And bonus points if the person is just so great that everyone wants them on their list."

She nodded. "I don't know Bob Bullard," she said. "Does this mean I lose?"

"He's a scientist," I said. "And no."

"Okay . . . Bill McKibben," Veronica said.

"Nice." We bounced around the room—DeRay Mckesson, Dolly Parton, Missy Elliott, and then I said Colin Kaepernick, and Veronica laughed.

"What? What's wrong with Kaepernick?"

"Oh, nothing's wrong," she said. "That cat survived all right."

"What?"

"He's with us."

"No." I stared at her. "*Colin Kaepernick* is with your group?"

"Sure. But it's no thing. He's not Kaep anymore, you know? He's just Colin."

"Wow." I sat back in my chair.

"He stands with Kaep," Penelope gave me a pat on the shoulder. "He's got the T-shirt and everything."

"Well sure," I said. "It's my favorite shirt. It was my favorite." I turned to Veronica. "I get it, that he's just Colin, but still, that must have been exciting. When you met him for the first time."

"Celebrity is just a machine," she said. "That's all. You put in people and it turns them into a product. Problem is, some people believe it. They become the product, and they lose everything that made them a person. You got to let the machine do its thing, yeah, but you watch from outside, don't let them touch anything that's true about you. Missy Elliott—she's the same girl she was before she went platinum. Colin, same thing. Don't believe your own hype, that's all."

It was that moment, as Veronica rose to put some more wood in the stove, that I suddenly knew where I'd seen her before. I'd stared at her image for hours as I sat with Hannah in her room, swapping songs back and forth, from her Auto-Tuned stuff to my old-school hip-hop. Tacked up on Hannah's wall alongside Frank Ocean and Tyler, the Creator and Childish Gambino was a poster of our host.

"You're Nasica," I said. "Oh my God, you're Nasica."

She closed the woodstove's door and stood. "Used to be," she said. "Sure."

"Who?" Penelope asked.

"She's a hip-hop star," I told Penelope, then, stupidly, I told Veronica as well. "You're a hip-hop star. Hannah loves you."

"Who's Hannah?"

"Our daughter. The reason we're going to California. We're going to get our daughter."

"Yeah?"

I was staring like an idiot. Maybe it was the hype, maybe I was starstruck, maybe it was just that it brought Hannah flooding back, all the time we spent sitting on her rug, leaning against the side of the bed, her Bluetooth speaker next to us, those sweet years when she was old enough to have developed her own taste in music, but young enough to want to share it with me.

"She's not going to believe it," I said.

"I look forward to meeting her," Veronica said.

"Can I ask, it's homage, right? Why you incorporate Nas's name?"

"Hell yeah. You know, I moved from Oakland to the Bronx. But, no lie, it's marketing too. You like Nas?"

"I mean, obviously."

"Top five?"

"For sure."

"All right," she said, sitting back at the table, "let's hear the rest." She turned to Penelope. "You too?"

She held up her hands and said, "Music is *his* thing. Some jazz, maybe a little Marvin Gaye, that's it for me."

"Okay." Veronica stared at me. This was surreal. I felt genuinely nervous, that taking-an-exam shiver from my youth.

"Mobb Deep," I said.

"Yeah?"

"One thing you have to understand, I'm all East Coast, New York."

"Hey, it's your list."

"Okay, then. Big L." Was I trying to impress her? Of course I was.

"A deep cut!"

"He would have been bigger than Jay-Z."

"Okay, that's three."

I looked up at the ceiling and bit my lip as I thought.

"It's okay, fam!" She laughed. "You know you want to say Eminem, maybe the Beastie Boys. You can do it. I won't judge you."

"I'll go with Gang Starr, but that one might change, depending on the day."

"You got one left."

"I saved the best for last. Speaking of collectives, I'll take the ferry to Staten Island for the Wu-Tang Clan."

She sat back. "Not bad. No bad choices in there."

"Really?"

"One question: you gotta pick one member of the Clan, who's it gonna be? Ghost? Raekwon? The Genius?"

"Method Man," I said immediately.

She nodded.

"I have this theory." My mouth was dry. "That emcees, maybe like poets, I guess, have a lot of emotions, but they all have one where they're at their best, just fire. Like, Meek Mill when he's rapping about Lambos and stuff, it's fine, but when he lets himself get angry, it just . . ." I made a blowing-up gesture with my hands. "And for Method Man, it's self-deprecation. The emotion, I mean. He understands that in a profession based on bravado, that not taking yourself too seriously is the realest strength there is."

She was nodding, but I couldn't tell whether it was in agreement or not. Her face wasn't giving much away.

"Like, when he's rapping about cartoons or the bunion on his toe," I said.

Penelope could tell I was nervous. She was laughing at the whole thing.

"I'm guessing," Veronica said. "Given that you are a woke, upper-middle-class White dude, that you love *The Wire*."

"Is that bad?" I asked.

"Nah, man, it's cool. I'm just saying you're predictable, is all."

"I do love *The Wire*."

"Do you know how Method Man got cast in that?"

"I don't."

"He auditioned," Veronica said. "Just like anybody else. And he got a role. And all these other guys in hip-hop, they were like, *Yo, can you get me on The Wire*, but he didn't pull any strings, ask for any favors. He earned it."

"'Fuck the world . . .'" I started the line, and then she finished it, and held out a fist to bump.

We spent the rest of the day eating and drinking water. Veronica ducked out for a little while, and we offered to go with, but didn't insist when she said she was good on her own. I kept falling asleep on the couch, thinking I was awake, and then waking up when Penelope shifted because she had fallen asleep too. And then that night, Veronica broke it all down for us. We cleared away the plates and spread a map of Nevada on the dining room table and stood over it, the three of us, leaning on our hands. Candles held down the corners, illuminating the landscape that was to come.

"So Hannah is in Bishop," Veronica said. We'd told her about The Revival, the radio call, everything. "That's over here." Her finger stabbed just beyond the margin of the map. "You could take 80 all the way to Sacramento, loop down, come at it from the other side. But you wouldn't make it over the Sierras until spring. That's some Donner Party shit there. And you get trapped in the snow, you die."

Penelope and I looked at one another. "So that means you're coming at Bishop from the east, and that means Nevada. And Nevada is fucking scary, yo. I mean, biblical shit." She looked up at us. "I don't mean to scare you, but you need to know."

"It's okay," Penelope said. "We've been through a lot already."

"No cap, I get that. But this is different. High desert. Hot during the day, freezing at night. Your car breaks down in the wrong place, you die."

"What about taking 395 south from Reno?" I asked.

"Same shit. Everything east of the mountains. Might be worse."

"So what do we do?"

She stared at the map. "I would say night driving with no headlights, but if you slide off the road, that's it. You're done. No use waiting for help, because ain't nobody driving around Nevada that you want stopping."

I could feel the silence in the room as we waited for Veronica to continue.

"Okay," she said. "I'm cruising in that beater out front to blend in, you feel? But we need to get you something with horsepower. You head straight for Bishop, you watch your six, and if they start coming at you, you fucking fly."

"Who's they?" Penelope asked.

"It's all that bullshit," she said. "That White militia nonsense."

"Proud Boys?"

"Yeah, Three Percenters, Boogaloo Bois, all that shit. But they organized now. They claimed all this territory, which was fucking stupid territory to claim, but . . ." She shrugged. "There's different groups but the headquarters is there." Her finger stabbed. "Round Mountain. There's an open-pit gold mine there. They're enslaving people to keep it going."

The candles flickered, and the faint spider-webbing of roads crossing the desert seemed to shiver and dance.

"The conspiracy theories run so deep, nobody can follow that shit, which is the point. It's QAnon, but then another dude named V. They think he knew the truth about the virus. You know, all that New World Order, Jewish cabal, all that bullshit. They call themselves the QV Company. That's who runs Nevada."

"The QV Company."

"QVC," she said.

"Like . . . the home shopping network?" I couldn't help myself. I laughed.

"Yeah, they think that Q and V were sending coded messages. On the network. Preparing for the fucking end times."

"Oh my God."

She shrugged. "I ain't say they were smart."

"Are they going to try to sell us a Snuggie?"

Veronica leaned forward on her palms. "Listen to me. They dangerous. I'm telling you now. The only language they understand is power."

"Okay," I said.

"They got some crazy theories. Like, you have to maintain immunity to the virus."

"Okay," I said again.

"Which they think they can do by drinking blood from people who dipped."

The dining room was silent.

"What if we say that we didn't dip?" Penelope said.

"Either way they put you to work in the mine. And you never come out again."

Around us, the house made the little noises that a warm house makes—we could hear the wood crackling in the stove, we could hear wind rattling the windows in the frames, the same wind that had swept across the long desert we were about to cross.

"Like I said, you got to be ready to fly."

The next day, while Veronica was off scouting, Penelope and I walked the empty streets, looking for cars. It was strange, how quickly we'd gotten used to living in the empty remains of America, the bones all around us: the houses clad in vinyl siding, the pickup trucks, the swing sets rusting in the yard. Nothing would get better, nothing would even be maintained. It would all slide toward oblivion. The weeds that were forcing their way already through the cracks in the asphalt—they owned the town. We saw an occasional face in a window, once we saw a man in his side yard splitting wood. We raised our hands in greeting, he looked up and saw us, but said nothing, and the ax fell again. We kept walking, past sedans and trucks, all of them slow, slow, slow. Back in Dobbs Ferry, Al was tooling around town in his Maserati, unless he'd succeeded in wrapping it around a telephone pole. And Carlos was in our house, warming himself at our fireplace, keeping the radio frequencies open in case we reached out from the other side of the world. We stayed together, looking for a car that could go, that could carry us through all the danger to Hannah.

Finally, we resorted to walking up driveways, pressing our faces to garage-door windows. We saw lawn mowers and workshops and Jet Skis and more economy cars than we could count, and we were about to give up for the day when we strode up to one last unpromising candidate, a detached garage alongside a double-wide trailer home. There, in the darkness, almost invisible, a jet-black Chevy Camaro.

"That will *work*," Penelope said.

The garage was locked.

I rapped the trailer door, but it was like knocking on a marshmallow. Squinting through the window, there didn't seem to be anyone home. Just darkness, but when I put my hand on the knob, it turned, and the door swung open. There wasn't any smell, other than closed-house funk, and so when I stepped inside and my eyes adjusted and I saw the desiccated corpse leaning back in the La-Z-Boy, I made a noise that brought Penelope to the door.

"It's okay," I said. "I'm okay." And I was okay, that was the horrible part. It would have sent me running a year ago, calling someone, anyone, frantically. It would have haunted me. Now it was just another dead person, and I went through the kitchen drawers, looking for keys. The corpse stared at the television set, its metacarpals still resting on the remote. In the third drawer I checked, a key with masking tape and the word GARAGE, and a bright Chevy key fob as well.

I stood for a moment in the doorway, one foot in the sun, the other in the darkness.

"Thank you," I said.

The corpse said nothing, of course. And we drove back to the house where Veronica was already home, starting the fire.

The next day dawned wet, and Veronica said it was auspicious, that we might be able to make it across the vast desert plains cloaked by the rain. By the time we'd had breakfast though, the skies were scoured clear, not even a cloud. It didn't matter. We packed the car—food, water, and jugs of gasoline. All provided by this young woman who had once been a hip-hop star beloved by our daughter, this miraculous figure without whose curiosity about the Boars Tusk we might already be dead in the Wyoming scrubland, and Hannah would never know that we came for her, she would never get to mourn, and we would never get to know whether she escaped The Revival, or maybe found peace there, maybe they actually did have the answers.

Somewhere in the middle of the country, the nature of our mission had changed. We were still going after Hannah, we were still on a rescue mission, but it was unclear who was being rescued. Maybe we were the ones who needed help.

"You've got the atlas," Veronica said.

"We do." There was a time we'd almost died for a road atlas. Now she'd given us one freely, as though it were nothing.

"Remember, the only thing they understand is power. You get caught, don't beg for mercy because it's not coming."

"Should we bring a gun?"

"You could. Break into a few places here in town, you'll certainly find them. But they'll have you outgunned no matter what. Speed is your friend."

"You told us you were looking forward to meeting Hannah some-day," Penelope said.

"Yeah."

"Does that mean we can join you? Join your collective?" Penelope asked. "After we find her?"

"Sure."

"Even me?" I asked.

Veronica turned to look at me. "Dividing people up, excluding them, that's your peoples' thing. You can join, we got some White folks. The only thing is this: they have to recalibrate their think-ing. Nobody wants to hear what you have to say, just because you're White. You gonna have to be comfortable with Black women leading the way."

"He'll be fine with that," Penelope said, and Veronica laughed.

"Meet us in Grand Junction, Colorado. That's where we're going to settle in for the next few months, see how it is, then maybe head further east."

"Grand Junction."

'You got it."

We all stood in the driveway. Smoke was curlicuing from the chimney. Her truck sat in the driveway, our Camaro pulled up on the curb. The wind spun a few leaves in lazy arcs before they settled back on the ground.

"I've got to be moving on with the day," she said.

I could see Penelope swallow, her nerves as palpable as mine.

"Thank you," I said, and Penelope stepped over and pulled Veronica in for a long embrace.

We were in the car, the engine rumbling, when Veronica pulled out of the driveway and alongside us, her window down.

"Hey," she called. "Don't worry. The world may have ended, buuuut . . ." She paused.

"But what?"

"But Wu-Tang is here *forever*!"

Her laughter lingered after she drove away. I put my hand on the gearshift, and Penelope put her hand on mine. We sat there for a moment, looking through the windows at this abandoned Wyoming town, Rock Springs, a ghost town. Then we looked at each other, and I said, "Ready?" and she nodded.

I put it in gear and tried to slide away from the curb, but only succeeded in stalling. Penelope just looked at me.

"Oh, boy," I said.

The Camaro engine didn't ease into things. It required commitment. This time, I stomped the gas, the car leapt, and we were off toward the highway headed west.

CHAPTER 11

A house in Vermont was the first vacation we took after Hannah was born. I couldn't remember the name of the family who'd accompanied us. We'd counted them among our closest friends, then drifted apart for no real reason, texts never returned on one side or the other, missed calls, so when they moved away, we didn't even know they'd gone. But Penelope was pregnant during the window of our friendship, and during dinner at their house I would stare at their two children, the toddler mouthing blocks and the little boy begging to watch television, like I was trying to divine my own future as a father. On the big day, they came to the hospital with balloons.

What I remembered from Vermont was the terror in Penelope's voice as she cried out from the bedroom. I was frying bacon, up early and staring into the snow-muffled landscape, our sleep schedule a random scattering of hours in response to Hannah's colicky mood. Penelope was shouting my name, again and again, careless of the other family, and I sprinted from the kitchen, the bacon burning into the skillet behind me as the fat popped and jumped. Hannah was awake and screaming too, her face purple, and I couldn't figure out what was wrong, Penelope was saying *Her heart, her heart,* and when I placed my palm against her little chest, I could feel it like a hummingbird, so fast the beats bled into one another, so fast it made my own heart hammer as though we were one.

Whatever the name of the other family, I was calling it now, and the father came thundering into the room, and in that moment I wanted him to roll his eyes and tell us all babies did this. That was the sort of people they were, the illusion of perfection, they never shared their own struggles, just made it seem as though they were born parents, so when I stumbled upon the mother hissing recriminations at her son in the hallway, it came as a tremendous relief.

When his hand pressed against Hannah, he didn't tell us we needed to chill out. Instead, his eyes went wide and he said, "Oh, Jesus," and I ran outside to start the car, stumbling and sliding on the new snow powdering the ice. Penelope strapped Hannah into the car seat and draped herself over it, squeezed between the back of the front passenger seat and our daughter, staring at her as I stomped the gas and we fishtailed out of the driveway and onto the road, my hand crumpling a page of MapQuest directions to Dartmouth-Hitchcock hospital against the wheel. When I reached the highway, I pressed the accelerator to the floor and kept it there. The car shuddered and the needle swung past vertical into areas of the speedometer I'd never visited before, over a hundred miles per hour, the posted limits meaningless, and my hands squeezing the life from the wheel.

I really thought she was dying. *Prayer* wasn't the right word for what I was doing as I drove. Bargaining, maybe, and I didn't even know with whom. I was ready to offer my own twisted muscle of a heart in trade.

And she was fine. We endured a few horrifying hours of tests and received like a gift the diagnosis of supraventricular tachycardia, the name they told us was the most probable and desirable outcome when we arrived. The mantra we repeated and begged for while the machines whirred and the doctors looked at charts and results. I'd never heard those words in my life, and now they were all I wanted. Supraventricular tachycardia. Treatable. Excellent prognosis. Probably our drive to the hospital had been more dangerous.

For a moment, we'd penetrated the veil, the illusion of normalcy that hung over our whole American way of life. Not for us famine. Not for us the artillery of civil war hollowing out our buildings. Not for us warlords. On a grand time line of human existence, we lived inexpressibly pampered lives, but the truth lurked behind it all: nasty, brutish, short, and all that. People still died. Children still died.

How many days had it been since we left to drive west? A week? Two? Time no longer had meaning, sure, but it went deeper than that. I could see now my naivete, my foolish insistence on maintaining the shape of a lost world. Why had Penelope left Dobbs Ferry behind so easily? Because *she* understood that it no longer existed. When we planted the garden, I only tilled to the edge of our property, as though Arlo and Jeff were still alive next door to prune their rosebushes. Driving through New Jersey, Pennsylvania, Ohio, I'd set the cruise at eighty and called it caution, but I could see now it was one last vestige of innocence that needed to fall. I had performed my young man's nightmare: becoming my father, afraid of change, living in the past, trying to impose some lost social order upon the wildness of the world. The truth was radical simplicity, as though Marie Kondo invented the Shark Flu as a gift to us all. Everything will be stripped away, existence not a blade-edge but the piercing tip, singular and terrible and beautiful. All our lives, we'd been chasing balance as though it were the key. Balance, balance, balance. I preached it to my clients, and they chased it too.

Balance *what?* There was nothing left except what I loved most: my family. Anything else was a needless hindrance, a jutting tumorous thing that interrupted the aerodynamic beauty of our purpose, arrow-thin. We were in the home-straight now, racing west, our Camaro low to the ground, teeth grinding at the bit, windshield raked back. When I stepped on the gas, the engine howled in response, and on the long straightaways, I hit 130, just so I knew I could.

There was one piece of my innocence left, if I was honest. I remained a virgin: I had never killed. That was the one last illusion of grace I wanted to retain, the river of blood I hoped never to cross. The world glittered with knives wherever you looked, but maybe I was right that violence only begat violence. Maybe this one moral remnant acted like the spoiler on the back of the Camaro, holding it to the ground so it didn't suddenly soar and flip and kill us both.

We drove through the last miles of Wyoming, and up into the Utah mountains. I downshifted and slowed as we wound upward, the highway torquing itself into sweeping turns as it rose. We kept the gas tank full, stopping often, mindful that the time might come when we needed to run, needed to outlast someone.

I saw everything differently now, scanned the hills and crags alongside the road for potential ambushes. When Penelope took the wheel, I was no less alert, both of us trying to make the most of the limited visibility the car offered, the windows just slits through which we craned our faces to see, as though the Camaro were a tank, but armor-less, nothing to shield us from attack.

The car was warm, but when we stopped and stepped outside, the cold surprised us, biting, reminding us of the thin air. And then a line of snow swept across the road, a squall so sudden and complete that we were nearly blinded, and Penelope slowed to a near-idle, the car nosing through the blinding flakes that left as quickly as they came, the road still black and wet, but the stubby trees and hillsides around us now white. A few more miles and we started the long downhill slalom toward Salt Lake City, and the brown and faded green returned, the crumbling bluffs, the whiteout in our past, like a hallucination we had driven through to get to the other side. Runaway truck ramps began to appear, their angles opposite to the highway's plunge. A ruined semi sprawled on one, like a dead brontosaur jackknifed and still.

Salt Lake was a low city on the plain, dwarfed by mountain ranges on either side. Not like New York, jutting ostentatiously into the air. Flying into Utah, you would marvel at the peaks, not the skyscrapers you pressed your face to the porthole to see as you descended to LaGuardia or JFK. Of course, flying was a thing of the past now, something human beings had briefly mastered before the continents separated themselves again. Planes, in the end, had been a virus distribution method, the key to their own demise.

We were out of the city as fast as we'd entered, the plain so flat on the other side that we could feel the marble-arc of the earth beneath us. Tangled cloverleafs of entrance and exit ramps broke the monotony, and then suddenly the lake that gave the city its name appeared to our right, long and glittering back at the sun. In the distance, mountain peaks seemed to sit like islands. We weren't talking much, but I said *Look*, and Penelope said, *I know*.

The highway narrowed to two lanes with a wide median between us and the eastbound side, and it ran absolutely dead straight through a stark white landscape of sand. I could have taken my hands off the wheel for miles except at high speed the car seemed alive, any little shimmy tugging at my hands, which gripped the wheel at ten and two. On the far side, an exit appeared reading BONNEVILLE SPEED-WAY, and I turned to Penelope.

"That was the Bonneville Salt Flats, where they try to do speed records." For a brief moment, I was a tourist. "Not sand at all. Salt."

"Wow." She gave me the same look I used to get when I insisted on recounting some highlight from the basketball game the night before. I laughed.

"What?" she said.

"Nothing."

The highway began to turn and rise as it passed through an outcropping of blasted rock and into the town of Wendover, and then a sign appeared on the right reading WELCOME TO NEVADA, and below that HAZARDOUS MATERIAL PERMIT REQUIRED CALL (775) 687-9600.

I stopped smiling and pulled over to the side. My hands were cramping from holding the wheel so tightly. Without a word, Penelope stepped out of the car, got a gas can from the back, and topped us off. We spread the atlas on the hood and stared at it, though we'd already planned our route.

"That's our exit," Penelope said, pointing back.

I looked down below the highway where the ramp led to an underpass. "Yeah."

Our path swung south, strung like a rope through the state of Nevada and straight to Bishop. Four hundred miles. In our car, four hours. We could be there in four hours. It took my breath away to think that the distance between us and Hannah could be measured not in days or lifetimes but hours.

"We don't even have a plan," I said. "For what we do in Bishop."

"We have to get to Bishop first." She was still staring at the map as though it might have something new to say. I'd never been to Nevada, never gone to Vegas. It had always occupied the theoretical place in my mind reserved for things about which I had opinions despite a complete lack of personal experience: casinos, prostitution, and, now, slave-worked gold mining. The route looked simple enough on the map, and we were different now, seasoned in apocalypse.

"We can handle this," I said. "We can make it."

Penelope gave me a tired smile. "There it is," she said. She folded up the map. "I'll drive."

She looped around and back to the exit. Down we drove through town, past casinos that probably seemed faded and sad even when the world was bustling. Now, they looked like gaudy coffins. We'd entered a strange landscape of grays and browns, rocks jutting from bare earth, and even the trees barely pretended to be green, their color washed out and spent. Low mountains serrated the horizon, but the road ran flat and true, the only corners gentle enough that Penelope barely had to turn the wheel. Even when we reached the rocky hills, they jutted from the plain like spikes, and the road's character didn't change at all, still flat, two lanes with a dotted yellow line between, with endless asphalt behind and endless asphalt ahead. Penelope drove fast, and it felt strangely safe to me. There was no place for someone to hide. We had horsepower to spare, and the only cars we saw were broken down and lurched onto the roadside dirt, abandoned.

The road rose, climbing into low hills, and the desert sprang into greener bloom, with scrub dotting all around us. The speed limit was seventy, which meant only that we could go as fast as we liked, Penelope's face tight with concentration, her shoulders high, her whole body leaning forward so I could see an inch of space between her back and the seat. We pelted on, a little airport appearing to our right, the wind sock limp and dangling, and then we were entering the town of Ely, and she slowed.

A woman was shuffling along the roadside as we passed an RV park, and the sound of our car approaching sent her scrambling back over a low fence and out of view. Then we were on into the town itself, a strange mix of gas stations and houses and strip malls sharing the same real estate, a trading post across from a low ranch-style home. Penelope turned onto Route 6, and now the road was winding through canyons, the hillsides rising at forty-five degrees on both sides, and I was scanning both directions for ambushes. There was cover, low trees, and behind every trunk, I imagined a man with a gun, his head leaning back against the bark, waiting to swing his barrel around.

"This is where I would do it," I said.

"Me too."

No one leapt out. No shots broke the desert silence. We burst through the other side, back into the sere moonscape, the road straightening string-tight as though pulled from either side, the landscape a smear of brown and gray as Penelope accelerated and the car roared in response. There was no sign of life, not even a circling buzzard. Maybe even the dead were gone. Maybe there was nothing. The road stretched so true that the opposite edges came together like a perspective exercise in art class, merging into one line at the horizon. We passed a derelict tractor-trailer perpendicular to the road, and then a scattering of burned-out automobile carcasses, and another tractor-trailer loomed in the distance next to the roadside, again perpendicular, its broad side facing us like a wall.

Alarm bells began to ring in my mind. It seemed like a thousand years ago, but I abruptly remembered the feminist collective in the Delaware Water Gap, the toll road, and the panel van they'd used as a roadblock. I knew what was going to happen before it did, I knew that we'd already driven into the trap, it had happened before we noticed anything, this was how it all worked, you thought the end was miles down the road but it was here, in the desert, waiting to surprise you.

The tractor-trailer ahead lurched to life, pulled across the road and stopped.

Penelope stood on the brakes. "Oh, no, no, no," she said. Before I could say it, she had jammed the transmission into reverse, but it was too late. Through the back window, a shimmer of smoke now rose from the tall exhaust pipes of the truck we'd just passed, and then it too pulled across to block the road and we were boxed in, trapped.

The dead cars in the desert made sudden and appalling sense. Thick low shrubs dotted the landscape, and between them the sandy dirt was soft enough that all the other cars had mired themselves immediately trying to run.

Nothing moved. No one stepped from the trucks. The one in front was still a quarter mile away, but there was nowhere to go.

Why hadn't we gone looking for guns? We could have tried to shoot our way out of this, though even as the thought ballooned in my brain, I knew it was a fantasy.

Penelope's breath was fast and shallow, and I could see her swallowing. I knew she was terrified, and I could see her fighting to master it. She took my hand and squeezed it so tightly it hurt. Our eyes met, and we held our gaze, the car quiet until her breathing slowed and she spoke. "Just follow my lead," she said. "Okay?"

"What are you going to do?"

She didn't answer, just put the car into gear and drove slowly up toward the truck. When we got closer, a man in camouflage body armor stepped down from the passenger seat and onto the roadway. He held an assault rifle in his hands. His head was covered with a BMX-style helmet, his face guard emblazoned with The Punisher's skull. The rifle rose to his shoulder and pointed at us.

We stopped about twenty feet away, and Penelope pulled the key from the ignition, yanked up the parking brake, and stepped out of the car. She was about to walk forward on the dusty asphalt when she leaned back into the car, took one last look at me, and said, "Take off your wedding ring."

Whatever I knew she was feeling, she walked toward the man with the gun as if she owned all of this, shoulders thrown back, as though whatever shenanigans he was trying to pull, they were barely worthy of her notice.

"Where do you think you're going?" the Punisher said.

"I am going to Round Mountain," Penelope said to him. "I have business with the QVC."

I was out of the car now, following a few steps behind her.

"That's right you do." He laughed. In the truck above him, another man looked down from the open window.

229

"Move your truck and let me pass," Penelope said. "Again, I have business with the QVC." Her voice, the voice I knew so well it was a part of me, rang out as flat and empty and distant as the desert all around us. If my eyes were shut, would I have even recognized it as hers?

"Bitch, I am the QVC."

"Good," she said. "I represent the New Black Nation. I am here on a diplomatic mission."

He squinted. "What?"

"The New Black Nation," she repeated. "I assume you know of us."

"What?" He lowered the gun barrel so that it pointed at our feet rather than our faces. "Curtis, what the fuck is she talking about?"

Curtis, up in the truck, just stared at us.

"Please take off your mask so we can talk," Penelope said.

"Don't tell me what to do."

Now Curtis opened the door and stepped down from the cab. "Just take off the fucking mask, Duane." He was fat, his belly hanging over his belt, his eyes raisins in the dough of his face as he stared at Penelope. "What are you going on about?"

"I represent the New Black Nation," she repeated. "I come on a diplomatic mission. Take me to your leader." She said this without any irony shading her voice.

"Where is the *New Black Nation*?" Condescension dripped from Curtis's voice as he said the name.

"Our stronghold is South-Central Los Angeles, but we now hold much of Southern California."

"I thought the wetbacks had LA."

Penelope smiled and raised an eyebrow. "They used to, yes."

"Jesus Christ Almighty," Curtis said.

We all stood in silence, the sun merciless overhead in the empty sky, though when I looked west, toward the California of the fantasy she was spinning, I could see storm clouds starting to smudge the horizon.

Curtis pointed at me. "Who's he?"

"He belongs to me," Penelope said without hesitation.

"What?"

"You would say, he is my slave."

"I fuckin' knew it," Duane said. His gun barrel swung in wild arcs. "I fuckin' told you, man."

Curtis spoke to me. "What's she talking about?"

I looked at Penelope. "She took me in," I said. "She gave me food and shelter and safety. And in return . . ." I shrugged.

"You want to walk, you can walk," Curtis said to me. "Right here, right now. Ain't nothing she can do about it."

"I am happy," I said. "My master treats me well."

Curtis spit in the dirt, wiped his face with his forearm. He looked at me like I was a bad taste in his mouth. "Goddamn," he said.

"Let me pass," Penelope said. "I have business with your leaders."

Curtis's eyes got even smaller as he stared at us. "I ain't stupid," he said. "Duane, zip-tie these two. We'll let the Dragon sort it out." He pulled a pistol from his belt and waved it at us. Duane swung the rifle around to his back and pulled two long green pieces of plastic from his pocket.

"You are making a mistake," Penelope said as he bound her wrists together, then mine.

"Shut up," he said.

"Take their car and get them to Round Mountain," Curtis said.

"Get in the back," Duane said to Penelope. She stared at him, shook her head, then climbed into our car's narrow little backseat, sitting sideways with her hands still bound behind her.

"You," he said to me. "Get in the passenger seat."

The bucket seat was not designed to accommodate arms tied

behind a back. I wedged myself in, but it hurt. Duane handed his rifle to Curtis, took the pistol in exchange, and dropped into the driver's seat.

"Goddammit." He got back out of the car. "It's a stick."

"What?"

"It's a fucking stick shift."

"So what?"

"I never drove one! Who drives a stick anyhow?"

"I drive a stick, that's who!" Curtis said. He took a long look at the front seat of the Camaro, and I realized he was judging whether he would fit. He came to the decision that he would not.

"You know I have to man the roadblock," he said.

"I can do the roadblock."

"The fucking truck is a stick too, Duane. You gonna drive that?"

"Well, what the fuck are we supposed to do then?"

Penelope and I looked at one another.

"Untie him, make him drive. But keep your eyes on him," Curtis said.

"Get out the fucking car," Duane said to me. I was moving too slow for him, and he grabbed the zip tie and pulled my arms backward. I stumbled out onto the road and fell. He stood over me. "Get up."

Penelope started to say something from the back, but kept quiet. I scrambled to my feet.

"Don't try no funny business." Duane pulled a knife out of a holster on his belt. He held it up to my nose. "I will not hesitate. You understand? I will not hesitate one fucking second. I will gut you like a deer."

I leaned my head away from the point. "I understand."

He stepped around behind me, slipped the knife between my hands, and I could feel the plastic wrench my wrists before the blade parted it and I was free. Curtis had the rifle aimed at me. There was nothing I could do, but I wasn't in charge here anyway. We were playing Penelope's gambit. I trusted her because I knew her, knew that even as her pulse thudded with fear, part of her brain had calculated odds, decided on a course of action. I climbed into the driver's seat, and Duane kept the pistol on me as he got into the passenger seat, closed the door, and leaned against it.

"No sudden moves," he said.

Curtis climbed back up into the truck and rumbled it to life. It backed off the road, and Duane pointed with his pistol.

"Go," he said.

His smell filled the car, sweat and unchanged socks and hate. After a mile, he shifted in his seat to face the road ahead, his hand still tight on the pistol in his lap, and he pulled down the shoulder belt and latched himself in. Any vision I'd had of pulling a cinematic stunt and deliberately crashing the car to watch him launch through the windshield was gone. It would have killed us all anyway. Even if we'd survived the crash, we would have been alone in the desert, our death postponed by a few hours, maybe a couple of days.

The green was gone from the brush tufting the ground. Nothing but brown, as though everything had given up. As we drove west, the clouds grew, tall and strangely reddish in color, blotting the sun so we were now driving in a half-light though the little clock on the dashboard read 2:32.

"Pull over up there," Duane said. A little blue rest area sign needled the roadside, but what it was marking was nothing more than a patch of dirt from which the brush had been cleared, a couple of old fifty-five-gallon drums overflowing with garbage there was no one left to collect. We came to a stop, and Duane unbuckled his belt, the pistol still staring at me. Before he opened the door, he said, "Gimme the key."

I handed it over, and he stepped a couple of paces from the car. He unzipped his pants, and stood there, his little flaccid penis just poking out of his fly. Nothing happened.

233

"Stop looking at me," he said. "What are you, a faggot?"

I looked in the back at Penelope. A spattering hiss said that he'd found success. Her face was impassive, but I could see her hands clenched tight. Her ruse depended on him being just the right amount of stupid. Dumb enough to buy what she was selling, but not so dumb that he would kill us, deliberately or accidentally.

He stepped back into the car and handed me the key, which was wet with sweat or piss, it didn't matter which. I put it in the ignition and wiped my fingers on my pants.

We drove on. The miles disappeared, the landscape around us endless and forlorn. It began to snow, just a little, but the flakes didn't melt onto the windshield, they flew back up and eddied in the air as we passed.

It wasn't snow, it was ash. The clouds weren't clouds at all. It was smoke from the California fires Veronica had told us about, riding the wind eastward.

We turned north, and it wasn't long until we reached a dirt road and he pointed and said, "You got no fuckin' idea what's waiting for you," and laughed.

The wall that appeared in front of us was built of junked cars and corrugated metal and wooden poles. It stretched as far as we could see in either direction, and flags were snapping in the wind, so many flags. QVC. American flags fluttering next to Confederate ones. Thin Blue Line. Nazi swastikas and eagles. Campaign-style flags that didn't have a date or a running mate, but just the words TRUMP FOREVER. Sentries stood at the top of the wall with long guns, and loops of barbed wire too, and spikes.

"Home sweet home," Duane said. He stepped out of the car and waved. My palms were slick against the wheel, my shirt wet too, as though I were running a race. The gate began to swing open, and Duane sat back down in the passenger seat, gesturing forward with the pistol. I stalled the car trying to put it in first.

Duane laughed. "You can't drive stick for shit," he said.

I started the engine again, and we crept inside, the odd thing about the wall becoming clear to me once the gate closed behind us: the guns were all pointed inward. It wasn't a wall built to repel invasion, to keep people out. This wall was built to keep people in. We were entering a prison.

Duane held up a hand and I stopped the car. He took the key again.

"Get out," he said. "We going to meet the Dragon. You gonna love him."

My brain was scurrying like a trapped animal. I couldn't focus on anything, just seeing the world in flashes around me as Penelope and I stepped out stiffly onto the dirt and Duane zip-tied my wrists again, roughly, and gave me a kick.

The wall stretched so wide behind us it disappeared on both sides. There were low buildings looming, the air swirling with dust. We stumbled forward and a man stepped out and said to Duane, "New meat?"

"From the roadblock on 6," Duane said. "They was saying something crazy about the Blacks taking Los Angeles."

The man looked at Penelope.

"I represent the New Black Nation," she said. "I am here on a diplomatic mission."

The man looked at her for a good three seconds before his face creased and he began to laugh. "That's a fuckin' new one," he said. "Take them to the Dragon."

"You heard him," Duane said. "Walk."

Maybe it was my arms pulling my chest back, but I could barely breathe, coughing with the dust and ash, my feet stumbling, and my eyes barely registering the images that swam into view as we walked, all of them reddened by the smoke-light sun: White men in body armor and Hawaiian shirts, eye black painted on their cheekbones like they were ready to play center field. Guns. All with guns. And cages. Open-air cages with metal bars and people inside, collapsed on the ground, some standing holding the bars.

"Help me," one of them was saying. He was clenching the bars tight, and as we walked by, Duane casually lashed out with the butt of his pistol, crushing the man's fingers. He fell backward with a cry, and we were past him, walking forward toward where the earth seemed to open and disappear into a yawning nothingness. As we stepped closer to the edge, the dust eddying on top, we could see descending in the distance a vast open-air mine like an inverted stepped pyramid. Figures moved, the rise and fall of pickaxes, and armed men walked between them. I heard a whipcrack. Colossal dump trucks and earth machines dotted the landscape, derelict. The scale was impossible, the people insect-like in their movements and number, crawling up the ridged sides, pushing wheelbarrows, slumping along in lines bound together. I felt my mouth falling open, felt my knees swimming and weak.

Through it all, striding through the chaos, head held so tall she seemed to have grown two inches, my wife. I saw her looking down into the mine and her face didn't change at all. She looked at it like a picture in a book.

"You going down there," Duane said. "Gonna dig us some gold." He laughed.

Penelope glanced over at him. "Take me to the Dragon."

"Don't tell me what to do. I'm in charge here."

She just looked at him.

After a long moment meant to reestablish his authority, he said, "Well, get fucking moving. The Dragon's waiting on you."

We walked left along the edge of the pit, and an A-frame structure built of the same corrugated metal as the wall swung into view. The eaves were decorated with rope hung in shallow loops like Christmas garland, festooned with ornaments, and as I got closer, the ornaments resolved into skulls, jawless, the strand of rope running through the eyeholes. A whole skeleton hung from the roof edge like a physician's model, except smeared with bloodstains and flecked with old bits of gristle, hair still limp from the skull-top. My eyes swam, and a noise escaped from my mouth. As though in response, the skeleton suddenly moved, a hunched dance like one of those toys you might see clacking on the sidewalk. The feet flopping, the arms raised elbow-high and swinging. Atop the roof, a man was mimicking the dance, his limbs moving wildly, and I realized the skeleton was tied to him, that whatever he did the bones would follow. He leered at us, leaning forward, and the skull bobbed up and stared.

Penelope stepped past the horror without a glance and into the shade of the A-frame, and I followed one step behind her. Ahead of us, a man sat on a throne, and I had to squint for a second. It was the Iron Throne, from the TV show. Not an ironic one built of AK-47s or something like that, just a replica, the swords flimsy, but swords nonetheless. And in it sat a man with a clipped black beard and pale hard blue eyes. Not for him the bandoliers of ammunition the others stretched across their chests. Not even body armor. Just a Hawaiian shirt tucked into his camouflage pants, which were in turn tucked into boots.

He stared at us in unblinking silence, and I felt myself wilting. Duane said, "We caught these two at the roadblock on 6." The man on the throne stared at Penelope. I was standing next to and a step behind her, and I could see her eyes locked with his. Neither of them spoke. The distant sounds of shovels and axes striking earth and the cries of voices rose from the pit. The wind stirred the red air, and one of the men standing near the throne put down his rifle and coughed.

Duane couldn't tolerate the silence. "They got their own country, she says, the nigg—"

Duane caught himself just as the Dragon held up his palm and looked at him. His face flushed.

"A war between the races is coming." The Dragon was looking at Penelope again, his voice higher than I expected. "Q told us that from the beginning. But that's no excuse for being racist. My apologies for my friend here. Black and White. It doesn't matter. They all work the mine."

The men standing around the throne laughed.

"I represent the New Black Nation," Penelope said. "You are the Dragon?"

He inclined his head.

"We propose an alliance . . ."

He held up the palm toward Penelope, pointed at me. "Who are you?" His eyes felt hot on my skin.

"He speaks when I tell him to speak," Penelope said.

"And why is that?"

"He belongs to me."

We were surrounded by a loose semicircle of men, and a ripple passed through them, guns shifting. "The fuck is this," one of them said.

The Dragon stared at us until the muttering stopped and then he finally spoke. "I knew this would come to pass. God created the races, and in his wisdom he put them on separate continents. They cannot mix without subjugation. Slavery was not a choice. As soon as the Blacks arrived here, it was an inevitability. You see"—he looked around the circle of his men—"this is what we fight against. This is why we must win this war. One must play the master and one must play the slave. And I will never be a slave."

Penelope had misjudged. It was over. The edge of the pit seemed to swim closer, and I could feel myself swaying.

"I do not deny that a war is coming," Penelope said. "But it is not the war that you think."

He was looking at her again.

"A new power is rising in the south," she continued. "Surely you

238

have heard this. A wave is coming, and it will break on us with terrible force. All the Spanish-speaking countries allied together, marching north to destroy us."

The shelter went silent.

"We took Los Angeles from them, but we cannot defend the border alone."

"The wall . . ." one of the men said.

Penelope didn't look at him, just kept her eyes on the Dragon. "The wall is nothing to what is coming. They will sweep over us like a wave, moving north, seeking cooler climates."

"It's a trick," one of the men said. "They trying to trick us."

The Dragon just looked at Penelope and said, "How do I know you aren't lying?"

"Send out patrols," she said. "Go to the border. You will see what we see." Her hands, which had been calmly clasped behind her, tightened. "But I must return to my people to let them know if you will consider our offer of alliance."

One of them men started to say something in protest, but the Dragon held up his hand for silence.

"Illegals," he said. "It never stops. Eternal vigilance is the price of liberty."

He stared at Penelope as though waiting for her to break. She was microscopically still. I couldn't even see her breathe. From behind, her eyes were invisible, but I knew she wasn't blinking.

"Fine," he said. "You can tell your people I will consider their offer. But I make no promises."

She inclined her head and bowed ever so slightly.

Before my heart could leap, the Dragon pointed to me. "But he stays."

"He belongs to me."

"Not anymore he doesn't."

The bottom fell out. My brain churned uselessly, my bowels

loosened, I might shit myself there in Hell, the red sky looming overhead. This was where I was going to die. Darkness overtook my vision, I could feel myself swaying, and then like a pinprick of light, I knew that both of us getting across the country had been a wild dream. Not only wild. An irrelevant dream. All that mattered was one of us finding Hannah, holding her close, telling her one more time how much she was loved. It turned out, it was going to be Penelope, not me.

"I need him," Penelope said. "To drive my car and protect me. And he will not agree to stay."

"Let him talk," the Dragon said, but before I could say anything, Penelope continued.

"I offer a gift instead," she said. "A token of respect."

"What gift?"

"Let him fetch it. If it's not to your liking, then I will leave him instead."

The Dragon nodded.

She turned to me. "Bring the gift." Her eyes were wide, and I understood immediately what she wanted me to get from the car.

I turned and said to Duane, "Give me the car keys."

"No," said the Dragon. "Go with him."

We walked back toward the car, past the cages. "This is some bullshit," Duane said. "The Mexicans ain't coming. They wouldn't dare."

"They are coming," I said. "Whether you believe it or not."

"You're a fucking disgrace to the White man," he said. "You're a . . . you're a . . ." His jaw hung open, his face red and working, and then he found an answer and his jaundiced eyes lit up. "You're an Uncle Tom."

I just kept walking. When we got to the car, he squinted at the key, then pressed a button. The horn bleated across the emptiness.

"My hands," I said.

For the second time, he cut me free, his knife nearly spraining my wrists.

I opened the door, then bent to the glove box.

"Watch yourself," he said. The pistol was aimed at me again. He crowded behind me to see what I was doing, so close that I could feel him pressing against my butt. When I turned, a paper bag in my hand, he didn't move, so our faces were inches apart.

I didn't say anything. He waited a couple of seconds, then feinted as though to butt his forehead against mine. I flinched, and he laughed. "He's never gonna let you leave," he said. "Whatever you got in that little bag don't matter."

We walked back to the shelter where Penelope and the Dragon were waiting in silence.

"A token of respect," she said, and I pulled Manny's gold bar out of the bag and held it high in the air.

"Holy shit," one of the men said. "Would you look at that."

"We have taken the Jewish gold reserves in Los Angeles," Penelope said. "And we propose to share them with you in return for your alliance."

Down in the pit, they had a thousand slaves working for thumbnail flecks of gold. I stepped forward, the bar heavy in my hands, and offered it to the Dragon, and he hefted, inspected, pressed a thumbnail into it. Then a man to his left stepped forward and took it, putting a jeweler's glass to his eye. We all waited.

"It's the real thing," he said. "Super-high quality. It's Jew gold all right."

The Dragon took the bar back from him, looked down at it, as though it held answers. Then he looked up. "We accept your gift, but we will never follow you into battle. The White race was born to lead the rest."

"You have power," Penelope said. "That is why I come bearing a gift. We will not kneel, but we do not expect to lead."

"I already knew of the coming invasion," he said. "Q told us years ago."

"Of course."

"Return to Los Angeles," he said. "Tell them I will consider their offer of alliance to defend the United States of America."

"Is the gold acceptable in place of my man?"

I could hear my own heart in my ears.

"It is," the Dragon said.

Jubilation bubbled inside me, and Penelope nodded, a little low bow. "What the fuck," Duane said. I could see his mouth gape, and he started to storm away.

"He has the keys to our car," I said.

"Duane," the Dragon said.

He turned back, his face twisted into a mask of anger. One step toward me, and he narrowed his eyes, hocked sputum in his throat, and spit a glob of it onto my chest. "Fuck you," he said, and he dropped the keys into the dirt. I bent to pick them up. He stalked off, climbed into a pickup, and spun the tires as he squealed away toward the gate.

"I need your assurance of safe passage," Penelope said to the Dragon.

He stepped down from his throne and walked toward us. She did not move. When he got close, he leaned in and said, "If you double-cross me, I will march on Los Angeles and take the Jew gold myself."

She nodded. From two feet away, they stared at one another. Finally, he said, "You will have safe passage. I guarantee it."

The skeleton hung limp as we walked away, the dancer staring at us from the roof. All the way back past the pit and the cages and the men staring at us, my body wanted to run, but instead I matched Penelope's slow steady stride. When we got to the car, she climbed into the passenger seat and looked straight ahead, waiting.

I got into the car and started the engine. We waited for the gate to open, and when it did, I put it in gear. This time, I didn't stall. I stepped on the gas, and we surged out back onto the road, the wall disappearing behind us into the haze.

I could barely keep the car steady as we pelted down the road. Penelope didn't say a word, like a Method actor staying in character. I kept looking over at her, even though we weaved across the yellow lines when I did.

"Are you—" I started, and she said, "We're not free yet."

She wasn't wrong. Duane was waiting for us just a few miles down the road, the truck stretched across both lanes, a rifle in his hands.

I started to swerve toward the desert, and Penelope said, "Don't, he'll shoot." So I slowed instead, coming to a stop twenty yards from where he stood.

He walked over to the driver's-side window, bent down, and rapped it with the muzzle of his gun.

"Lower it," Penelope said.

He was sweating, a vein throbbing in his forehead. "What did you do?" he said to Penelope.

"What do you mean?"

He looked like he was in pain. "I can't figure what you did back there."

"I made an alliance," Penelope said.

"Alliance my ass," Duane said. "What did you do?"

Penelope said nothing.

"You can't fool me. I know a liar when I see one."

"The Dragon has guaranteed us safe passage."

He looked at me. "Get out of the fucking car."

"Do not get out," Penelope said. She placed a hand on my forearm, the first mistake she'd made in this whole charade. He saw it.

"This is fucking bullshit," he said. "Get out the car."

I shook my head.

"Get the fuck out the car."

I didn't move. If he'd clenched a fist, I would have been able to ready myself. Instead, he swung his elbow through the open window, colliding with my jaw, and my skull seemed to explode, stars constellating in my vision and a high whine in my ears. I fell sideways.

"We were guaranteed passage," Penelope kept her voice calm, but I could hear her panic.

"I know what you was told."

"Then let us pass."

"You remember your place, bitch."

My eyes began to refocus, the red sky looming through the windshield, Penelope next to me, and Duane's breath close to my nose as he leaned in to whisper into my ear, so close I could feel the flecks of spit on my skin, "I don't know what the fuck is going on here, but you disgust me. Have some fucking self-respect."

He strode back to the truck like he'd proven something, his shoulders back and the gun cradled in his arms. Before climbing into the driver's seat, he aimed the gun out into the vast desert and held down the trigger, a long string of gunshots like hands clapping faster than they could clap. Then up into the truck he went, the engine raced, and the wheels spun as he stomped the gas and skidded sideways before lurching down the road and out of view.

I could barely see, stars still blooming on the edges of my sight, but I stepped on the gas and started driving away from the nightmare, the ringing in my ears loud enough that I could barely hear Penelope saying in her real voice, "Oh, baby, please tell me you're okay."

"I'm okay." I started to look at her.

"Don't stop. Keep driving."

It wasn't until we were back on Route 6 headed west that her voice asked me to pull over, and when I did, she stepped out on the dirt and vomited, and I opened my door and started to step around the car to hold her shoulders, rub her back, but the gorge rose in my throat too and I staggered and fell to my knees as my stomach rejected everything in long dizzying retches.

I could see her bent over and shaking, and when I stood, my body felt so light that I stumbled trying to walk. She looked up.

"Are you really okay? He hit you so hard."

Pain bloomed when I moved my jaw, but it was only pain. We were alive. We were driving west. "I'm fine," I said.

"I can drive," she said, but her face was utterly spent. Whatever it had taken to do what she'd just done, there was none of it left.

"I got it." The vomiting seemed to have helped clear my vision, and I got a gallon of water from the car. We rinsed our mouths, spitting water to the ground where it scattered and held together in pools and drops coated with dust. To the west, the sky's red was deepening. There were no shadows to grow long, but darkness was beginning to fall. We got back into the car, and Penelope's head slumped back, her eyes closed.

I drove easy, the headlights on. We were only a few hours from Bishop and Hannah. All I had to do was keep the car in its lane, keep us rolling forward. I didn't know if Penelope was asleep, but I said, "How did you know that would work?"

I thought she wasn't listening, but then she said, "I didn't."

"If they knew that we were married . . ."

"Then we were dead," she said.

"But why your slave? I worried it was going too far."

She didn't open her eyes, her face still empty and gaunt with exhaustion. She said, "It's the only logic they understand."

CHAPTER 12

Penelope sleeping beside me. A moonless, starless night, though I knew if I turned off the headlights, my eyes would adjust from white brilliance not to darkness, but a lurid red glow in the sky. Ash spun like dry snow flurries, dusting the road and the empty chaparral desert. We were driving on the Grand Army of the Republic Highway, the occasional green sign told me, and I said it out loud, under my breath, *Grand Army of the Republic*, my whole body wrung out and exhausted, my blood still trying to filter the adrenaline that kept my eyes wide and staring. Mountains loomed on either side of the road as we began to turn south, not seen so much as felt, and I expected a huge banner at the border with California—WELCOME TO THE GOLDEN STATE!—but it was just a cattle guard running under the two lanes instead, with a little sign that I only really saw because I'd slowed for the grid the tires rattled over. Simple barbed-wire fences extended into darkness on either side of the road.

"We made it to California," I said to Penelope, but she was truly asleep now, not hearing anything I said. "We made it."

The road bent south, and there were patches of green in the desert now, occasional trees, and I saw my first road sign giving the distance to Bishop, and time warped, miles passing without any awareness, and we were there, we were in Bishop, the exhaustion coming on so utterly and quickly that I began to weave drunkenly across the yellow line. A dirt road appeared, and I pulled off, just far enough that we couldn't be seen from Route 6. Penelope already had her seat thrown back, and I got the blankets Veronica had given us from the back and tucked her in. She muttered something I couldn't hear. The driver's seat didn't go flat, but it didn't matter, I pulled a blanket tight around me and sleep came for me as unseen and sudden as Duane's elbow swinging through the open window.

When I woke, light filled the car and Penelope was looking at me, her face cocooned by the blanket.

"My poor love," she said, and she reached out a gentle hand not to touch my face, but to shift the blankets away from my jaw. Her eyes opened wide, and she said, "Oh no, baby."

Does it look bad?

That's what I was going to say, but as soon as I opened my mouth, an explosion of pain began in my jaw, the shock waves sweeping over my whole head. I pushed up from the seat, grabbed the rearview mirror, and craned it down to face me and the puffed bruise of my cheek, chipmunk-swollen and purple. My teeth were all in my head, but my tongue ran along them and felt one tremor.

"Do you think it's broken?" she asked.

"It hurts," I said, the *t* a slur.

"Can you eat? We haven't eaten in a long time. You need to eat."

"We're in Bishop," I said, and her eyes widened.

"We're . . ." her voice trailed off.

"We made it." As though we shared one body, our eyes dampened at the same time, I could see it, tears welling up, and our hands met on the gearshift, and we lay in the cranked-back seats of our Camaro in Bishop, California, the sky boiling above us, the whole journey like an absurd shared dream.

"I love you so much." After decades of marriage, saying *I love you* was habit, it was pro forma, it was call-and-response, but I said it differently, as forcefully as my jaw would allow, like I was trying to tell her something she didn't know.

She heard me. "Oh baby," she said. "I love you too. We made it."

We needed to eat. She was right about that. We got out of the car, and she went through the food we had in the back, settling on canned peach halves. She cut them for me like I was a child, little pieces that could slither down my throat without chewing. I drank the syrup, chased it with water. My blood sugar rose, and I could feel myself unfold like a desert plant after rain.

After eating, we sat on the hood of the car to make a plan. Low trees surrounded us, and a little stream cut through the flatness of the valley floor. I knew from the map that we were cradled by peaks, the White Mountains to the east, and west the great granite spires of the Sierras. But the smoke that turned the air red and congealed in my nose and throat hid them from view, curtailing our vision. From Dobbs Ferry, Bishop had seemed like an absurdly precise target, a dot on the map so small that Hannah had to be standing in the middle of it, waiting. Now it sprawled around us, and there were no flashing signs at the side of the road, THIS WAY TO THE REVIVAL.

We needn't have worried. Route 6 became Main Street, leading us straight into town, and it was alive. I'd forgotten what a living town felt like. Not that the businesses were open, not that electricity was flowing, but there were people. People everywhere. People standing in the parking lot of the Vons, distributing food. People watching children play in a park. People standing on the sidewalk in conversation that stopped as they turned to look at the black Camaro rolling through town. The simple fact of *people* was so overwhelmingly strange that it took me a minute to realize they were all wearing the same clothing, the same rough tunic and pants, men and women and children, all the same faded tan burlap color. They looked at the car with neither malice nor fear. We could have stopped, begun a conversation, but it all felt so surreal that we just kept driving. We didn't even speak to one another. Finally, I turned off the main drag, drove into the gridwork of homes, and it was Dobbs Ferry all over again, though not Dobbs Ferry as it was now, nor Dobbs Ferry as it had ever been, really. A simulacrum, as though we'd vibrated into the uncanny valley of an alternate universe. All the houses were alive, figures moving in the windows, but a faint ash drifted over everything, and it wasn't just the outfits all the people wore, it was something in the way they looked at the car, something in the way they moved.

We stopped outside a cheery split-level home, a woman bent over and weeding the garden in her side yard. She heard the engine and looked up, using the back of her wrist to push her hair from her face. We stepped out and onto the sidewalk, and she rose and walked over to join us. Her clothes were the same as all the others, hand-sewn neatly, boxy and plain.

"Welcome, strangers." She said the word *strangers* as though it had particular meaning, and there was an empty smile on her face.

"Thank you," Penelope said.

We all stood in silence that the woman seemed like she might never break.

"We're looking for The Revival," I said stupidly.

"You've found us," she said. "You've found the truth."

"Oh, good."

We all looked at one another.

"How many families are there here?" Penelope asked, looking around at house after living house.

"One," the woman said.

Penelope cocked her head quizzically.

"We are all one family."

"Oh, sure," Penelope said, "I just meant . . ."

"We are one family," the woman said again, her voice falling in gentle condescension. "One family in the light." As she said it, her hands caressed her stomach, pulling the tunic tight enough that we could see the protrusion of her pregnant belly.

Penelope's face softened. "How far along are you?"

"Five months."

"Your first?"

The woman nodded.

"That's wonderful," Penelope said. "You're going to have a child."

"The child will not be mine."

"What?"

"My womb belongs to God," the woman said, her finger raised in correction. Her forehead was sticky with sweat, hair plastered to it, but also falling into her face once again. She blew upward from the corner of her mouth, her eyes closing involuntarily. It was a little human gesture, a mar in the android nonsense of her demeanor.

Behind her, the door to the house opened, and a man stepped out to the stoop. He said nothing. Just looked at us.

"We want to join The Revival," I said.

"You already have."

This didn't seem to obey any of the laws of conversation. I had no idea how to respond.

"None of this is a choice," the woman said. "The water follows the riverbed to the ocean. Go west past the field of boulders and you will find what you are looking for."

It took me a moment to realize that her last sentence was not an expression of spiritual invocation, but instead actual directions.

"Oh, okay," I said. "West."

"You will see the signs," she said.

I wanted to ask if we were talking about road signs or metaphysical ones, but the man said something to her, and she turned to her garden.

We drove back to the main road.

"You're weeding," Penelope said. "And a White guy and a Black woman pull up in a Camaro. They're filthy, and the man has a spectacular bruise on the side of his face. Wouldn't you have questions? Wouldn't you be curious? It's like she was lobotomized."

I just shook my head.

The titles of the last movies ever to be shown still decorated the faded marquee of the theater downtown, although individual letters had begun to fall like leaves. If we'd still been in Nevada, ratty casinos would have dotted the streets, every restaurant billing itself as something more, but we were in California and so we passed instead the desert West's strange mix of crystal healing studios and animal feed stores. The Toggery, with its LEVI's sign and cowboy boots. We turned right onto West Line Street, passing a police station, its windows dark, the clouds seething above. We didn't know what we were looking for. The low eternal buildings of a high school appeared on the far side of athletic fields, and on the baseball diamond, kids in Revival uniforms were playing catch. They did not look at the car as we passed.

When I started wondering if we were headed the wrong way, a hand-painted sign appeared on the side of the road. LOST SHEEP, it said, with an arrow pointing straight ahead. I knew we were the sheep it referenced, though the sign made it seem as though we were approaching a lost sheep depot, maybe a lost and found.

Another sign pointed us off West Line Street and onto a dusty side spur. The mountain slopes began to appear in the distance, hovering in the smoke like striding giants. Rattling on the dirt road, the car slowed, and the first monolithic boulder appeared. The sandy desert flat, snarled with brown tangles of dry brush, and studded with tremendous stones, some as big as houses, scattered across the landscape. I pulled onto the shoulder and said, "We need to make a plan."

"We don't know if she's up there," Penelope said.

I shook my head again.

"But if she is, they're not going to let us waltz in and take her," she continued. "Remember what she said on the radio? I've thrown my old life on the fire?"

"Only one of us should go," I said. "The other stay here."

"I can do it," she said.

As soon as she said it, I knew that the opposite was true. "It has to be me," I said. My whole life as a father had been leading me to this moment. Every time I took Hannah to the playground, I sat with other parents on the benches, chatting away, and when I stood up and called her name and she came running, I endured their stares as the little Black girl and the White man walked away hand in hand. Penelope and I decided early on that Hannah looked more like me, but that didn't matter to the onlookers at soccer games whose eyes flicked back and forth between my daughter and me, to the teachers who couldn't hide their little double-take on Back to School Night. I could walk into The Revival and they would never suspect a thing.

We pulled the car behind one of the big boulders, bumping along the dirt and then brushing away the tire tracks as best we could. It was two boulders, actually, a smaller one leaning against the larger like a tired child. Beneath them, a little cave hollowed out of the earth, so sheltered from the wind and rain that the white chalk from rock climbers still decorated every edge and pocket in the stone.

Two days. That's what Penelope was going to give me. Two days to see if I could find Hannah, convince her to leave, and, on the morning of the third day, if I wasn't back, then she would follow my path up.

What time was it when I set off, my jaw throbbing a little with each stride? The sun was smothered, all the light ambient. Still morning, that much was clear. As soon as the sweat began on my back, the smell from my clothes rose again, even over the wood-ash stink of the air. My hair hurt when it moved, an unshowered phenomenon I'd never understood. I'd eaten what I could before I set out, walking through the stones that disappeared when I began to climb the brush-studded slope. The road ran through the valley beneath me, switchbacking up the slope as it climbed. I was on a ridge looking down and hadn't gone far when a broad flat area opened below, tucked into the mountains' hemline, and in it was The Revival's camp. A few cars, parked in a line, a wide long building, one story, with some sheds and outbuildings like dice scattered around a deck of cards. A garden. I could see two men guarding the road, could make out the guns they carried slung around their shoulders. Even through the thick red air, I realized how visible I must be, looking down from the slope, and I dropped behind some brush, staring down at the people moving busily around the building.

Their clothes were what I'd expected, the same Revival chic. They were digging something, a trench on the far side of the camp in a broad semicircle. Its long arms embraced the whole compound, as though to divert a flood they expected to roll down the hillside. My brain was working slow, but it clicked: a firebreak. The mountaintops beyond were invisible in the smoke haze that hung like low cloud cover, and everything was shaded a diabolical red, as though a movie gel was coloring the scene.

My vision was decidedly in its fifties. When I played golf, the ball seemed to disappear after about 150 yards, and I'd occasionally find myself sheepishly reteeing after a drive I thought was sliced into the woods only to catch my younger playing partners staring at me strangely. *You're in the middle of the fairway*, they would say. Put that together with the visibility, and The Revival people all looked the same. Would I even recognize Hannah if I saw her? Was she Hannah anymore? Or had she become one of them entirely? Joined this new family and left ours behind? I'd had three thousand miles to plan this conversation, and I'd used none of it. My mind was empty.

I had a colleague who actually specialized in cults, in deprogramming. But she was dead, and her knowledge had died with her. If Hannah had lost herself, I had no idea what I would say. She could be pregnant, I thought suddenly. She could be *pregnant* with a grandchild she would claim had no relation to us, belonged only to God.

I dropped my face, my forehead against my hands, my lips almost touching the dusty ground. I could climb down, try to slip in among them, but even if the guy with the giant bruise on his cheek wasn't noticeable enough, how could I get a set of their outfits? And what would I do when I got there? It was not clear to me whether the guards were there to keep people out or keep them in. If I entered the compound, I might never leave, and if Hannah wasn't there, that would be the most bizarre and ignominious possible end to this journey: get all the way across the country, three thousand miles, just to wear a burlap suit and dig a ditch in a Revival compound while Hannah was somewhere in the town below, her smile blank and anonymous and empty.

I was about to give up, head back to Penelope so we could ponder our options, when a bell began clanging in the valley below me, and as one the diggers laid down their shovels and pickaxes and began to move toward the building. Only the guards on the road did not move.

My eyes didn't recognize Hannah so much as my body did, my lungs forgetting for a moment where they were in the whole inhale/exhale cycle because while her face was a blur, there was her gait, her long swinging stride, two steps, and she jammed her shovel into the ground so it vibrated there like a tuning fork behind her as she strode toward the building, and it took everything not to leap up, calling her name, stumbling down the hillside.

The noise from the shovels and pickaxes ringing against stones in the dirt was gone. Wind moved through the valley. Smoke rose from a squat aluminum chimney in the main building. The guards spoke to one another, and I knew what I was going to do. My indecision, my hopelessness felt like something I'd experienced in a dream, one that could be shaken off and forgotten in the light of morning.

I crawled back out of sight, moving quietly, then looped down the slope to the road. I didn't have to pretend to be a beggar, starving and wounded. That's who I was. I could feel my heartbeat throbbing in my swollen cheek. My lip was still cracked and puffed too, from the accident in Kansas that had happened a thousand years before. A gelatinous stink rose from my body as I climbed the switchbacks and began to sweat.

One of the guards saw me coming, said something to the other. The guns migrated into their hands. I held my arms up, palms flat toward them, and when I got close, I dropped to my knees in the road.

One of them spoke. "Are you lost?" he asked, and I knew what he meant.

"Yes, I am. I am lost."

"Have you come to join the flock?"

"I have."

"Nothing of your life can follow you here. Are you prepared to let go and submit to the will of God?"

"I am."

He patted me down roughly, though I could tell from the look on his face that he didn't want to be doing it. His lips pursed, as though trying to rise to block his nostrils. There were no weapons to be found, but I knew he was looking for more than that. There was nothing personal to be found either. I'd been stripped bare. All that was left of my wedding ring, somewhere in the car's glovebox, was the white circle looping the base of my finger. Only a year before, I would have felt naked without my phone, keys, wallet, and the mask I still wore when I was on the train. Did I ever leave the house with empty pockets? Now, there was nothing to hide. That wasn't true. San Cristóbal still hung around my neck beneath all the crusted layers of clothes, but the guard didn't notice him.

"Okay," he said. "I'll walk you up." He exchanged a nod with the other guard, and then I followed him through the empty yard toward the double doors of the building where I could hear a man's voice preaching, high-pitched and penetrating.

The first thing that hit me was the heat. The smoke I'd seen from the chimney rose from a big open fireplace on the far wall, and as I blinked, my eyes adjusting to the dim humidity, a figure took a stone from the fire and dropped it into a tub of water where it hissed and a new wave of steam rose into the jungle air.

Everyone was naked. That was the next thing I saw. Not fully naked. They all wore the same white boxer-style underwear, the women as well as the men, but their outfits were all in a single heap at the front of the room. They were all sitting crisscross applesauce, the room was full of them. They seemed to sway back and forth as one.

The voice was coming from a skinny bearded man, extra tall because he stood on a little dais at the front of the room. My entrance did nothing to interrupt the flow of his words.

"God is light," he was saying. "God is a beam of light without which the world is only darkness. We think the light is there to shine upon us, to help us see, but we're wrong. We *are* the light. God and his Creation are one and the same. Without creation there is no God, without God there is no Creation. And every atom is an expression of that light."

He paused and smiled. "Aral," he said, and a woman stood. She was about my age, her hair gray. She seemed unembarrassed by her bare chest, standing with her arms hanging loose at her sides.

"You studied science," the man said.

"Lara did," she said. "Lara studied science."

He smiled. "That's right. What is light, Aral?"

256

"It's complicated," she said.

"What in life is not, other than God's love?"

"Light is a particle and a wave," she said. "At the same time."

That was what he'd wanted her to say. "A particle and a wave," he repeated. "The mystery at the center of it all. We are particles, bodies moving through space, yes, but we are also part of a wave. A wave is movement, a wave is without individuality, without form. A wave is an expression of feeling, that's all. A wave is God."

"This man," and now he was pointing at *me*. I looked around. "Even this man is part of the wave that is God." He waved me forward, and I stepped into the room. It felt like I would stumble and fall, I could feel all the eyes on me, and in the group somewhere was Hannah, naked like the rest of them. I heard a gasp, a sharp inhale, and it had to be her recognizing me, I wanted to call out, I wanted to look, I wanted our eyes to meet, but I kept my discipline and stepped up in front of the man, my back to the mass of lightwave-people behind me.

"Why are you here?" the man asked.

"I have traveled across the country to find you," I said, my voice loud and ringing around the hall, loud enough that my jaw hurt when it moved. I was speaking to Hannah, of course, all of my consciousness reaching backward toward her.

"The journey is always long," the man said.

"You are the only thing that matters to me." I could feel Hannah behind me. If I listened hard enough, could I pick out her breathing?

"Are you prepared to throw your life on the fire?" the man asked.

I couldn't help it. I looked over at the blazing hearth, and he laughed.

"Don't worry," he said. "Not literally." And his laugh seemed to give permission to the flock, and they all laughed too.

He held up a hand and they fell silent. "Are you prepared to be made new after the sacrifice?"

"I will do anything."

He waited, as though I hadn't yet said enough.

Maybe a decade before, I'd been out for a walk with Penelope, the sun warm, the two of us holding hands. My phone rang in my pocket, one of my poker buddies, calling to figure out whether we had a quorum for the game that week, and I was distracted as I spoke, feeling Penelope next to me, her palm against mine, our fingers interlaced, and so when he said, *All right I think we're good* and we were saying goodbye, I said, my voice full of feeling, *I love you.*

There was a pause, a hiccup, and then he and Penelope, one in my ear and one next to me, simultaneously whooped with laughter, and a half second later I joined them, all three of us understanding precisely what had happened, my brain mistakenly saying out loud what my hands were feeling, and I knew this moment would live on for years, would be a story to be told around the card table again and again, knew as well that it was true: my center of gravity, the place around which all the rest organized itself, was love for my wife and daughter.

This time, I knew what I was doing, and I looked up at him as I spoke, but reached out backward toward Hannah with all my spirit, half shouting, "I love you."

He looked at me, and for just a second, his demeanor cracked and I could see him thinking, *So this filthy half-wit is what passes for a new recruit these days.*

"What is your name?"

"Bill. I'm Bill."

He turned. "Nek," he said to the gunman still standing in the shadows, "Take Lib and show him to a room."

I didn't look back, just followed Nek down a hallway roughed out with plywood rooms. The cooler, dryer air made the sweat prickle against my skin. Galvanized nail heads dotted the wood like lines of silver ladybugs. He stopped at a door and swung it open. Inside, a little cot and a chair filled the space, and a set of Revival togs sat folded on the blanket.

"Get changed," he said.

I waited for him to leave, but he didn't move.

"Can I . . ." I started.

"There is no right to privacy," he said. "We have nothing to hide from one another." But he clearly didn't want to see me in my altogether because he turned and looked down the hall as I took off my clothes and joined the flock. The neck of my new shirt was wide enough that San Cristóbal's chain would have been obvious, and there were no pockets—what was the point of a pocket when you had nothing to keep? Cristóbal had gotten me here, he'd done his job already, but it just seemed wrong to leave him coiled on top of my old clothes, waiting to be discarded. I shoved him deep into my sock.

"You done?" He turned back around to face me.

I nodded.

"Follow me."

He led me outside, looking up at the long uphill slopes of the Sierra's broad apron, thick with low brush and pale dry grass beneath the red sky. The meeting must have ended because people were streaming out, clothed again. There was no way they could have picked their own clothes out of the pile, and that was why the outfits seemed so ill-fitting: they were communal, not your shirt and pants. They were just Shirt. And Pants. The underwear and socks, people got to keep, so on a microbial level, The Revival seemed to make some small concessions to individuality. Maybe they just knew that even the most devoted follower might balk at sharing underpants.

Nek put a shovel in my hand.

"We show devotion through labor," he said.

He started to walk away, but I said his name and he turned. "When do I get to go down to the town?"

"When you're ready."

"When is that?"

He took a long look at my face, then touched his own cheek, as though in sympathy and said, "Someone got you pretty good, huh."

"Yeah."

"You stay here until you've made your full commitment," he said. "Until you're truly one of us."

Whatever hours were left in the day, I spent them there, on the hillside, my hands blistering on the shovel handle, coughing, papery ash descending and the color deepening bloody in the sky as the sun began to set. I was hungry, exhausted, pained, and ebullient. Floating and overjoyed. Hannah was still here, which meant she had not made her full commitment. She wasn't pregnant, at least not visibly so. She wasn't too far gone. I could have been singing while I worked. Good luck to the goddamn Revival! Penelope and I had spent our entire parental lives trying to mold and guide this daughter we'd been given, and all we'd done was twist in knots ourselves and squabble like children. If there was one thing I knew about my daughter, it was this: she was herself, and always would be. Hannah. Beautiful, singular, palindromic Hannah.

When darkness finally overcame the landscape, Nek called us down, and I half ran, stumbling, back toward the mess hall and my daughter.

Whatever meal was going to be served, whatever ritual observed, I wasn't to be a part of it. They brought me to my room instead, brought me a jug of water and a bowl of oatmeal, hot enough that it burned my mouth as I began to wolf it down. The water was cold, and I held it in my mouth, stirring it with my tongue.

Then it was quiet. I tested my door and found that it was locked from the outside. There was a wildfire approaching and being locked in a wooden room would have felt terrifying, except it was all so flimsy, the door flexing at the bottom and the top. Even my old bruised shoulder would have been enough to send it flying.

I looked around the room in the candlelight. Perhaps eight feet by six feet. No windows. Just an unfinished plywood rectangle, anchored with more silver screwheads. A box. In the corner, a pail and a roll of single-ply toilet paper.

Before I could even begin to formulate a plan, a soft knock, and I could barely say *Come in*, so strangled was my voice by the certainty that this was Hannah, coming to see me. I would hold her in my arms, hear her voice.

The bearded man stepped into the room and closed the door behind him. I recoiled, sitting back down onto the cot. My body odor was intense enough that even I didn't enjoy being in the room with myself, but he didn't seem to notice, just stood for a moment, impassive, before reaching for the chair, turning it around so he could sit and lean forward onto its latticed back as he looked at me.

His eyes never seemed to blink. He wore the same clothes as everyone else, but while they were still wearing the sneakers and boots from their old lives, he wore open leather sandals, and his tunic was held in at the waist by a length of rope. There was no trace of self-consciousness in his stare, he held my eyes with a calm certainty that might have made me uncomfortable if I hadn't done the same thing with countless patients, sitting in my chair, allowing the silence, waiting for them to speak, as though nothing else existed in the world. A fever burned in his eyes, that was the difference. I knew he was The Nameless One.

"Let me see your hands," he said, his voice resonant enough to ring even when he spoke softly.

I held them out, palms down, and he gently turned them over, running his fingertips over my blisters.

"Sorry about Nek," he said. "He believes the path must be made straight through the wilderness. He believes the body must suffer to release its hold on the soul. And he's not wrong. We must mortify the body so its tyranny ends." He looked up at my face. "But you've already suffered, haven't you? I don't just mean your cheek. You've spent a lifetime suffering."

I didn't say anything.

"Why are you here?" he asked.

"Everything that I thought mattered . . ." I said. "Didn't. I've traveled a long way to get here, all the way across the country, and the journey has changed me."

"Are you ready to give up the self?"

"Yes, I am. All my stupid bullshit . . . sorry." I paused.

He laughed. "It's all right. I've heard all the words before. Used them too." He smiled, and I knew this was him humanizing himself, making himself just a regular Joe like me.

"Okay," I said. "I'm tired of the bullshit, tired of being at the center of my own life. Me, all my petty concerns, all my frustrations, all my grievances."

"None of those are real," he said. "They are all inventions of your mind, and they serve no purpose but suffering."

I nodded.

"May I ask if you grew up a Christian?"

"A little," I said. "We went to church on Easter and stuff."

"The seeds of the church's misunderstanding of Jesus were planted even when he was still alive," he said. "The born-again movement, a personal connection with Jesus—that only increases our loneliness, our mistaken belief that we exist as individuals and not atoms in the fabric of the world. Jesus suffered, died, and rose again not because *we* would do the same, but because *the world would*. And it has. Everything has unfolded as God told me it would. The world died for our sins, and now we must make a new one in the ashes of the old, we must rise again, in accordance with the Scriptures, but not as individuals, selfish, squabbling, but as one single collective body."

"Yes," I said.

"The lost sheep seeks the flock," he said, "because in the flock it ceases being lost, but it's more than that. It ceases being the sheep. It *is* the flock."

"How do you know all this?" I asked.

"I speak with God." His tone was as matter-of-fact as mine was when I said things like *I like toast.* "Like Moses and Jesus before me," he went on. "Some men are given a heavier burden than the rest."

Most cult leaders predicted apocalypse and then, when the sun rose on another worldly day, had to perform recalculations, find a new date for Armageddon, but I looked at this man in my room and realized he was the case study: What happened when the world *did* end? When a cosmic coincidence reinforced your own messianic impulses? He sat in the chair, staring at me with embers for eyes.

"You are not worthy of God's love. God loves the world, not us. You love an ant not for who it is, that would be absurd, but for the role it plays in the world that you love."

I nodded, and he stared at me in silence for long enough that I had to blink.

"You aren't ready," he said as he rose from his chair.

"No! I am!" I thought for a moment he was going to send me away, away from Hannah.

"Don't worry," he said. "Rest. There will be more work tomorrow. You'll stay here, working and learning, until you're ready. And then you can move down into town. You will be a member of The Revival." He stood. "And make sure you use some rags to wrap your hands before you dig again."

"Thanks," I said, and he stood.

"Rest," he said. "Sleep." He blew out my candle before closing the door behind him, which left me in coffin-complete darkness. As though the world had stopped existing. I heard the lock snick shut.

There was nothing to do but what he'd said, and as I lay down on the cot, I scanned my body to find a part that didn't hurt, couldn't seem to find one. And then I was out, not even The Revival snoring coming from adjacent rooms able to keep me awake.

My next awareness was the clatter of people in the hallway and Nek bringing me a morning bowl of oatmeal. This time I poured some of the water into it, cooled it down so I could eat fast. My cheek reflected in the surface of the jug looked spectacular as a flower, but it felt a little better. No one had taken my old clothes— they were still heaped in the corner. I pulled out my T-shirt, ripped it in sharp tugs, then wrapped my hands in the rags. No one had to tell me to pick up my shovel again. I just walked out back and got to work. The air was even thicker than it had been, the sky more malevolent. It wasn't just ashes sifting down now, but sparks, red embers riding the wind. There were people with hoses standing on the roof, spraying it down in long continuous arcs of water. The loud rattle of a gas generator rose above the scene. Given the candle-powered lifestyle in the building, I realized it was there to power the well pump, pressure the water in the hoses. The Revival was making their stand here. The fire was coming, spreading east toward us and the desert on which it would break like waves on the sand. But before it died, Bishop might go with it. There was a frantic tempo to the digging now.

I couldn't see Hannah, though with the way figures dissolved in the miasma, she could have been twenty yards away and I wouldn't have known. Was she looking for me too? Were we feeling our way through the haze toward one another? My blisters popped almost immediately, soaking the rags, my hands raw. Trees on the distant hills exploded into flame, burning like giant candles on the horizon, while the sharp red edge of the wildfire began to work its way down the slope like a snake. The Revival people dug like mad, widening the firebreak. The smoke boiled, and I choked on it, coughing. An ember landed on my sleeve, stuck there, smoldering, and I whacked at it with my palm.

Maybe she was in the ditch. I worked my way over, dragging the shovel along the ground with my fingertips, but once I'd clambered down, I found myself alone. No one to my right, no one to my left. The only people I could see were the ones with hoses perched high on the roof.

The air was better down here, the smoke swirling above. I leaned on my shovel. Once I caught my breath, I turned to climb back out, to keep looking, when she slid down the slope on her hip, a pickaxe held high like a ski pole.

I couldn't help it. I stumbled toward her, my arms outstretched.

She turned away and swung the pickaxe, sparks flying as it hit a rock, saying in an urgent hiss, "They're watching."

I stood staring at her, my jaw hanging. We made eye contact and she shook her head. "Dig, Dad," she said. "At least pretend. God."

As soon as I began digging the lip of the shovel into the ground, flipping a little dirt, she asked, "What happened to your *face*? Are you okay?"

"I'm fine!" I was smiling but it was lopsided, half my smile wasn't working, and I could feel drool on my cheek. "Hannah, I'm so—"

"Is Mom . . ." She cut me off, her eyes wide. "Is Mom . . . ?"

I suddenly knew what she was thinking, me arriving here alone.

"Oh God, I'm sorry, she's fine! She's great. She's down by the boulders, waiting for us."

"Waiting for us," Hannah repeated.

I'd told myself to remain calm, to let her be in control of how this went. I'd told myself *This is like dating*, which I hadn't done in thirty years, so that wasn't very helpful, but I knew at least that if I pushed, she was likely to recoil. I needed to be calm and loving and let her make a choice. Zero pressure. This was my plan, I was determined, but now, lightened by the sheer buoyancy of seeing my daughter, I immediately and utterly abandoned it.

"We can go now!" I found myself saying. "We can slip away, no one can see us in all the smoke. She's right down the hill . . ." My shovel slipped from my hands, and I looked around wildly.

Hannah's face, which had been wide open with concern, closed like a slammed door. She swung her pickaxe in an enormous looping arc and dug the tip deep in the dusty earth.

"What?" I said.

"So you're here to take me away. That's your big plan."

"I don't have a *plan.*"

"Well, *that's* obvious."

I took a deep breath. The wind was swirling, so the ash spun around Hannah, seeming to rise up out of the ditch.

"When you radioed—" I started to say, but she interrupted.

"Let me guess, it took you guys about three seconds to decide you'd better drive across the whole fucking country because God forbid your daughter make a choice you don't like."

"That's not fair."

"Not fair? Really?"

We'd abandoned all pretense of digging.

"We just want you to be hap . . ." My voice trailed off as I saw her mouthing the words along with me.

"To be happy. Yeah, I know," she said. "This is so fucking classic."

"How is *this* classic?" I waved my arms at the Armageddon-haze of the cult encampment around us, but I knew precisely what she meant. Like a tsunami casually obliterating a seaside resort, our domestic drama was sweeping over the firelit scene and drowning it. A man with a rifle could have dropped into the ditch, barking orders and firing warning shots into the dirt at our feet, and we would have spun toward him in unison and said, "God, do you mind, we're *talking*!" until he backed away, apologizing, palms up.

"One month!" she was saying. "I'd been at Irvine for one month when you guys visited for the first time. I'd barely gotten to know anyone, and now I had to spend the weekend showing you around.

And Mom just happened to have talked to the admissions people at Amherst and found out that they would welcome a transfer application. I mean . . ."

"She just . . ."

"Why couldn't you get hobbies like normal people? Why did micromanaging me have to be your hobby?"

The old grooves of argument were so familiar that we slipped into them without effort, like it was eleven on a school night and I was standing outside her bedroom door, about to check on her homework even though I didn't give a shit about her grades, just because if Penelope did it, an immediate shouting match would ensue, but thirty seconds later my own voice was raised and Hannah was half in tears, yelling at me to get out of her room.

"Hannah—"

"And you think we can just walk out of here? Really? Do you understand *anything*?"

"I just thought—"

"They have *guns*, Dad," she said. "If they let people walk away whenever they felt a little uncertain, there'd be nobody here. And when you arrive, they assign you a Shepherd."

"A what?"

"He doesn't take his eyes off me! There's no way he lets me walk out of here."

"Then we'll stay."

"What?"

"We'll join The Revival."

She stared at me. "Right."

"No, Hannah, I'm serious."

"*Mom* is going to join The Revival?"

"Yes." Penelope and I had talked about it before I walked up the hill as we shared one last meal in the cave beneath the boulder, huddled together beneath a blanket. What if she wouldn't come with us?

What would we do then? And the answer came shockingly easily for something so . . . well, shocking. We would join The Revival. And not as some reverse-psychology ploy to get her to leave either. We would really join. Just so we could be together again.

"You recognize how fucking ridiculous that is, right?" she asked. "The whole point of The Revival is that you give up your family."

"I recognize the irony."

"What about Dobbs Ferry? What about the house?"

"It's just a house."

"Not to me it isn't! Did you ever stop to think that the best thing you could have done for me is to stay there? That in all this chaos, that was the one thing that was keeping me together?" Her voice cracked as she spoke, and she pulled a rough forearm across her eyes, the way she used to do when she was little. When I was a child myself, we moved a thousand times, my father gaining and losing jobs like hands of poker, and so I sometimes forgot Hannah had only ever known our home in Dobbs Ferry, an anchor so rooted in her ocean floor that it had become a part of it.

"I'm sorry," I said. "I know—"

"Did you ever think how hard it would be for me to radio and hear *Carlos's* voice instead of yours? To know you were just gone?"

"Wait, you radioed again? After we left?"

She shook off my question like it was a horsefly circling her head, and when she spoke again, I had to take a step forward to hear.

"Why is Carlos in the house?"

She looked so young, her voice so quiet, that the threat of unseen eyes barcly kept me from stepping forward and pulling her into my arms.

"Oh Hannah, I'm sorry," I said. "That must have been so hard, to reach out and find us gone."

"Why is Carlos there?" she repeated.

"Well, you remember Jen. She used to babysit for you sometimes.

She . . . she didn't make it, and he needed someplace new. Without all the memories."

She stared at me, and then the bell began to ring in the building. Though from the ditch we couldn't see the other diggers, the ring of pickaxes on rock ceased. The Nameless One would have his say, even as the flames crawled down the hillside, their smoke and ash and embers swirling in the air. The hose-bearers on the roof we could see, and they weren't going anywhere, the feathered spray of water still rising and falling. Hannah closed her eyes, pinched the bridge of her nose between two fingers.

"We have to go inside," she said. "And don't call me Hannah, whatever you do. They call me Nah."

"Nah," I said.

She turned and climbed back out of the ditch.

The feverish orange air was cold, but the fire pulsed with heat, sending embers spinning high to drift down. Hannah was halfway across the yard when I thought of what I should say, the words came to me, and I stumbled into a run after her, stopping only when a sudden spray of water pockmarked the ground in front of me. I looked up, and there was a guy on the roof saying my name.

"Lib."

"Yeah?"

"I been calling your name. I guess you weren't listening."

"Sorry. I was distracted."

We stood like that for a moment, my head craned back. His hose had a nozzle, a hand sprayer, and he took the pressure off the trigger. Water dripped from the end, and he squatted to get closer to me. His toes were almost in the gutter, he was right on the edge.

"I'm Eel," he said. He was young, early twenties maybe, White, with a face as empty and flat as his palms, a broad forehead over eyes drawn a little too close to his nose, as though by a magnet. His hair stood tall in a short-bristled buzz cut, a 1950s-style cut.

"Good to meet you."

"They said I should clean you off."

"What?"

He nodded at the hose in his hand. "Like a shower. Then you can join the others for the Word."

"Seriously?"

"Yeah." He walked along the roof-edge, flipping the hose as he did so the coils wouldn't drag on the shingles. He got to a little ladder and tucked the sprayer into his armpit to use his hands as he climbed down. We met in the dusty yard, my ears full of the roar of the wildfire, the high tones of The Nameless One starting his homily.

"I think I'll pass," I said.

"Have you smelled yourself?" He said it with a smile. "No offense."

"Okay, fine, I got it." I reached for the hose.

"Gotta be me," he said.

"Why?"

"That's how we do it."

"But . . ."

He held up a finger. "Give me a second."

While he ran inside, I wanted to summon the energy to resist, to demand the hose myself, but my body was exhausted, and all my struggling brain could do was stare at the fact that Hannah had radioed again after we left. I circled that fact like it was a sculpture on a dais I needed to interpret. And so when Eel came back out holding a towel, I'd figured out nothing to say to him, and there was no fight in me. He gestured at my clothes, the two of us out there on the dusty ground, the sparks whirling in the air around us like swarms of angry insects, and I stripped, making sure that when I pulled down my sock, San Cristóbal came down with it, still hidden inside. And then I was naked, the air brisk enough that I hopped from foot to foot, my arms folded against my chest, and he said, "You ready?"

I nodded, and he looked down at the nozzle in his hand, his forehead wrinkling as he adjusted the spray.

"Sorry I don't have no soap," he said and pulled the trigger. The ice water hitting my body made me dance, my hands cupping my crotch, my eyes squeezed shut. It felt good, actually, there in the swirling heat of the coming wildfire, knowing the sweat lodge that was to come. I turned around, let the spray hammer me. I actually let myself enjoy it.

It stopped, and I opened my eyes. He stood looking at me, his face impassive. My skin stung, the water running from my hair down into my face. I reached for the towel, and he took a half step back.

"I lost everything," he said. "All my brothers and my sister, my parents. All dead. I dipped, the worst fever you can think of, and when I came back from it, I found them. You got no idea what that was like."

I stared at him.

"I couldn't clean that up, no one could. I just left. So I lost my home too."

"I'm sorry." I said. "That sounds terrible." Again, I held out a hand for the towel. The air was cold, and my body gave a spasmic shiver and my teeth began to rattle.

"I think I deserve something good in my life," he said. "I think I'm owed that. Don't you think so?"

The way he was talking, with the fire behind him and the sound of the incantatory sermon from inside: fear began to climb in my gut. My arms were wrapped around my torso as though they could keep me warm and I shifted from foot to foot.

"So I'm here," he said. "And what happens? I'm Shepherding this girl. A girl who just can't seem to get with the program. And I could be down in the town by now, I know how to talk the talk. I could have a little house, I could have already started a family. But there's something about this girl."

Now the alarm bells were ringing, the rhythm of my pulse accelerating with my breath.

"Why are you telling *me* this?" I said.

"Because you know her," he said.

I stared at him, and I knew it took me too long to respond, but there was nothing I could do. "What are you talking about?" I finally said.

"You don't care about The Revival. *She's* the reason you're here. It's so obvious. The rest of them, they may not notice, but I do."

"I don't know what you're talking about." I was shivering harder, even my voice was coming out jagged.

"I haven't told nobody," he said. "Yet."

"Can I have the towel?"

He held it toward me, and I reached for it, but then he pulled it back. "She belongs here. She belongs with me."

"Are you talking about that girl in the ditch?" I asked. "I was just helping her with a rock, that's all."

He rolled his eyes. "I ain't stupid," he said.

"Okay."

"And I'm not a bad guy. I take real good care of her. When I get her on the program, they'll put us together in a house down in town, and we can make a go of it. I think that's fair. There's nothing wrong with that." The sparks were spinning around him as he spoke, and behind him I could see the feathered spray of the other hoses still whipping around the building's roof.

"I don't know what you want me to say. I don't know her." It was weak, and we both knew it. I took a step toward him, and he clenched the trigger. This time, the water wasn't refreshing, it was ice I could feel in the center of my chest, the breath gone, so even when it stopped, I wasn't shivering, I was shuddering, my whole body, and I couldn't stop.

"I missed a spot," he said.

Now he held the towel out again. When I took it, he didn't let go. We stood holding either end, and he said, "All I have to do is say the word, and you'll never see her again." He let go suddenly, and I stumbled backward and fell in the dirt.

"Watch your step, old man." He turned and climbed his ladder without looking back.

CHAPTER 13

I was a stone in the center of my cot, my body pulled tightly into itself, knees pressed to chest, chin tucked. My hands were touching my feet, except I couldn't feel either, they might as well have been touching nothing at all. And my mind had collapsed to a pinprick of thought, just the word *cold* like a black hole pulling all my light inside. The room, the world was nothing but the squeaking of the cot's metal coils as I shook, pain sparking in my jaw with every twitch, but it hurt even worse to clench it tight, to try to stop my teeth from chattering.

I'd barely managed to dry off, my arms not working and my body lurching, so I staggered inside wet and filthy with dirt. The moist heat of the prayer room against my skin felt like pressing my palm to a red stove coil, burning without penetrating the skin, my abdomen a brick of ice. The homily was already ending, The Nameless One sending them back out to battle the coming flames, and I staggered down the hall to my room where I fell into the cot, pulling on the clothes I'd arrived in and the Revival outfit over the top and the blanket pulled tight and it didn't matter at all. I wasn't reduced to an animal, animals were alive with curiosity and hunger and the drive to protect their offspring. I was just an elementary particle in the absolute darkness of the room, the only thing left the fear in my gut, the most basic fear a mammal could feel: *I can't get warm.*

I barely noticed Hannah slipping into my room. The candle she was carrying made the walls swim with light.

"Dad, what happened . . ."

I tried to say *Eel*, but I couldn't, my voice was shaking.

"I'll be back. I'll be right back." Her hand against my cheek felt feverishly hot.

How long it took, I didn't know, but she was back with more blankets, she was piling them on top of me, and then she was crawling in next to me, the springs groaning beneath our combined weight, and she spooned me from behind like I was a child, drawing her body as close to mine as she could. Her breath was on my cheek, and she was talking into my ear, *You're going to be okay, I'm here, you're going to be okay.*

My body's shuddering kept pushing her away, but she held firm against me, her mouth inches from my ear telling me to breathe, and that's all I focused on, trying to slow my lungs, and I began to inch back toward the world, following her voice.

". . . and we went to see the seals at Laguna Beach, remember, they were just lying there in the sun, it was so strange, they were just a part of nature, with people walking past not even looking, like they were squirrels or deer or something . . ."

She was talking about that weekend, when Penelope and I visited her at Irvine for the first time, early October in Southern California.

". . . and then we went to Taiko for sushi. Mom had uni for the first time. Do you remember her face? But we had to hurry, you kept looking at your watch because you were so excited to get back to the beach, the sun was starting to go down and you wanted to see the green flash when it hit the ocean, remember . . ."

"We . . . we . . ." I could find my voice again, but couldn't get past that first syllable.

"We made it," she finished the sentence for me. "And didn't see anything. The sun set against the water, and we were sitting on the beach all together, and there were surfers riding the waves in and walking back up past us, their wet suits half peeled down and their boards under their arms. I'd always wondered if I made the right choice, going west, and that's when I knew it was right. We were there in my new world, and you were there with me."

For a moment, she was quiet. My breathing had slowed, and we'd unconsciously found the same rhythm. "I've still never seen the green flash though," she added.

"It's . . ." I finished in a rush. "It's . . . a thing."

"I'm just saying, I've never seen it."

The frozen part of me had started to melt. My hands and feet no longer numb, but painful, as though they'd fallen asleep but prickling harder than I'd ever felt before. Sweat beaded on my forehead. When I felt like I could move again, I rolled over so I was facing Hannah, our heads on the edges of the same pillow. The candlelight was playing on her face, making it seem like it was moving even when she was still. We could have been back in her room when she was a child, a little faux tent set up on the carpet, a little lantern inside. Her books and stuffed animals lined up. A snack, just in case either of us got hungry.

"I'm sorry again," I said. "That we weren't there when you radioed."

"I get it."

"We thought you'd cut us off."

"I mean, I did." She shrugged. "I did cut you off. It just didn't take."

"It sounded like you were on something."

"Oh, I was totally fucked up."

"What did they give you?"

"Them?" She laughed. "They think the Light of God should be enough for anyone. I'm perfectly capable of getting fucked up on my own."

Above us, the shingles drummed with the water from the hoses. There were heavy footsteps too, the ceiling creaking with them.

"Eel . . ." I started.

"He did this to you?"

I nodded.

She took a long breath through her nose, her jaw set.

"Is Angie here?" I asked.

"I haven't seen Angie in weeks. She's down in town somewhere. Probably pregnant."

"Do you want to stay?"

"Did you even hear what I just said? Angie is probably *pregnant*. Do I want to have sex with, like Eel or somebody, and have his baby? Umm, no."

"Do you want to go?" I knew this wasn't the same question as staying.

"If you mean, do I want to go back to my old room and come down when you guys say it's dinnertime and have you tuck me in . . ." She raised an eyebrow and looked at me.

"I get it," I said.

"I just want to live my life. I want to *have* a life."

We were looking at one another, our eyes together, and I could see her pupils lose focus as she retreated into thought. The room was quiet.

"I wanted to want what these people do," she finally said. "I wanted this to be enough for me. I mean, if you're happy, you're happy, right?"

She looked at me like it was a real question, and I nodded. "Sure," I said.

"Why does it matter what makes you happy, if it makes you happy? If it gives you a sense of purpose?"

I nodded. I was trying to listen like a father, not a psychologist, usually she was so sensitive to the difference, even if I couldn't feel it.

"It's not like I think I'm better than anybody. I mean, to be honest, I used to. When I was in high school I looked down on everyone, but especially all the earnest strivers, with all their competitive bullshit. I was above it. Like acing chem justified your existence. Stupid. Just pathetic. That's what I thought. But when Keisha got into Yale, she was happy, Dad. Like, really happy."

"I know."

"What's wrong with that?"

"Nothing's wrong with that."

"So then what's wrong with me? I could have gotten into Yale or somewhere. I mean, I could see *how* you did it. But it all seemed so ridiculous. And taking your sense of yourself from some external validation . . . I thought it was pathetic."

"Hannah," I said, "you think for yourself. That's a good thing."

"No, Dad, it's not." She caught her voice rising, and reduced it back to a whisper. "I was being judgmental. It was bullshit. I was taking my own shit and making it some higher quest when I wasn't any different. Not really. And college was more of the same, and it's only now that I look around at these people and see how beautiful it is. How simple. If you're happy, you're happy. That's not something to disparage. That's good, that's a good thing."

"Yeah," I said. "I see that."

We stared at one another, the silence filling the room.

"But does this make you happy?" I asked.

"No." She dropped her face, and I could barely make out her voice. "I want to feel what they feel, but I can't," she said. "I really tried."

"Maybe . . . and Hannah, when I said we would join The Revival,

I meant it, we will . . . but maybe if you have to try so hard, it means this isn't the right thing for you."

"Something being difficult doesn't mean it's the wrong thing to do. It might mean it's the right thing to do."

I recognized my own words, probably uttered before some endless swim practice she wanted to avoid.

"Okay, you got me. But that doesn't mean you have to join a cult."

As soon as I said the word *cult*, I braced myself for a spasm of anger, an accusation of judgmentalism, but Hannah didn't dispute the word.

"They're trying to build something," she said.

"They make you share pants."

She closed her eyes and I worried for a second that I'd gone too far, but she was actually laughing. "It's so gross. Especially if you end up with Nek's pants. He sweats, like, *so* much."

"They're not the only ones trying to build something." Her eyes opened and I told her about Nasica and Grand Junction, but that led into the quads and the desert and the nuclear missile. I told her about the Delaware Water Gap, and the stoners, and Manny. I told her about the man with no pants. I told her about the man shot dead on the highway. I told her about the QV Company. I told her about Penelope.

"We're sorry," I said. "Both of us. We both love you so much, and we got caught up in our own battles."

She looked at me for a long time. I waited.

"I cry myself to sleep half the time because I miss you guys so bad," she finally said. "It's all so scary and insane, I can't even figure out what's happening. You think I didn't wish I was at Bennington when everything fell apart? I could have *walked* home from there. But this is my life. I need to do something with it. I can't go backward. But I don't even know what forward looks like."

"I don't know either."

I thought she was going to say something, but instead, her eyes drifted again. Heavy steps moved over the roof above us, the hiss of water. Whatever she was thinking, she didn't share, and I waited, watching her face.

"I'll go," she finally said. "But it doesn't mean I'll stay with you guys forever. I'm going to make my own way."

I closed my eyes and held her, my daughter. We lay like that until the footsteps over our heads jolted us into making a plan.

I said, maybe the fire is distraction enough, we can slip away, but she shook her head. The firebreak was doing its job, the hoses theirs. The line of flames would pass around this camp like a dream and then we would be trapped here in the scorched landscape. And Penelope would be walking up that hill in a few hours now. There was no time to wait.

So that's why I slipped outside into the surreal haze of smoke and sprayed water hissing into steam as it met the embers sifting down from the sky. The distant roar of the fire mingled with the coughing noise of the generator, a big old thing whacking away, uncovered, its belts spinning, straining against the bolts locking it down to the concrete pad. A chain-link fence surrounded it, a little square with a roof of sheet metal as protection. Jugs of gas were sheltered there, but I didn't need to blow them up to create a diversion. Just stopping the generator would be enough, that was what we'd come up with, that was how we were going to create enough chaos to slip away and run down the hill unnoticed by the guards who still stood in the road, unnoticed by Eel.

No longer was the fire just a scene in the distance. It was washing up against the break, the heat enough to make everything feel combustible, my shirt hot against my body. Everyone was working as a team, whipping the hoses in great arcs around the building, and there were others now with buckets, flinging their contents too.

The gate to the generator was locked. I held my shovel up high, brought it down against the padlock, but it was hopeless, a doomed idea. Instead, I flipped the shovel around, put the wooden handle through one of the chain-link's diamonds, but I came up a foot short of the whirring belt. I needed to throw it, which meant I needed to separate the handle from the spade. I held it high above my knee, parallel to the ground, and paused. If I didn't bring the shovel down with enough force, it would bounce and maybe break my knee. Doing this without full commitment meant not doing it at all, so I brought the shovel down with all the strength I had, half expecting my leg to snap instead, but the wood shattered and the blade came free in my hand, flipping backward and impaling itself in the soft ground.

I shoved the handle through the fence, held the end and tried to slow my breath. I had one shot at this, and if it went wrong, then I would have lost my stick, and with it my chance of stopping the generator.

Calm in the face of chaos. The rhythm of my breath. I thought of Penelope sitting in the cave, waiting for the sun to rise. I thought of Hannah. And then I thought of nothing at all, just lost myself in focus on the stick in my hand. I slid it back and forth through the fence, getting a feel for the weight of it, like a pool player rocking the cue forward and back before taking his shot. All the noise disappeared, the fire too, and all I could see was the generator, lurching and working like an animal, and I threw the shovel handle forward, my aim miraculous and perfect, the wood shaft flying into the void around which the belt spun. It hung there for a moment, then dropped onto the belt, which grabbed it and swung it up against the flywheel in an explosion of wood shards, the belt shrieking before it snapped, whipping into the air, a wriggling snake, before falling to the ground. The generator shuddered like a dying animal, like the cow I'd hit with the car a million years before in Kansas, then made one final bellow and fell silent.

Nothing seemed to happen at first. The hoses still sprayed water high in the air, and I thought perhaps I'd miscalculated, this generator wasn't powering the well pump after all, but then the arcing water slumped and stopped, the hoses limp, and shouts were rising above the sound of the fire roaring, and I ran down toward the guards shouting, "Help, help! The building is going to go!" I wasn't lying, the embers were already smoldering on the roof, and people were throwing dirt now to smother the flames, cutout figures against the pestilential light of the coming fire. The guards ran toward the others, and I stood in the road where they'd been, looking for Hannah. The people all blended together in the scarlet darkness, and I had to stomp on my desire to run up there too, to look for her. I needed to trust my daughter, to wait here where we said we would meet.

And then she came, around the corner of the building, at a quick jog, looking behind her at the turbid scene, and she was alone. We could move down the road, no one would see us go. We were free.

Closer now, I could see the concentration on Hannah's face, the focus. She looked just like her mother. I was going to call to her when over her shoulder, I saw Eel dash around the edge of the building. His mouth was open, he was yelling and pointing at us, trying to catch the attention of the guard running the other way. He tugged at the guy's sleeve like a little kid. The guard glanced back toward us, then waved him off. The roof was catching now, its flames rising to meet the fire falling from the sky.

Eel took the gun. The guard ducked as the strap slipped over his head, then ran on toward the building, and Eel swung the rifle to his shoulder, aiming it at me, but Hannah was in between us. For a moment, we existed in a line, Eel and I staring at one another and Hannah moving between us like a bead on a string. Then he broke to his right, sprinting toward the line of cars The Revival kept on the edge of camp.

Hannah could see in my face what was happening without even turning around. She caught my hand, accelerating now, pulling me with her, her arms pumping. "Come on!" she shouted, and I was running too, stumbling as I tried to keep up. All those times when she was little, her legs flailing as she ran and I jogged alongside, and now I was running as hard as I could, and she was waiting on me, slowing down, trying not to lose me.

The squeal of the car's tires sounded above the pandemonium, headlights stabbing the night, and Hannah was shouting, "Hurry, Dad! He's coming!" I couldn't look back, I would have been blinded by the light that now was flooding around me, my shadow suddenly stretched out, slender and wild against the road ahead as the car loomed behind.

He was not going to let Hannah go. I could hear the engine revving. He would run me down without a second thought in his pursuit. I ran as hard as I could.

A switchback loomed ahead. Hannah dove to her left and I followed, the two of us stumbling down the scree slope as Eel gunned his engine and flew into the corner. I tripped and tumbled and she was by my side, half lifting me as we ran back onto the road, the car starting to catch up again as boulders began to appear in the desert around us.

"This way!" I pulled Hannah's sleeve and we broke off the road, running through the sudden darkness, my ankles twisting on the little rocks and brush grabbing at the rough cloth of my pants. All the boulders looked the same in the lurid glow of the fire, hulks looming ahead of us like ships wrecked on the shore. None of them were right. No cave, no Penelope. The car lurched off the road behind us, and the stones threw giant shadows that swung back and forth as he tried to find a way through. Then the lights swung upward, disappearing into the sky, and I knew he'd lurched into a ditch somewhere, and now he was on foot. A gunshot rang out, percussion sharp against the roar.

"Where are we going, Dad?" Hannah cried, and I didn't answer, just kept running forward, my head swiveling back and forth as my eyes strained the darkness looking for the Camaro, the boulders leaning on one another.

My ears heard Penelope before my eyes saw her, a voice in the wilderness shouting my name, and we ran left around a boulder and there was our car, not black anymore but red, the firelight dancing on its glossy paint. Penelope was standing there, looking in the wrong direction, and Hannah cried, "Mom!"

They fell into one another's arms, a deep guttural noise rising from Penelope's throat, and I ran up to them, my eyes wide and staring, looking for Eel in the darkness. If we got into the car, we could stomp the gas, take the chance that he wasn't very good with a gun. I was about to say that, to pull them in that direction, when I saw a flicker of movement. He was just off to the left, prowling, moving slowly, working methodically through the field of stones.

"The cave!" I whispered, and Penelope tugged Hannah down beneath the rock, into the darkness.

"Nah!" he called. He was turning around, the gun was pointing at the sky, he was scanning the landscape. "Come back!"

We didn't make a sound, we were tucked into the cave, Hannah and Penelope holding one another.

"Don't do this to me, Hannah!" His voice was harsh, like he was fighting not to cry. I saw him see the Camaro. Not that I could make out his face, but his figure turned and froze, and I knew what he was looking at. Now he moved even slower, the gun at his shoulder. Hannah and Penelope were huddled together behind me and I hunched by the low entrance to the cave beneath the boulder. Closer, Eel walked closer, and as he did, I could see his face in the red glow. His eyes were narrow, his jaw working as though he was chewing something.

"Come out!" he called. "Hannah! Come out! I've come to bring you back home."

Penelope held Hannah tighter, as though she could wrap her

whole body around her. Eel stepped closer to the car, close enough that I could no longer see his upper body, just his legs, his feet scuffing through the pebbled sand.

"Hannah!" his voice cracked. "You belong with me."

Hannah pulled herself free from Penelope's embrace and looked at me as though to communicate something. Without a word, she ran to the far side of the cave, and wriggled her way out from beneath the boulder, onto the sand, and out of view. Penelope opened her mouth, reached for her, but she was gone.

For a moment, all was still. Then Eel began to squat, he was going to look in the cave, and Hannah's voice rang out from off in the distance. "I don't belong to anybody!"

A rock flew out of the darkness too, lopsided and spinning. It missed Eel by a foot. He spun in that direction, away from me, and now I understood Hannah's plan, what role I was meant to play once she had him distracted.

"Don't make me do this," Eel said, and I launched myself out from the cave, my arms wrapping his knees and knocking him forward, the gun skittering out of his hands and his body landing heavy on the ground. As quickly as he fell, he started to rise, a wild man, all thrashing limbs as we rolled. Penelope was calling my name. Eel's body went still for a moment, then he threw me off with a single propulsive jerk and he was scrabbling forward, looking for his gun, and all was going to be lost if he found it, we would have gotten to the finish line only for Hannah to watch us die.

From where the idea came, I don't know. Maybe from the pain as San Cristóbal dug into my foot as we plunged hell-bent down the twisting mountainside road. I reached into my sock and snatched him out on his chain and then threw myself forward and landed on Eel's back just as his fingers touched the gun. One spasm of movement, and I had the chain looped around his throat and I leaned back, pulling so hard I disappeared into pulling. I was nothing but a pair of hands, bleeding and raw, on the chain. Eel made a gurgling, coughing sound like a piece of meat had lodged in his windpipe. The gun fired once, twice, he was trying to wave it back toward me, but I was too close to his body, our torsos one struggling mass in the darkness. I felt the skin tear on his throat, felt the blood run warm over my hands, and I prayed for the chain to hold. All I needed was for the chain to hold itself together, for San Cristóbal to give me one final miracle. Eel's body lurched as he tried to free himself, the gun fired again and again, and I pulled even harder and we rolled, now he was on top of me and I stared up and over his bristled hair at the fire falling from the sky, the red rain coming down as I strained, his blood mixing with mine, and he went still, jerked, and then still again, but my hands wouldn't stop pulling, my breath coming in ragged gasps, and Hannah was there, touching my face, saying, "Dad, he's dead. Dad."

Penelope too. She was there, and they were touching my arms, loosening my fingers, and pushing Eel from my body. He rolled with a thump, his limbs sprawled and dead, and his face was dead too, and staring, his blood already pooling in the sand, and my blood with his. My hands were shaking, and my breath coming in uneven gasps like sobs.

"We need to go," Penelope was saying. "We need to go."

I tried to stand and I couldn't. I fell back onto my knees, and they had their arms under me, they were lifting me up and I stumbled between them back to the car, where they got me into the passenger seat. My teeth were chattering again, as though I'd never gotten warm, and as they rattled my jaw flared in waves of pain. Hannah ran around and climbed into the backseat, like we were going to drive her to a friend's house, maybe to practice. I wanted to reach out to her, to hold her hand, but all I could see was Eel's sightless eyes staring up into the fire and my arms shook even when I pressed them to my body, held myself close.

Penelope turned the key, and the engine roared.

She looked at me, looked at Hannah.

"Are you ready?" she asked.

I managed a nod. And from the back, Hannah said, "Let's go."

Penelope stepped on the gas and the car surged out over the desert, back onto the road, The Revival encampment a pillar of dark smoke rising behind us, and she turned the wheel east under the pestilential sky, the sky torn asunder, and we drove, together again, toward Grand Junction somewhere ahead of us in the darkness.

ACKNOWLEDGMENTS

To my agent, Henry Dunow, thank you for believing in my voice from the beginning, and thank you for the brilliance of your editorial mind. This book would be a shell of itself without you. Thank you to the equally brilliant Sara Nelson, whose instincts are unerring and who saw what this book could be.

Thank you to Arielle Datz at DCL, and to the whole team at Harper: Katie O'Callaghan, Martin Wilson, Jessie Maimone, Zoya Feldman, Edie Astley, Mary Gaule, and all the many people who have worked behind the scenes to make this book a reality.

I'm grateful to all of those who read drafts of this book and offered insight that made it so much better, especially Del Case, Greta Doctoroff, Michael Forbes, Pearce Green, and Lisa Waller.

To the teachers who changed my life in so many ways: Danny Paul, Tom Donnelly, Sue Benston, Kim Benston, and Michael Ryan—thank you. And to the many generations of my students: you have been a part of this from the beginning, and your talent, zeal, kindness, and moral fiber teach and inspire me every day.

ACKNOWLEDGMENTS

Thanks to all my Irvine peers, especially Matt Thomas for reading my first short stories and telling me I was a fiction writer. And to Andrew Tonkovich at the *Santa Monica Review* for publishing one of those early stories. Those early seeds of belief sustained me for many years.

Thank you as well to the friends and family who supported and encouraged me along the way, especially my sister, Abby; my mother, Betsy; and my father, Alan.

And to Greta: to say that this book wouldn't exist without your love, support, belief, and insight doesn't go nearly far enough. How could I be so lucky to be with you?

And last, to Daphne, my daughter: I am impossibly proud of you, and you have my unconditional love forever. I would travel around the world and back for you.

ABOUT THE AUTHOR

A graduate of UC Irvine's MFA program, CHRISTOPHER M. HOOD is the director of the Creative Writing Program at the Dalton School. He has published short fiction and essays in various literary journals. *The Revivalists* is his first novel. He lives in the New York area with his wife and daughter.